Teenage Love Affair

Also by Ni-Ni Simone

Shortie Like Mine
If I Was Your Girl
A Girl Like Me

Published by Dafina Books

Teenage Love Affair

Ni-Ni Simone

Dafina KTeen Books
KENSINGTON PUBLISHING CORP.
http://www.kensingtonbooks.com

DAFINA KTEEN BOOKS are published by

Kensington Publishing Corp.
119 West 40th Street
New York, NY 10018

All Kensington titles, imprints, and distributed lines are available at special quantity discounts for bulk purchases for sales promotion, premiums, fund-raising, educational, or institutional use.

Special book excerpts or customized printings can also be created to fit specific needs. For details, write or phone the office of the Kensington Special Sales Manager: Attn.: Special Sales Department. Kensington Publishing Corp., 119 West 40th Street, New York, NY 10018. Phone: 1-800-221-2647.

KTeen Reg. U.S. Pat. & TM Off.
Sunburst logo Reg. U.S. Pat. & TM Off.

ISBN-13: 978-0-7582-4189-4
ISBN-10: 0-7582-4189-5

First Printing: April 2010
20 19 18 17 16 15 14 13 12 11 10 9 8

Printed in the United States of America

*To my first teenage love
Michael Jackson—
you will forever be missed.
And to my little cousin Korynn,
who sat in church and chatted away with me about this
book,
who texted me every day for more and more pages:
You are so smart, so beautiful, and so gifted!
Stay as you are and
I assure you that the best is yet to come!*

Dear Reader,

You are about to partake in the journey of my love life, my home life, my mistakes, missteps, and everything in between that makes me . . . well . . . me. In these pages you will see that it's hard work being a seventeen-year-old diva, and that's for certain. I swear, what I thought was love had turned out not to be. Then there was the time where I changed my mind midstream and decided that love, relationships, and endless drama just weren't for me.

Heck, I felt like I needed a break from my own life. For real–for real, no lie, I've gone to Heaven and Hell at least twice only to land somewhere in between. But along the way I learned some very valuable lessons that I want to share with you.

For one: Love feels good. Period. Anyone who tells you anything different is played. All of these sad songs that say I want you/I need you/and I gotta have you back is because someone messed up and mistreated someone else. That's not love, that's nonsense.

And if by chance love is more difficult or complicated than that—we can learn that later, after teenage life. Feel me? But, anyway, as I was saying, love—true love—never feels bad and it doesn't make you feel worthless.

Oh yeah, and it doesn't send you on a cat-and-mouse chase and have you sweatin' some dude or some chick who plays you to the left.

Along my journey I also learned that our parents deserve a chance. I know that sometimes they seem, to us, to be buggin' or trippin', and always want to take charge over what we feel is *our* life. But they do this because they love us and want what's best. I'm not trying to sound like an afterschool special, I'm just saying that parents can be cool people, and besides they love us unconditionally—teenage flaws and all.

Last, I learned that the most important type of love is the love you have for yourself. If you don't love yourself, then other people won't. I know you've heard that a thousand times before but it's *sooooo* true.

I went through a time in my life where I thought my boyfriend putting his hands on me was love, but it wasn't. And if you're in a relationship where either you or your dude are hitting on one another, putting the hands up, bumpin', boxin', throwin', or whatever you call it, then the two of you don't need to be together. Let me say that again. "YOU DON'T NEED TO BE TOGETHER!"

All it takes is for someone to fall, hit their head the wrong way, become seriously injured or worse—die—and then what? Both lives are ruined. And it doesn't matter if he or she tells you they love you, because if they hit you, they don't love or respect you. And please don't think you can change them, because you can't. Don't fall for their apologies and don't accept any gifts from them. Just get out of the relationship. Love yourself enough to bounce.

And if you're the one hitting on your boo, then you need to stop and get yourself some help, tell your parents, and don't be afraid to go to counseling.

Counseling is for anyone who feels they have issues or problems they want to work out. Counseling is not played, and it doesn't matter what anyone else thinks. What matters is becoming a better you. As a matter of fact, here are some cool people who can help you: National Domestic Violence Hotline: 1-800-799-SAFE.

So, to wrap this up, just remember this: Life is what you make it, and love is great when it's drama free. If you are good to yourself and respect yourself, then everyone else will get in line. And if they don't, then tell them that Zsa-Zsa said, "Lose yourself! You don't need the hassle!"

Remember love is good, easy, and free, and only when you understand these things will you enjoy the true essence of a teenage love affair!

Now let's turn the page and do the damn thing!

Peace!
Zsa-Zsa

PROLOGUE

June 2004
Newark, New Jersey

Zsa-Zsa

Understand this: I'm grown—no two or three ways about it. I've been grown since last year, once I realized that the daily bruises on my mother's face and her busted lip were not from her walking into the front door but were instead courtesy of my daddy's left hook. Then I came into womanhood.

Don't sleep. I knew how to cook, clean, and pretend that my mother liked to wear sunglasses indoors, and that my daddy wasn't drunk, he just smelled bad. I knew not to open my mouth and question my mother when she called the cops. My daddy would beat her one day and the next day my mother would drop the charges and bail him out of jail.

I knew it all, which is exactly why I was not impressed by the note that had mysteriously landed on my desk with the words "You wanna be my girl? Circle yes or no" written in block letters.

I knew it was from my classmate Malachi, although he

didn't sign his name. We lived in the same building and would sometimes walk home together. He'd told my two best friends, Courtney and Asha, that he was checkin' for me. That turned me off. Although I loved him, I didn't need anybody else knowing that. So I stopped talking to him . . . but that only seemed to light his fire even more. This explained why he was giving me the up-down with his eyes while I was sitting on the cement bench in the playground with my friends.

I turned to Courtney who, although he was a boy, only played with girls, had a high-pitched voice, and a swish. "I need to go handle this," I told him.

"Well." Courtney smacked his gums. "Me personally, I wouldn't even go through the changes. I would just get with homeboy."

"Ill." Asha frowned, her ebony microbraids swinging as she spoke. "Don't listen to him. He thinks Jay-Z is cute. Look at Malachi." We all turned our heads. "He's chubby, has a zipper running across his teeth, and let's not even discuss that pimple sitting in the middle of his nose. Can you say yuck?"

"Hatin' is so unattractive." Courtney flung his wrist and twisted his mouth to the side.

I didn't say a word. There was no way I could admit that despite the extra weight and the braces on his teeth, Malachi's cinnamon-colored skin and almond-shaped eyes were the prettiest things I'd ever seen.

I circled my answer quickly on the note, pushed my shoulder-length hair behind my ears, and walked over to where Malachi was standing by the monkey bars kickin' it with a few of his friends. I could hear Courtney and Asha running behind me.

"Malachi." I placed my hands on my hips. "Don't be dropping notes on my desk." Before he could respond, I continued on. "I don't appreciate you being all in my face with your childishness. What kind of man writes notes? Now lose yourself." I tossed the note at him and as I turned to walk away, a bunch of oules and ahhhs created a choir behind me.

"Zsa," Courtney said, as we returned to the bench. "You love him, don't you?"

I couldn't hold it in any longer, so I giggled and fell onto the grass. "I sure do." I smiled. "I sure do."

"Y'all just nasty." Asha frowned while standing over me and Courtney, who had just fallen beside me. "Real, real nasty."

After lunch I finished my classwork with the quickness and found myself daydreaming about me and Malachi getting married. I wrote Mrs. Malachi Askew with hearts all around it on small scraps of paper. I found myself naming our unborn children: a girl named Zsa-Zsa, after me of course, and a son named Malachi, after his father.

Once I floated back from my daydream, I looked up and saw Malachi staring at me. I don't know what got into me but I gave him the biggest smile in the world. I was cheesin' from ear to ear, and for a moment I thought I could see hearts floating around Malachi's head. He blew me a kiss and I blew him one back. As I started giggling to myself, the bell rang. "Okay, class," my teacher said. "Have a good weekend and see you on Monday."

See you on Monday? For a moment I was confused. I looked at the calendar and today was Friday. All day long I hadn't thought once about what today was. Had I remembered it was Friday, I would've stayed at my desk all day

and sulked. I hated Fridays. I hated them. Fridays were
when my daddy would get paid and my mother would act
as if all that mattered in the world was the money he gave
her, the weekly Chinese food he brought home for us to
eat, and the attention he paid her. Friday also meant that
my daddy would be drunk at an earlier time than he was
any other day.

I couldn't believe I was caught so off guard. I watched
my classmates pack their backpacks and brag about the
weekend they were due to have. I wished that I could
change bodies and be one of them, because Fridays for me
didn't say time off from school and endless playdates with
my friends. It said pain, tears, and nightmares. Not laughing, not fun, but bombshells of, *"Whack!* Get off of me,
Zach! *Whack!* I'm tired of your drinking, Zach! *Whack!*
I'ma call the cops! *Whack-whack!"* This is why I hated Fridays. Mondays through Thursdays were my saving grace.

"Zsa." Courtney interrupted my thoughts as we left
school and started walking down Clinton Avenue and
headed home. "How come we can't ever come to your
house and play?"

"I've been wondering that too," Asha followed up.

Instantly, I was a mix between embarrassed and pissed.
Pissed because they had the nerve to want to chill in my
crib. And embarrassed because I didn't know how to say,
"You can't come to my house because we don't have nothing. All of our furniture is cheap, tore up, and mostly broken. I'm not sure if the apartment is going to be clean, or
worse, I don't know if my daddy is drunk and has already
beat my mother because of something 'she asked for.' So,
no, you can't come to my crib because if you really knew
how I lived, you might not want to be my friends."

Since I couldn't say any of that, I said what my mother told my aunties and cousins whenever they wanted to visit. "Don't nobody want a buncha hood rats tearin' up their stuff!" I placed my hands on my hips. "My parents work too hard for me to be bringing a whole lot of company home. So, no, you can't come home with me. My mother won't allow it."

"Oh," Asha said as if she didn't know what else to say.

"I'm not no hood rat," Courtney complained, jerking his neck from left to right. "You got me all the way twisted."

"That's what they all say," I said as we reached the front of my building. "Now beat it. See y'all later." I shot 'em a two-finger peace sign and entered the lobby. But no sooner than I walked past the same crackheads I flew by this morning did tears streak down my cheeks.

After a few moments of whimpering in the hallway, I had to get myself together. I wiped my eyes with the back of my hands and headed up two flights to our apartment. I could hear the radio playing as I twisted the knob and opened the door.

My mother, who was the color of the evening sun with hazel eyes and dark brown shoulder-length hair, smiled at me as I walked in. Most people said that I was my mother's twin, except my complexion was milk chocolate.

My mother opened her arms for a hug and I walked into her embrace. "Hey, Zsa-Zsa," she said while kissing me on the forehead. "How was school?"

"It was okay." I hunched my shoulders.

"Well, you have to tell me about it later." She released me from her embrace. "But for now, go wash your hands while I set the table. Your father brought home Chinese."

I hated Chinese.

"You see I brought your favorite," my daddy, who resembled Denzel Washington, said as he walked out of the bathroom. "Shrimp egg foo young."

I hated shrimp egg foo young.

"Thanks," I said, watching him take a beer from his six-pack and pop it open. I was careful not to step on my five-year-old sister, Hadiah, who was rolling around on the floor playing with her dolls as I headed to my room.

"Wassup, Zsa?" my brother, Derrick, said as he headed toward the front door to leave for the evening. Leaving had become a new habit of his. I couldn't wait for the day when I could escape.

"Derrick," I heard my mother say as I unloaded my book bag on my bed. "Why are you always running out of here on Fridays?"

Before I heard my brother's answer, I sucked my teeth. I swear that was the dumbest question I had ever heard. If nothing else she knew why he was always leaving. I knew hitting was wrong, but the truth be told that question alone made me want to slap her.

"Ma," Derrick said. "I'm sixteen now."

"You're still not grown," my father interjected.

Derrick was silent for a moment and then I heard him say, "See ya later, Ma. I love you."

After an hour of eating, my parents laughing and talking about the news, my daddy had licked off the bottle of Hennessy and finished his third beer. "Do that dance, baby," he said to me, while turning the radio on. "Do that dance they teach you down at the community center." He sipped his beer.

I fought the frown that had inched its way on my face. I didn't see this as my daddy being interested in me dancing. I saw this as the steps he took toward slapping my mother.

"Jazmyn." He smiled at my mother. "Get her to do that dance for me."

"Go on, Zsa-Zsa," my mother urged. "You know we love to see you dance."

Reluctantly, I put on my tap dancing shoes, stood in front of the TV, and as the music played I started to groove.

Believe it or not, for a moment . . . a brief moment . . . as my feet moved in a swift melody, I felt free, as if I didn't have a care in the world and all that mattered was the singing of my feet. When I was done, both of my parents were giving me a standing ovation.

My father popped his fourth beer open and my mother said, "You don't need to be drinking all of that!"

Why? Why did she say that?

"Who the hell are you talking to?" my daddy snapped.

There was no turning back now. It was officially on.

My mother tried to back out, but it was too late. "I don't know why I even said anything to you!"

Me either.

I turned on my heels and went into my bedroom. For a moment I thought about taking off my clothes and putting on my nightgown. But then I remembered that if she called the cops I needed to be dressed so that I could go with her to the police station to press charges. So I changed my mind and instead laid down and waited on my wall to start thumping.

BAM!

The wall jumped and scared me out of my sleep. I didn't even know I'd fallen asleep until I heard the weekend music that makes my mirror shake. *BAM!* There it was again. "I'm not gon' let you beat on me!" I heard my mother scream as the entire apartment felt as if it were convulsing. I couldn't take it. I hated this. If only she would learn to keep her mouth shut!

BAM!

I looked over to my sister, who was stirring around in her bed. Tears were running down her cheeks as I touched her on the shoulder. "Shh," I said as I sat on the edge of her bed. "Don't cry. It'll stop in a few minutes."

"I'm scared." She wrapped her arms around me.

"Don't be. We can stick this out."

The more the room shook, the more Hadiah cried. I did my best to comfort her but after a while I couldn't take it anymore, so I took her by the hand and we crept out of the apartment and up the stairs.

Malachi and his family lived in the apartment directly above us, so he was the only one who really knew my story. His place had been my retreat for the last year. One Friday he heard my parents fighting and the next day when he saw me coming back from the police station with my mother, he whispered in my ear if I ever wanted to get away I could come to his place. He claimed his parents slept hard as a rock and seeing that they didn't wake up the times Hadiah and I came into their place, I believed him.

As always, during times like this the door was unlocked. Me and Hadiah walked in quietly. The apartment was small so we didn't have to travel too far down the hall to get to Malachi's room. There were a few boxes in the way that hadn't been there before, but I managed not to trip over them. I eased into Malachi's room, and he was asleep in his bed.

I looked down on the floor, and the pallet of blankets that he made for Hadiah was lying there, and as if this had become our second home, Hadiah laid down and fell asleep. I eased onto the bed next to Malachi. He slid back to give me room, shared his cover with me, and eventually we fell asleep.

A few hours later when I heard sirens blaring I woke up. That was the cue my mother had called the police. "I have to go," I said to Malachi, who was now awake. "I'm sorry about how I acted earlier today at school."

"It's okay," he said as a stream of light came into his room from the street lamp. "I want to give you something before you go, though," he said.

"What?" I picked up my sleeping sister from her pallet.

He handed me a gold-plated ring with a heart on top and the word *wifey* written in small letters in magic marker. "It's a permanent marker, and it won't come off." He hunched his shoulders in defeat. "That's if you ever decide to be my girl."

I smiled. I couldn't help it, I swear I was cheesin' hard. "Didn't you read the note?" I asked him.

"No." He hunched his shoulders. "I figured you said no."

I shook my head. "I said, 'yes,' silly. Of course I'll be your girl." That was the extent of me admitting my feelings. I couldn't stand being sappy too much longer so I grabbed Hadiah's hand, hurried out of his room and down the stairs. Just as I was entering the apartment, the police were slapping handcuffs on my daddy. "My kids shouldn't have to see this!" my mother shouted. I wondered if she even noticed that we'd just come back into the apartment. "I'ma be right behind you pressing charges, officer," she said with confidence as she grabbed our hands and said, "Let's go."

When we arrived at the police station, I was beyond embarrassed, especially since the officers knew us by name. "How are you, li'l Miss Zsa-Zsa and sweet Hadiah?" the officer, who we saw every week, said to us as he handed us each a lollipop. He looked at my mother. "Another weekend, huh?"

"I just can't do it" was her response every time. "I get tired of trying to make this work for my children, and it ends in disaster."

"So are you going to follow through with the charges this time?" the officer asked.

"Yes. It has to stop," my mother said as she filled out paperwork, wrote down her recollection of the event, and handed the forms to the officer.

"Your court date will come in the mail."

"Thank you," she said, grabbing us once again by the hand and leading us out the door.

The ride home was a short one, and the sun was rising by the time we got there. I was quiet as we headed to the apartment, and like clockwork as soon as my mother opened the door, I could hear the telephone ringing. I looked at her. The shiners on her face gleamed like black and blue gold. I wondered what she would think of herself when she looked in the mirror.

She turned her head once she realized I was looking at the marks on her cheeks and forehead. The phone continued to ring as my mother said, "Don't answer it." So I didn't. I simply sat down in the chair next to the phone because I knew that the phone would ring again.

Brrrrrnnnngggg . . . I didn't even look at my mother. I simply answered the phone. "You have a collect call from," the recorded operator said, and then paused as my daddy said his name. "Zach."

"Will you accept the charges?" the operator continued. "If so, press two. If not, hang up."

"Press two?" I asked my mother, knowing she would say no but meant yes.

"No. Hang up that phone!" She paused. "Know what? I can't put you in the middle of this. Press two and give me the phone."

I handed her the phone. I started to go into my room, but then I remembered I had to keep my clothes on for when she dropped the charges.

"Zach," my mother said into the phone, "I can't keep going through these changes. I want more than the constant fights and arguments." She paused. "But you say that every time." She paused again. "I love you too, but I need more than love. I need respect. I need for you to keep your hands off of me." She paused. I knew he was offering gifts, because she started to grin. "You don't have to buy me diamond earrings, just do the right thing. . . . Okay, I'ma give you one last try and that's it. If you put your hands on me again, you got to leave and that's all to it."

My mother's smile was so wide that the bruises on her face ran into her curled lips. "I'ma drop you and Hadiah off with your aunty Grier. Me and your daddy need to talk."

My aunty lived around the corner so it only took us a few minutes to get there, and judging by the look in my aunt's eyes when we arrived, she knew what my mother was up to.

"Did you look at yourself before you came here?" my aunty said to my mother as she opened the door for us to come in. My twin cousins, Seven and Toi, were standing behind their mother as me and Hadiah walked past her. "What happened?" they whispered. "They were fightin' again?"

I nodded my head as my aunty continued on. "Jazmyn, all it takes is for one person to hit their head the wrong way. And then what?"

"Why are you in my business?" my mother scolded. "Why? All I asked you to do was to keep my girls until I returned. What me and my husband do doesn't concern you. Worry about yours and his mistress."

My aunty slammed the door in her face, and I could hear my mother storm down the stairs and jump into her car.

"It's okay, Aunty." I tapped my aunty on her thigh. "They always make up."

"No man is supposed to put his hands on you," she said to me sternly. "You hear me? No man."

"I know, but he's always sorry," I said, taking up for my daddy. "You'll see, he's going to buy her something pretty."

My aunty stood silent, her eyes combed my face and seemed to say something to me that perhaps I was too young or too naive to understand. And although I didn't know everything about life yet, I knew enough to know that she could talk to my mother until she was red in the face, Jazmyn and Zach Fields would never change and Friday nights would always be the same.

"Aunty," I said, breaking the troubling silence, "I need to change my clothes. I have had these things on for two days."

"I knew I smelled something," my cousin Seven said, laughing and running into her room.

"I'ma get you!" I laughed while running behind her. "I'ma get you!"

For the next few hours we played with my cousins, and before we knew anything my mother had returned with an even wider smile and the prettiest diamonds I'd ever seen dangling from her ears.

"Mommy," I said, "those are pretty."

"Thank you, honey." She looked at my aunty Grier. "He said he was sorry."

"He does every time."

"Look." My mother grabbed me and my sister by the hand. "I have to go."

"I'm sure you do," my aunty said as we walked out her front door. "I'm sure you do."

The next few weeks at home were surprisingly calm. There was no Chinese food, beer, or Hennessy. We even saw my brother more. I'd never been this happy and prayed that things stayed this way. We had a lot of fun together, and what I discovered during that time was my daddy had a sense of humor. Can you believe it? He was funny. Oh, and my mother could sing. I never knew any of those things. I hardly watched TV anymore because we'd become masters at entertaining one another.

It was the last day of school, and I was sad that I wouldn't be seeing my friends every day for a while. I mean, I knew I would see them every now and then on the block, but it wouldn't be the same as daily.

Besides, I hated goodbyes, and this is exactly what today felt like . . . the end.

We all signed each other's autograph books and wrote crazy messages to one another. This was it for sixth grade, and we were on our way to junior high.

From where I was standing I could see Malachi watching me from across the room. I thought about going over and talking to him for a quick moment, but then I changed my mind. There was no way I could let anyone, besides Courtney and Asha, know I was in love with him.

When the bell rang and everyone gathered their things, I lagged behind so that I could say bye to Malachi, especially since my emotions and embarrassment wouldn't allow me to say goodbye in front of anyone.

Once the classroom was cleared and everyone rushed into the hallway, I walked over to Malachi and stood in front of his desk. I didn't know what the heck I should do or what I should say, so while the teacher's back was turned I did what I'd secretly been dreaming about for weeks. I planted a wet one on his lips, and then before he realized what had happened to him I took off running, leaving nothing but the echo of my Nikes behind.

By the time I arrived home I was completely out of breath. I could hear music playing as I opened the apartment door, and spotted Chinese food on the dining room table. My heart immediately fell to my chest. Hell on Earth was back again. I swear I hated Chinese food.

My mother looked at me and smiled. "Hey, Zsa." She held her arms out for a hug. "How was the last day of school?"

"It was okay." I hunched my shoulders.

"Well, tell me about it later." She smiled. "Your father brought Chinese food."

"I see," I said, looking at the table and then glancing at the case of beer and bottle of Hennessy on the counter. It was official. Our dysfunctional routine was back in motion. Derrick didn't waste any time leaving. I felt as if I was waiting on an inevitable car crash.

"What's wrong, Zsa-Zsa?" my mother asked while I finished up my food.

"Nothing," I said, watching my father drink his fourth beer.

My mother followed the direction of my eyes, and she snapped. "Zach, don't you see Zsa-Zsa is upset with you starting to drink so much again?"

My eyes bugged out of my head. I couldn't believe my mother did that! Now the argument was about me? It was my fault? Now I knew for sure when the wall thumped I would be the cause. "Ma, I didn't say that."

"As long as she knows," my daddy said, slurring his words, "not to do what I do, but to do what I tell her to, she ain't got to worry."

My father belched and my mother started screaming, "What was that?"

I couldn't believe it, just like that we were upside down again, and this time it was all my fault.

"You startin' again, Zach?" my mother said. "Keep it up

and you gon' be right back in jail!" She stormed into their bedroom and a few minutes later he stomped in behind her.

It didn't take long before the wall was jumping again. I tried to comfort my sister, but after a while I couldn't take it anymore. I grabbed Hadiah's hand and we headed upstairs to Malachi's. I twisted the knob on Malachi's apartment door and it was locked. My heart started beating like a drum. I twisted it again and nothing. I nervously started biting my bottom lip.

I swallowed the lump in my throat and knocked softly. Tears filled my eyes as I found my knocks growing harder and louder with each passing minute. My stomach was churning and my knees started to buckle. I didn't know if I was getting sick or if I had to pee really bad. I started pounding on the door again. I needed Malachi to be home now more than ever. I pounded and pounded and pounded until the sides of my fists were turning red.

"Hey, sweets" interrupted my banging. I turned around and it was the woman next door. "What are you doing up here alone this time of the night?"

"I was looking for Malachi." I wiped my eyes.

"Oh, honey." She waved her hand. "Malachi and his family moved."

"No." I shook my head. "He wouldn't leave me."

"Well, honey, I hate to be the one to tell you, but he is gone. He and his family moved to Murfreesboro, North Carolina."

At this moment North Carolina sounded as if it were on another planet.

"And Murfreesboro, North Carolina," the neighbor carried on, "is a long way from here, so you better go on back home. I'm sure your parents are looking for you two."

I felt frozen, as if someone had just turned me into ice and then without warning I melted, and before I knew anything I'd slid to the floor with a crying Hadiah leaning against my shoulder.

1

Daydreamin' 'bout you all day in school, can't concentrate . . .
—ALICIA KEYS, "TEENAGE LOVE AFFAIR"

Five Years Later, 2009

> *"Can't wait to get home, baby, dial your
> number . . ."*

Zsa-Zsa

My Armani stilettos clicked against the tile floor as I
placed my hands on my curvaceous hips and Naomi
Campbelled to the front of the classroom. I was due to
give a report on self-esteem, but after a week of sneaking
out of the house and spending nights with my boo, Ameen,
I had nothing prepared but my hair, nails, and fresh gear.
So, I figured I would wing it. When I applied myself I got
all As anyway, so why not apply myself now? Besides, I
wasn't beat to argue with this old chick; I rolled my eyes
toward my health teacher and shot her a fake smile.

The drama of getting Saturday detention for lack of
preparation simply wasn't worth it.

"Miss Fields." My teacher, Ms. Raymond, sat behind her desk and called my name. "Where is your paper?"

"I don't need it," was my attempt to play it off. "I can recite my report from memory."

Ms. Raymond's eyes narrowed. "Now, Miss Fields, if you have memorized a report I will be quite impressed. So please, proceed."

"Alright." I cleared my throat, pushed my gum to the side of my mouth, and popped my MAC-covered lips. "My report on self-esteem." I looked to one side of the classroom and then to the other. "Do you all know what it means to have a positive self-image?" I asked the class, only to receive blank stares and dumb looks.

Pitiful.

But I would bet my last dollar if I asked them if they knew how to do the Pop-Lock-and-Drop-It or the Stanky Leg they would all be at military attention.

I sighed loudly. And to think this was Science High. "Listen, in order to get anywhere in life you have to be comfortable with who you are and know where you are going."

I looked around the classroom and everyone was obviously bored. Even my homeboy, Courtney, was yawning. So, I had to bring it to 'em in the only way they would understand. "Excuse me." I snapped my fingers. "Do y'all birds even know what self-esteem is?"

Seeing no response, I continued on. "Well, self-esteem is like . . . when you got it like that. Like, when you know that deep down inside you're really fly and it's not just a front for the cats around you. Dig?"

"Oh," one of my classmates yelled, sounding proud of himself. "It's when you got it goin' on."

"Exactly, you feel me?"

"Yeah, I feel you, Zsa," Courtney agreed.

"See, Courtney, we here." I pointed from my eyes to his and back again. "But understand we as young women and li'l dudes don't need to be playin' ourselves for these li'l ghetto hoods around here. We need to have dreams, explore our talents, and be determined to go to college. Plus these hoods around here, they don't have no money."

"For real," my newly emerged amen choir in the back of the room said.

I snapped my fingers. "They have no style."

"Umm . . ." the amen choir carried on.

"No fly gear."

"Tell it now!"

"No rides."

"Preach!"

"And for real." I was so into my report I had to stop myself from getting the Holy Ghost. "They can't do nothin' for you. So what's the use of wasting time on them when it's more important things in life to attend to? Don't be gettin' fooled by these donkeys lookin' to trick you outta ya li'l Burger King dough. Don't even do it to yourself."

"Miss Fields," Ms. Raymond interrupted, "this sounds like a sermon from the church of slang. What does this have to do with your report on self-esteem?"

"Ms. Raymond, we need to speak to each other in a language that we understand. All I just said to them was believe in yourself and don't let anyone use you."

"You just said that?" she said in shock.

"If you would listen and stop interrupting her," Asha commented. "God-lee."

"She always interrupting people, too," somebody in the back of the room added.

"Continue," Ms. Raymond said, "and class"—she eyed
Asha—"last warning, watch your tone. Next step is out the
door and Saturday detention."

"Okay." I popped my lips. "See y'all need to grow up
and be like me. Understand this, my boo, Ameen, is the
truth." I hit 'em off with a moment of silence, and then I
went on. "He's nineteen and his pockets are always fat." I
opened my arms wide and pointed my hands like guns,
and said, "Boom. Now peep this, 'cause this is some real
ish, I'm his number one friend on MySpace."

"That . . . is . . . so . . . sick. . . ." Courtney drooled while
snapping his fingers in a Z motion. "Oh, my God."

"You haven't heard a thing. I'm the screen saver on his
iPhone and when it rings, it's my voice saying, 'It's me, li'l
daddy, pick up the phone.' "

A series of dangs rang throughout the room.

"That's my homegirl right there!" Courtney said in a
proud excitement.

"Now, don't you think that means something?" I tapped
the ball of my foot and placed my hands on my size 10
hips. "Of course it does, and if you don't agree, you're a
hater. And you know what I say to haters? Hi, hater." I
waved. "Bye, hater." I hit 'em with a salute. "See, my
mother raised me to know that I'ma leader, not a follower,
which is why I recited my report from memory, 'cause I
know that all y'all wannabes gon' try and copy that.

"Needless to say, I believe that I can accomplish anything I want in life, 'cause I'm too fly not to succeed. I
don't look like Ciara for nothin'." I did a booty drop and
popped back up. "So, just look at me and see what it
means to have self-esteem."

I looked at Courtney and we popped our lips, gave each other fist bumps, and I sat down.

Just as everyone started telling me how good my report was, the bell rang. Forty-five more minutes and I'ma be like deuce-deuce baby.

"Miss Fields." Ms. Raymond called me on my way out the door. "On Monday, I expect a written and less creative report."

This chick knew she was trippin'. I didn't even respond to that. Instead I headed to honors algebra and allowed my teacher, Mr. Watson, to bore the heck outta me.

After three pages of mixing my first name with Ameen's last name with hearts, clouds, and bubbles around it, class had finally ended and I was on my way to fulfill my destiny.

I walked down the hall, mixed in with the first-period lunch students, walked out the side door of the school, and there was my baby sitting in my black '97 Honda Accord. He crashed his onyx Escalade last month, so being the caring and supportive woman that I am, I let him stunt in mine.

My man's whole presence was fiyah: Five foot eleven, a muscular build that put 50 Cent to sleep—scratch that, it put 50 in a coma—he had a fresh Caesar with thousands of brushed-in waves, and his swagger was so serious that anybody looking at him knew he was nothing to play with.

Lil' Wayne's throwback "Lollipop" was bumpin' so loud inside the car, it looked as if the tinted windows were jumping. I slid in and Ameen looked at me with a sexy glare on his face. "You're late." He tapped the digital clock on the dashboard.

"I had to go to algebra, baby. That was the only way I

could cut without anyone noticing I was gone." I reached over to kiss him and he pushed me back.

"So what you sayin'?" he asked seriously.

"I'm sayin' I had to go to school." I couldn't believe he refused my kiss.

"So school comes before me, that's what you sayin'?"

"No." I hesitated. "Nothing comes before you."

"It better not, either." He ice grilled me and pointed his finger in my face.

"Don't be mad." I pecked the tip of his finger and he twisted his lips. "You know I love you," I said.

"Yeah, ai'ight," he said as we pulled off. My baby was always jealous. Sometimes it was scary as hell, but cute. I eased back into the smooth black leather of my worn seats, and out the corner of the rearview mirror I spotted a shopping bag with Gucci written on it. It couldn't be. I turned around in my seat and oh . . . my . . . God! The boots I wanted. I threw my arms across Ameen's chest and started hugging him.

"Slow down, Zsa." He laughed as he swerved across the yellow line. "I'm driving."

"I can't believe you bought them!" I screamed, holding one of the candy apple red wedged heel boots in my hand.

"Yeah," he said as I hugged the boots. "I felt bad for the misunderstanding we had the other day when I thought you were letting that dude kick it to you."

"I don't wanna talk about that." I quickly swallowed the lump in my throat, as the thought of how he yoked me by my collar flooded my mind.

The last thing I wanted to think about was how frightened I felt with my collar in his hands and the look of rage in his eyes. I mean . . . I knew I had no business talking to that dude, although I didn't know him and all he did was ask me for directions to Springfield Avenue. But still, I knew Ameen had had a bad day and all I did was aggravate it. So . . . in a way . . . I guess I asked for it. But my baby made my day once again with these thousand dollar kicks. "I swear you the truth." I planted a wet one on his lips as we headed to his spot.

Ameen lived with his mother, her boyfriend, his sister, and her baby. His house was ran nothing like mine. For one, he paid rent. Rent, can you believe it? Your mother taking money from you. Now, what kinda bullshit is that?

Wait, that's not all of it. You know I can chill in his room, right? Door closed, slow jams playing and everything, and Ameen's mother has never knocked on the door or asked what we were doing. She really didn't seem to care. As a matter of fact I don't even think she knew my name. I would always speak and ask everyone how they were and they would respond by looking at me like I was stupid. Whatever.

I walked behind Ameen into his room and before long we were doing things that I knew my mother would've had me drowning in holy water for.

Two hours later I was showered, dressed, and ready to go to work. I grabbed my car keys off of Ameen's nightstand. "Call me later."

"Where are you going?" He hopped out the bed. "Hol' up, wait for me."

"I have to go and pick up my little sister."

"So, what? I can't use your car?"

"I didn't say that." I hesitated. Lately, Ameen had been using my car a little more than I really wanted him to, but then again, he was my man. "We have to hurry, Ameen. She doesn't like being at the neighbor's too long."

He smiled. "You know I got you."

As we drove down Clinton Avenue toward Highway 78 West, I swear this mofo had stopped at least a hundred different times to speak to just about every dude he knew on the street. If he wasn't blowing the horn like crazy, he was slowing down to kick it with someone. I was getting pissed by the minute.

He slowed down for the umpteenth time and yelled across the street at a guy standing there. "Yo, come 'mere!"

After a few minutes of Ameen kicking it with his friend, a guy pulled up next to us on the flyest 2009 royal blue and white Suzuki motorcycle I'd ever seen in my life. I waited for him to pull off since the light had turned green, but he didn't. Instead he took his helmet off.

Damn! Can you say fine?

Imagine Idris Elba at seventeen, or better yet, Souljah Boy completely muscled out and looking like a man. Six feet tall with toasted almond colored skin, a crazy nice build, muscles everywhere, tattoos in all the right places, sexy dreads that hung midway down his back, and a shadow beard and mustache that would make the saneness chick hurt somebody. I hoped like hell that Ameen didn't notice me starin', because if he did, he would see that for a split second I was in love with somebody else.

"Hey, yo." The guy on the motorcycle called for my attention.

Hey, yo? Last I checked, my birth certificate said Zsa-Zsa La-Shae Fields, not "Hey, yo." So I turned around and looked at Ameen, because just that fast I'd been turned off.

"You know him?" Ameen asked as his chiseled jaw clinched tightly.

Before I could say no, the guy on the motorcycle said, "Zsa-Zsa." I turned back around and this cat had the nerve to be smiling, and that's when it came to me, exactly who this was. I hopped out the car. Tears of joy filled my eyes and my heart raced in my chest. "Malachi?!"

"Yeah, it's me, ma. What's good? I been looking for you since I got back in town," he said, hugging me tightly. The ring he'd given me years ago hung around my neck and pressed against his chest. "I missed you so much," he said.

"I missed you, too!" I couldn't help the tears falling down my face. I felt like such a dork. "I can't believe you're here!"

"Yeah, I'm back here for good." He wiped my eyes and continued to hold my hand. I knew for sure that Ameen was probably pissed. "You look beautiful."

"Pardon me," interrupted our moment. "You wanna introduce me to your friend?" Ameen said as he leaned over the middle console.

"I was waiting for an introduction myself," a pissed female voice chimed in. I looked up and a chick that I knew from school was standing there. I just hoped this wasn't his girl.

I turned to Ameen and said, "Ameen, this is Malachi, and Malachi, this is my boyfriend, Ameen." They gave each other a fist bump and I turned to the girl Malachi was with and said, "Don't I know you? What, are you two related?"

"This is Staci," Malachi said. "My girl."

I felt like I'd been stabbed. I swallowed, and Staci rolled her eyes at me. "Whatever," she snapped. "Can we leave now?" She hopped on the back of Malachi's bike.

"Yeah, whatever," I said, getting back into the car.

Malachi looked at me and his eyes seemed to apologize. Suddenly I remembered how it felt when he'd left the first time.

"So I'll see you around," Malachi said.

"Yeah," I said dryly, watching them take off and head down the street. "You do that."

I turned to Ameen and was greeted by the palm of his hand. I tried to move, but Ameen palmed the entire side of my face and pressed it against the window. "You gon' disrespect me!" Ameen screamed.

"Get off of me!" I tried to swat his hands, but he grabbed my wrist with his free hand and said, "I dare you to move. Move." He paused and looked at me. "Do it and see don't I pimp smack you!"

"What are you doing?" I screamed again.

"You cheating on me with that dude? Huh? You cheating on me?"

"Would you chill, Ameen?" *I can't believe this.*

"Who the hell was that?"

"Malachi!" I screamed. "He was my best friend."

"Oh, now you got best friends? So what am I? Nothing? You have to be crazy disrespecting me!"

"We were best friends when I was a kid!"

"And here I bought you a thousand dollar pair of boots trying to make up with you!" he screamed toward my ear. "And you gon' disrespect me? This is the same thing you did the other day when that dude asked you for directions." He mushed me again before letting me go. "As a matter of fact"—he grabbed the Gucci shopping bag—"these are going back." He opened the car door.

"Ameen!"

"Don't be calling me now." He took my car keys and tossed them toward me. "Call me when you know how to act!" He slammed the door behind him and disappeared up the street.

Tears filled my eyes, and all I could do was hold my hand over my mouth and cry silently.

A few minutes later I started my engine and placed the car in drive. I felt like my heart was underneath my back tires. I hated that my mind kept rewinding what had just happened, but I couldn't help it.

Everything inside of me said I was stupid for taking this. I knew I needed to walk away, especially since I grew up on my father's saying boys not 'spose to hit girls. The problem was I also grew up on, don't do what I do, do what I tell you, because every Friday night, before my father died from cancer, he would beat my mother like she stole something.

But then again this isn't really the same thing that my parents went through. I mean . . . we don't live together . . . and we aren't married. Ameen is nothing like my daddy was when he would get drunk. Ameen only yoked me up once or twice . . . okay and maybe he just mushed me . . . but still, there are times when I did defend myself. I'm not all weak like my mother.

I turned the radio up to drown out my sorrows and that's when I looked at my gas gauge and realized it was on empty . . . oh . . . my . . . God . . .

2

I couldn't wait to get home and cry in peace. The fight with Ameen was messing with every part of my being and I felt like . . . like . . . I couldn't think straight and if I didn't get my relationship back on track I was sure to wither into a thousand pieces.

I parked my car and walked to my neighbor's house to pick up my ten-year-old sister, Hadiah, who resembled a young Raven Symoné and was way too grown for her age. We were close, though, especially since more times than not my mother wasn't home and it felt like all we had was each other.

I rang my neighbor, Ms. Lucinda's, bell. She was a sweet old lady who kept Hadiah a few hours after school until I picked her up. A few seconds later Ms. Lucinda opened the door and Hadiah was standing there, giving me the eye as if to say "what took you so long?" But hmph, she would have to understand I was going through some things.

"Thank you, Ms. Lucinda," I said.

"You're welcome, baby." She smiled.

Hadiah waved and Ms. Lucinda closed the door.

"Yo," Hadiah said to me as I unlocked our front door and we walked inside. "Ms. Lucinda had me in there watching *Wheel of Fortune* and learning how to knit. I swear I can't take it." She wiped her brow. "What in the world took you so long?"

"Ms. Lucinda is a nice lady. Plus me and Ameen had an argument so I am not in the mood for your sarcasm."

"You two are always arguing," Hadiah said, exhausted. "And I may only be ten, but when Michael, my boyfriend in class, kept wanting to argue and every time I turned around he was showing off on the school playground, I dumped him. Maybe you should think about that."

"When you're seventeen you can talk to me about my boyfriend. Until then, do your homework."

"I finished my homework."

"Okay, well watch some television."

"I can't. I keep hearing *Wheel of Fortune* music in my head. I need to do something else."

"Well, you figure it out while I warm up the dinner Mommy cooked."

Hadiah followed me into the kitchen, sat down at the table, and proceeded to tell me the happenings of fourth grade as if anything they were going through compared to my drama.

Not for one minute can I tell you what she said. My mind was too busy replaying the argument I had with my man.

I warmed up the dinner of chicken, corn, and collards that my mother cooked and left for us in the refrigerator.

Lately, leaving cold dinners behind was all my mother was sure to do. Anything other than that was up for negotiation. She was never home on time or at a reasonable hour. True, she was a corrections officer for Northern State Prison, and, yes, she worked evenings, but it seemed as if we never got to see her anymore.

She was never here to know what we were doing, how we were doing, or what was going on. I used to fill her in on my day until she started falling asleep on me and then I figured if she wasn't interested, then to hell with it. Besides me and my moms never really kicked it like that anyway.

I always felt angry with her, as if she was the cause of most of my problems. Like how, after my dad died of cancer last year, she up and moved us into this house. She didn't ask how we felt or what we thought, she just moved us, and I felt like she was in a rush to leave my dad's memory behind in that dusty apartment. That's when my brother, Derrick, joined the army and never came back, leaving me and Hadiah here with my mother by ourselves.

And no, my dad wasn't the best, but he was mine, and up until he died he was always here when we came home; he always seemed interested in what we did and what we had to do. But, as I sat there with my sister in that lonely house, with tears sitting at the base of my eyes, I realized more than ever that all we have in this world is one another.

I watched my sister eat because with tears dancing on my tongue, I couldn't put a morsel of food in my mouth. "I'm going to bed," I said to her.

"Me too." She cleared the table and then looked at the

chore chart that hung on the pantry door. "Tonight is your night to wash the dishes."

"Well, it'll have to wait until tomorrow because I'm tired."

I rose from my chair, practically ran into my room, and as soon as I closed the door tears slid down my face. I looked at the clock and counted the hours that had passed since me and Ameen fell out. I couldn't fight it anymore. I needed to call Ameen at least once . . . yeah, that's it . . . only once, and if he doesn't answer then forget it. I definitely won't be sweatin' him.

I picked up my phone and called him only to get his voice mail. I swallowed the ache in my chest and tried my best to make it go away.

I changed into my silk pajamas, cut the radio on, and laid in my bed. Then it hit me, if I called Ameen one more time, he just might answer . . . so I did . . . and nothing. I hung up. A few seconds later I called again. . . . No answer. Forget it, I'm done. If he doesn't call me then, oh well, his loss.

I laid still for a few moments, and then I turned back over and looked at the phone. Okay . . . maybe just one more time and he'll answer. One more time ended up being a thousand times, and the last time I called the phone didn't even ring, his voice mail simply picked up. Which could only mean one thing; he'd turned his phone off.

I felt so stupid.

I returned to staring at the ceiling, and the last thing I remembered before I fell asleep was the radio playing slow jams and wondering how long it would take to put my life back together again.

* * *

"Zsa-Zsa La-Shae Fields, get out that bed!" stunned me
out of my sleep. Instantly I sat straight up. I felt like I'd
been fighting a war instead of coming around from being
asleep. My eyes felt heavy, and my heart was racing. I
couldn't see clearly, but I could swear I heard my mother's
voice.

"And I mean get up right now!" Now I knew for sure
that was my mother. I still couldn't see clearly, but I could
see well enough to read the electric red numbers on my
alarm clock, which said 2:00 AM. I didn't respond to my
mother's invasive voice because obviously, unless this was
an extreme emergency, the chick was trippin'. I grabbed
my pillow, snuggled under my blanket, and closed my
eyes.

"I know you heard me!" She snatched the covers off of
me and then yanked the pillow.

Now it was on. I turned over and sat up. "Are you for
real, comin' in here like this?!"

"You better shut your fresh mouth and get up to wash
those dishes! It was your night to clean the kitchen and
you just left it a mess!" She clinched her jaw. "I want you
up and those dishes washed. Now!" She flicked the light on
and I swore I went blind.

I fell straight back on the bed and prayed out loud.
"Lord Jesus, help me with this lady here because she is—"

"Excuse me?"

"Gettin' on my nerves!" I sat up. "Why would you wake
me at this time of the morning?" I looked her over. She still
had on her dark brown and tan corrections officer uniform. "You know you're not at work, right?" I said. "You
know I'm not one of those prisoners on the cell block?" I

popped my eyes open wide. "So why are you in here acting like you can't tell time?"

"I'm a little sick of your fresh mouth."

"You wake me up at two AM. What did you think we were going to talk about, the weather?"

"You know what? It's to the point where I just don't know what to do with you. Ever since your father died you just act as if I'm the enemy."

I rolled my eyes to the ceiling. I had bigger fish to fry than this: like losing my boyfriend. "Please don't act like the victim." I shook my head. "That's what you always did; you always acted like the victim when you were always the one to start it. So just go in your room so I can go back to sleep."

Apparently she didn't hear anything I just said because now she was screaming. "You don't tell me what to do! And you don't talk to me like that, I'm the mother around here!"

"Then act like it. I do everything and what do you do?! Huh? Nothing but work and ignore the hell out of us as if you are on the countdown for us to turn eighteen. So don't come up in here because I didn't wash the dishes. Acting as if you are Justine Simmons, mom of the year."

"What are you guys yelling about?" Hadiah came to my door, wiping her eyes.

"Nothing," my mother said. "Go back to bed."

Hadiah stood there.

"I said go back to bed!" my mother said, enraged.

Hadiah looked at me, and I said, "It's okay, Hadiah, go back to bed."

"You sure?" she asked with a worried look in her eyes.

"Yes." I nodded. "I'm sure. I got this."

My mother's mouth hung open, and I could tell she was a mix between being extremely pissed and her feelings being hurt. I grabbed my comforter and pillow from the floor, pointed to the door, and said, "That's called stay home more." Not that I wanted her around, but Hadiah needed her.

"I will not have you disrespecting me," my mother said. "I swear ever since your father died everything around here is turned upside down!"

"Oh, now you wanna blame daddy? Here you go again being the victim."

"I was a victim! Your father beat the hell out of me!"

"Well, now he's dead so you don't have to put up with him! All you did was call the cops on him anyway!"

"We had problems, and he had no right to put his hands on me!"

"Then you should've shut your mouth and kept quiet. Then he wouldn't have been stressed behind you, got cancer, and died. You couldn't even wait for the ink to dry on his insurance papers before you ran and bought this house. And you only bought it so that there would be no memories of him here! You ain't slick, I know your tricks and you don't have to hold your breath because when I'm eighteen I'm out of here! Now cut my light off and you're dismissed!"

WHACK!!!! Have you ever seen shooting stars in the middle of your room? I could've sworn that my mother's backhand across my face sent me to the edge of the Big Dipper, but I'm not sure. All I knew is that my ear was ringing and the left side of my face was burning. The same side that Ameen had left a bruise on.

"Let me tell you something!" My mother walked up so

close to me that I thought she was going to push me through the wall. "You don't know anything about what me and your father have gone through. You don't know how many nights I cried and begged and pleaded for him to change, for me to change, for us to change! You think I like what we went through?! But you know what, I don't have to explain anything to you, you're a child. You will get it together, come hell or high water you will learn to respect me."

I started to repeat the same things back to her, but I didn't. I simply turned over toward the wall and within the next few minutes I heard my door slam. The tears that had been haunting me all night had returned and were now sliding down my cheeks. I thought about Ameen and wished for a moment that I could share with him the argument I had just had with my mother. So I picked up the phone to call him, only to be greeted by his voice mail . . . again.

Don't look now, but my life was hell.

"Zsa-Zsa." Hadiah knocked on my door and simultaneously tipped into my room.

"Wassup?" I wiped the crust from my eyes and looked at the clock: six AM. Time to get up and get ready for school. I grabbed my cell phone but there were no missed calls, which meant that Ameen didn't think about me all night. "Yeah, Hadiah, what is it?"

"Man down." She placed her hands on her hips. "It's about to be a man down situation."

Life according to my sister was always a man down situation. So instead of responding I got out of bed and walked over to my closet to pick out my clothes for today.

For a moment the Gucci boots Ameen bought me and took back ran across my mind. "I want you to wear that soft pink Apple Bottoms sweat suit," I said to Hadiah. "The one I bought you and those white and pink air force ones. I'm wearing my True Religion skinny leg jeans and pink tee with my pearl accessories and Prada heels."

"Did you hear me?" Hadiah placed her hands on her hips. "I said Mommy is shuttin' the world down. She's on the phone with Aunty Grier right now crying and complaining about us."

"What? Complaining?" Now she had my attention.

"Yeah." She twisted her neck. "Said something about you being out of control and me being too grown. Can you imagine?" Her eyes bugged out. "Me being too grown? Hmph, she got me messed up."

"Are you sure she's on the phone with Aunty Grier, in Georgia?"

"Listen at this." She handed me the cordless phone she had in her hand. I pushed the talk button and my mother was complaining so much she didn't even notice we were on the line.

Hadiah and I placed the phone in between our ears and listened. "I just need some help," my mother cried. "I can't lose my girls. Derrick is already gone. He's in the army and he never comes back home. I just don't know what to do."

"Stop crying, Jazmyn," Aunty Grier said. "I know how you feel. When Tre left home I didn't know what I would do, but I made it and you can, too. You want to come down to Atlanta and move in with me, Noah, Man-Man, Cousin Shake, and his wife? We would love to have you.

The girls are in school and they come home every weekend. This house is huge and there is more than enough room."

"She better not say we're moving to Georgia," I mouthed to Hadiah.

"I will die if she does," Hadiah whispered back.

"You know I can't do that." My mother sniffed.

Thank you.

"Okay, well, the only other thing I can think of is Cousin Shake and Ms. Minnie coming up there. I know they'll be happy to help out."

Cousin Shake, oh, hell, no.

"You really think they won't mind?" my mother asked.

Why is she entertaining this?

"I know they won't. You know how he was when we were little."

My mother laughed. "Don't remind me."

"Well, he hasn't changed much, except now he has a new wife and unlike when we were young he isn't stuck in the seventies, it's now the eighties. . . . Oh, and the hearse still works."

The hearse?

I couldn't take it anymore so I clicked us off the line. Hadiah looked at me. "Don't you have enough money for us to bounce and have our own place?"

I shook my head no.

"I can't believe this," she cried. "I looked up to you and you're broke."

"We'll survive, Hadiah."

"No, we won't. Man down." She wiped her eyes. "Man the hell down."

All I could think to say was, "Don't cuss. Something will work out, but I can't allow you to cuss."

"Cussin' is the least of our problems." And she walked out my room.

I sat down on the edge of my bed and placed my head in my hands.

God must hate me.

3

If this isn't love, tell me what it is . . .

—JENNIFER HUDSON, "IF THIS ISN'T LOVE"

I called Ameen a thousand times before I left for school that morning, and not once did he answer. Of course I was pissed, and since I had no one to take my anger out on, I barked at Asha and Courtney. "For once," I snapped as they filed in my car on our way to school, "can you two be on time?" I looked up at Courtney, who had a hot-pink boa wrapped around his neck with the ends running down his white ruffle shirt. His red patent leather pants were Jonas Brothers tight, and all I could do was shake my head. He looked like a big ball of red grease. "And don't slam my door!" I said as Courtney climbed in the backseat and Asha, who wore Aeropostale jeans, a fitted purple tee, and matching accessories, sat in the front.

"Oh, hell, nawl." Courtney threw the ends of his boa to the back of his shoulders. "Not this morning. Trust me; you don't want it over here." He wagged his finger. "My mother told me off because I didn't clean my room. My daddy caught an attitude because he said I was holding my wrist limp for too long, as if he hasn't gotten the point yet. And my dog shitted on my floor, so don't"—he popped his lips—"even go there."

"Whatever," I said as I pulled off and we headed down the street.

Asha cut her eyes at me and proceeded to slide in a CD Courtney handed her, and within an instant Aretha Franklin's "Natural Woman" filled the car. If it wasn't for the truck behind me I would've come to a screeching halt. "What is this?!" I screamed as I turned off the CD.

"What is your problem?" Asha asked.

"Look, maybe you didn't hear me the first time," Courtney said, "but today ain't the day. I'm PMSing like crazy and I don't have time for your foolishness. Now if you are mad at Ameen we can discuss this. Otherwise cut my damn CD back on, because if I don't hear me some Aretha this morning it's gon' be a situation."

"Know what," I said, turning the CD back on, "I'm not gon' even argue with you this morning."

"Thank you for the consideration," Courtney said as the music came through the speakers and he laid his head back against the back headrest. "You don't ever mess with a black man and his music," he said as he closed his eyes.

After a few minutes of driving to school, Asha popped the gum she was chewing and said, "You may as well just tell us what happened, otherwise you gon' be buggin' all day."

"I don't feel like talking about it." I paused and then quickly decided that I needed somebody to confide in. "Me and Ameen had an argument yesterday," I confessed.

"Why?" Courtney asked.

"Because . . . remember Malachi from elementary school?"

"Yeah," Asha said.

"Well, he moved back here to Jersey, and when me and Ameen were together yesterday I saw Malachi. Ameen got mad because I hugged Malachi and said that I was showing off. He left me in the middle of the street, the car was running, I swear I was soooooo humiliated." I intentionally left out being mushed against the window.

"Have you talked to him since then?" Asha asked.

"No," I said somberly. "I called him but he won't call me back. And you know . . . like I'm just so tired of the changes."

"You said once before that you were thinking about taking a break. Why don't you take a break now?"

I could've slapped Asha; I hated it when she threw things up in my face. " 'Cause I wanna take a break when I wanna take a break, which is not now. Ameen is a good guy—"

"Who left you in the middle of the street—"

"He just has a jealous streak."

"You always have an excuse for him."

"I don't have to make up excuses for him. And I don't have to argue with you over my man."

"I didn't know it was an argument," Asha snapped. "All I'm saying is that if he has more jealous fits than anything else, then something is not right."

I sucked my teeth. "When you get a steady man you give me advice."

"And when you get a man," she snapped, "you let me know."

"Can you two retreat to your corners?" Courtney tapped his finger on the back window as I pulled into the school's parking lot. "And look at Jesus and His disciple."

Asha and I turned and looked out the passenger side window at two dudes parking their motorcycles next to us. When they took their helmets off, I realized that one of them was Malachi. He had on a pair of black Tims, slightly baggy True Religion jeans, a white tee with a skull in the center, and a black leather jacket. He held his helmet in his hand, leaned against his bike, and stared at me.

"Why are you blushing?" Asha tapped me on the shoulder.

"Please, don't even play me like that." I rolled my eyes, "I am not blushing, that's only Malachi."

"Daaaaannnng," Courtney said, "two snaps up and a fruit loop . . . would you look at li'l daddy here."

"And who is that other hottie?" Asha asked.

"I don't know." I hunched my shoulders, looking at the guy standing beside Malachi. I had to admit even in the midst of being pissed that the guy was a cutie: deep chocolate skin, spinning waves, almond-shaped eyes, and a goatee. "He is cute, though."

"I called him first," Asha said. "Now introduce me."

"Didn't I just say I didn't know him?"

"Go find out who he is from Malachi," she said to me, and then turned to Courtney. "How does my breath smell?" She blew air into his face.

"Oh, my." He placed his hand over his nose and fell back against the seat. "I've been shot with dog poo."

Asha playfully punched Courtney on the arm. "This is serious and you play too much."

Courtney laughed. "It smells ai'ight, but your lips need a li'l gloss." Courtney handed her his clear MAC gloss. "And how do I look, I look okay?" he asked.

"And who gon' be checking you out?" I had to ask.

"I just want to be in the atmosphere." Courtney took his pocket mirror from his pageboy bag, flipped it open, and batted his lashes at his reflection.

"You know what," I said, "I'm cold on this." I got out the car and I could hear Asha whispering, "Introduce me." I closed the door behind me, walked past Malachi and his mysterious friend, without speaking. Stank, I know, but so what? I was pissed and when my love life isn't right the whole world shuts down.

Once I walked through the doors the bell rang, and I headed to homeroom class. If only I could have gotten the memory of my fight with Ameen and the aching feeling to have left my stomach I would have been cool.

By the time the bell rang again, I'd slyly texted Ameen a thousand times but not once did I get a reply. I placed my phone back in my purse, wrote down the homework assignment, and headed to my locker to get the book for my next class.

I stood at my locker, exchanged books, and when I looked in the mirror that hung inside of my door I saw Malachi's reflection behind me. Don't ask me why but I was blushing like crazy.

"Crime to speak, ma?" He placed his head on my shoulder, pressed his cheek against mine, and looked into the eyes of my reflection.

"No, speaking is not a crime but stalking is," I snapped. I shook my head. There had to be a law against a man being this fine. I swear this dude was knocking me off my square. I diverted my eyes from his reflection and he stood up straight.

I did my best not to be nervous as I tapped the ball of my stilettos on the tiled floor, closed my locker door, and turned around to face him. Malachi slid the tip of his index finger through my belt loop, pulled me toward him, and kissed me on my forehead. "Damn, look at you." He joked. "You sweatin' already."

"Whatever." I waved my hand while praying that he couldn't hear my heart thundering in my chest. "I'm starting to get concerned, why are you following me?"

Malachi laughed. "I go to school here."

Why the heck am I nervous? "Isn't it a little late?" I rolled my eyes. "The first day was last week."

"What's with you and the attitude? And what's up with eye action—chill with all that. That ain't even for you."

He's right, I am being a li'l extra . . . but still.

He stroked my cheek. "Or are you mad because I made you wait so long. My apologies for holding up our life together, but I'm back now."

Was it me or was this cat bold? Didn't he have a girl? Or better yet, didn't I have a man?

"Malachi!" A loud male voice called him from down the hall, and immediately I took a step back. Instead of letting my belt loop go, Malachi held on to it.

"Yo." His friend nodded his head at me as if to say hello, then he said to Malachi, "You know li'l ma over there?" He pointed.

Instinctively I turned around and noticed that he was pointing to Asha. "That's my homegirl." I butted into their conversation.

"Yo, hook that up," he said to me, and then he looked back at Malachi. "Dawg, you see li'l shortie-rock? She pretty as hell, and man, she thick like a mug."

"And your name is?" I asked.

"This is my cousin, Samaad," Malachi said. "And Samaad, this is Zsa-Zsa."

Samaad smiled. "Oh, you're Zsa-Zsa? Heard a lot about you. Now, be a good in-law and hook that up."

In-law? That threw me for a loop. I stared at Malachi, and he fingered the ring dangling from the gold chain around my neck. "I see you missed me."

I took a step back. This was too much. I held my index finger up and told Samaad, "Give me a minute." I walked over to Asha, who was talking to Courtney. "My fault," I said to them. "I know I was buggin' earlier. I'm sorry."

"Yeah, you were buggin'," Courtney said.

"Exactly." Asha twisted her lips, and I could tell she was pissed.

"Awwl, Diva." I hugged her. "Don't be mad, you know I love you and you're my best friend."

"Whatever." She laughed. "Did you do the hook-up?"

"I didn't have to. He walked over there to Malachi already sweatin' you."

"Daaaang," Courtney said, "that's what I'm talkin' about. What did he say?"

"He was like"—I smacked my lips—" 'who is shortie over there?' "

"And you're sure he wasn't talking about me?" Courtney asked.

"You get a li'l carried away sometimes." I shook my head. "Asha, he's waiting on you."

"Waiting on me? He better come over here. I am not"—

she twisted her lips—"walking over there looking all easy and greasy. He has to come to me."

I gave her a high five. "And you know this."

I walked back over to Malachi, who was still standing next to Samaad and now Staci, who had worked her way in front of Malachi's locker. I couldn't help but suck my teeth. "Look," I said to Samaad, "my homegirl thinks you're cute but you know we don't run up on men." I looked over at Staci. "We ain't all thirsty."

"Who you talking to?" she snapped.

I ignored her and continued talking to Samaad. "Anyway, my friend's name is Asha, and she's expecting you."

"Good lookin' out." He smiled and left me standing there. Before I could walk away from Malachi and Staci, who had her face twisted, the bell rang again and everyone headed to class.

For the next three periods straight all I thought about was Malachi. Something was terribly wrong with this because I was supposed to be heartbroken over Ameen, not contemplating cheating. The problem was my heart kept forgetting what my mind wouldn't let go of.

I needed desperately to get back on track so I could maintain my focus: getting Ameen back.

I was in English class, and for the first time since school started I completed my classwork without the interruption of my vibrating phone letting me know Ameen was calling or sending me a text message. Utter silence was coming from my Prada bag, and I swore my love life was M.I.A.

By the time I got to chemistry, I was thinking and rethinking what I could've done differently about my baby

. . . and then suddenly, as if a light autumn breeze had come my way, Malachi and I were on his bike riding in New York—Central Park—kickin' it and holding hands, eating cotton candy and laughing at each other's jokes. We shared a soda, and just when he'd asked me to be his girl is when the bell rang and I realized I was daydreaming about the wrong man.

This was a hot mess!

It was lunchtime and I felt out of my mind. Ameen had yet to call me back and just for GP sake I walked to the side door and peeked outside, only to see nothing. Damn.

I walked into the cafeteria and thought I could cry my heart out to my best friends, but they were both preoccupied. Asha and Samaad were sharing a secluded corner and Courtney was arguing with this dude named Otis. "How you gon' get mad," I heard Courtney say to Otis.

" 'Cause somebody think you sexy? Don't that sound crazy to you? I have a right to my opinion."

I definitely wasn't about to become part of that conversation; besides, Courtney could hold his own. Instead I stood in the lunch line and grabbed a salad and a bottle of water. It's not that I was on a health food kick, it's that I didn't have an appetite, so there was no need to waste much money. I walked toward an empty table and "You don't see me sitting here?" floated my way. It was Malachi, and there was no way I could fight back the smile on my face, so I let it go. I walked over to the table where Malachi was and sat down.

"Why do you seem so mad at me?" he asked as I started sipping my water.

I blew air out the side of my mouth. "You really don't know?" I tooted my lips.

"No, and don't give me a riddle, I don't want to guess, I just want to know so we can move on."

For some reason tears danced on my tongue but I was able to fight them. "I don't wanna talk about it."

"We're not twelve anymore."

"You don't have to tell me that."

"Then why can't you express yourself?"

"For the same reasons you didn't tell me you were moving and when I went to look for you, you were gone."

"It was different then, Zsa. I had no choice."

"You could've told me."

"I was twelve years old. I didn't know how to do that," he said.

"Well, it is what it is."

"But it doesn't have to be."

"Excuse me, but don't you have a girl, playboy?"

"You concerned about my girl? 'Cause I'm damn sure not fazed by your man."

"So what do you think—we gon' all be one big happy couple? Not."

Malachi laughed. "Listen, Staci's family and my family are close. People expected us to grow up and be together . . . so we've been kickin' it off and on long distance for a minute. But now that I'm here in Jersey, I'm not so sure if I'm feeling the relationship anymore."

"And when did that change?"

"When I saw you."

Silence. I didn't know what to say or better yet what to do after that comment.

"Zsa, I'm sorry about leaving you. I am, but how long are you going to act like this?"

I couldn't help but blush. "I missed you, you know that," I admitted.

"Now I do." He took my water from my hand and had a sip. "So wassup with your boy?"

"Who?"

"The dude you were with the other day. Do you love him like you love me?"

I looked into his face and just as I had made up my mind to keep it one hundred with him, and admit that I loved Malachi more, I noticed Staci standing at Malachi's shoulder. "None of that matters now does it?" I stood up as the bell rang and walked away.

4

If I were a boy
I think I could understand how it feels to love a girl
I swear I'd be a better man . . .

—Beyoncé, "If I Were a Boy"

I felt as if I had weights pressed against my tongue. I hadn't heard from Ameen in three days, and I swear I could do nothing without crying. I couldn't eat, couldn't sleep, and I promise you I wanted no one—and I mean no one—who lived in my house to talk to me. Everything they said got on my nerves, and in return I greeted them with straight attitude. I wanted to scream, "Don't you see my heart is bleeding on the floor? Can't you see that I'm missing my man like crazy? Can't you see that nothing you say to me will be as important as what I'm feeling right now? Can't you just leave me the hell alone?"

But, no, my mother stayed in my neck about making sure the house stayed clean and the dishes were washed. And Hadiah was in my face every day telling me stories about what went on with her in school.

Can you say inconsiderate?

I laid faceup on my bed while slow jams serenaded me in the background, and I wondered why I couldn't have the perfect life. Why did everything have to be so compli-cated and confusing? Why couldn't Ameen understand me and be reasonable?

This was hell.

I turned on my side and wondered who I could call and confide my sorrows in, but I really didn't want to hear Asha or Courtney's opinion, and I most definitely would cut somebody if they even suggested that I quit my baby. So I decided that the only one who could handle my se-crets were the pages of my diary.

I took my sacred book from my nightstand and bled my sorrows onto the pages.

Dear Diary:
Life is so confusing. Sometimes I wonder if people are really happy or if they are just faking the funk and along for the ride. I feel so stupid with Ameen . . . like . . . like . . . I'm not good enough for him to treat me well and to love me right. I just want peace. I swear, I wish that Ameen could see that it's all about him. I wish I could see into the future, so I would know when this pain would be ending. Or better yet, I wish I had somebody to talk to . . . my friends are too opinionated and my mother. Paleeze.

Of course my mother was at work. Ever since my father died, finding other things to do besides staying home had been her answer to everything. And I guess I could under-stand it. I didn't like to stay at home either. But still . . . I was there sometimes. And talking to her? Not. Every time I'd tried to talk to her, her answer to everything was, "Pray about it." Or "pray for him, pray for her, pray for it." So I just stopped asking her anything. And now when she asked me questions as if she was actually interested in my life, I simply said to her, "I prayed about it already."

Anyway, today was typical, me in tears.

I held my diary to my chest, laid down with my face on the pillow, and cried . . . again.

An hour later, I turned over on my side and my heart throbbed. Ciara's "Never Ever" was playing, and as my mind absorbed each and every lyric I felt as if I had drowned in depression.

I reached over to my nightstand, flipped to another radio station. Beyoncé was singing about being a boy. I promise you, I had gone insane.

I felt bad enough as it was. I didn't need the radio pouring salt in my wounds. The memory of what happened between me and Ameen played over and over again at least a thousand times in my head, each time with a different ending and a different way I should've said what I had to say.

I looked at the clock and only fifteen minutes had passed. Yo, I was buggin'. I turned to lay on my back and stared at the ceiling. . . . Being without my baby was killing me and I couldn't take it. I picked up my cell phone and called him, but of course he sent me straight to voice mail. I hung up feeling even more pathetic.

It was official, I'd lost my mind. The clock was creeping time by, and forever was passing my way. I thought about driving over to Ameen's place unannounced, but then again maybe not. The last time I pulled that he made me get back in my car, call him on my cell phone, and ask permission to come to his house. I thought it was funny, so I did it. Only for him to tell me, "no," he was going to sleep. Not wanting to repeat that drama I quickly erased the pop-up-over-his-spot idea from my mind . . . but then again, I could always do a drive-by.

Just when I decided I should give up and let myself wither away, my phone rang. I didn't even look at the caller ID. I was too scared of being disappointed . . . but of course you know I had to play it off, so I flipped the radio to 105.1 where Jamie Foxx and T-Pain were singing about blaming it on the alcohol. "You rang?" I answered my line.

"Dang, girl," Asha said, "you sound good for somebody who's brokenhearted."

"You sure do," Courtney chimed in. "I would be crying my eyes out."

I sucked my teeth. "What y'all tricks want?"

"Whatever." Asha laughed.

"Especially since you're not doing anything but sulking behind Ameen's dusty butt." Courtney laughed.

"Don't call my baby dusty," I said defensively. This is why I hated to confide in them, because they always threw it back in my face at the wrong time.

"Did you talk to him yet?" Asha asked.

"No," I snapped. "Do I look like a donkey? I'm not sweatin' no man."

"Dang, girl," Courtney said, "you're real strong, 'cause I would be listening to a buncha sad songs, crying, and asking God why."

"Not." I faked a laugh, hating that he'd just described me to a tee. "Look, Ameen knows I am not the one to be chasin' him so when he gets over his tantrum he'll call me, but other than that I'm doin' me."

"Cool," Asha said. "So, come hang out with us at the Chocolate Bar."

"I'm not going there," I said. "You know er'body and their mama will be there, and I am not trying to see Ameen."

"Why you frontin'?" Asha said. "You know Ameen is exactly who you wanna see."

"Uhm-hmm," Courtney said, "so throw on your gear extra cute and meet us outside in a few minutes."

"Who's driving?" I asked.

"Me," Courtney said. "Granny let me borrow the Mary Kay Cadillac."

"Courtney, you don't even have a license."

Asha laughed. "I'm driving. I borrowed my brother's car."

Reluctantly I slid on a pair of tight Juicy jeans, a fitted Juicy tee, and a midriff denim jacket, with silver accessories and black stilettos. By the time I was done my friends were in front of my house waiting for me.

"Dang!" Courtney said, as I climbed into the backseat. "Why are your eyes so swollen? Oh, my, you've been lying to us. You been crying all night."

"Whatever," I snapped, knowing that tears were dancing in my mouth right now.

When we got to the Chocolate Bar the place was packed. We saw everybody from school and the hood in the place. We kicked it with a few people and then the hostess showed us our table.

The bad part about being there was that the food was slamming but I didn't have an appetite.

Courtney and Asha were talking about something—

what, I don't know—because of course my mind had wan-
dered back to my man, which is why when I heard, "Yo"
float over my shoulders, I thought it was my imagination.
At least until I heard it again. "Yo, Zsa." Now, that was
Ameen. I felt like screaming and jumping up in glee. It's a
good thing I always looked good when I went out—kept
this dude on his toes and gave him something to worry
about. I did my best to suppress my smile as I looked up
into his beautiful face, twisted my lips, and said, "May I
help you?"

The vein on the side of Ameen's neck was thumping,
causing the tattoo on his neck to rise. "Let me hollah at
you for a second."

"Nope." My eyes combed the menu.

"What did you say?" Ameen asked in disbelief.

"She said bye." Courtney gave Ameen a salute.

"See ya," Asha followed up.

"Yo," Ameen said sternly, "I'm not playin'."

I sucked my teeth, rolled my eyes, and turned to my
friends. "Just give me a minute to see what he wants. I'll
be back." I walked away quickly before either of them
could say something sarcastic.

Ameen and I walked into a secluded spot in the hallway
and instead of talking he stood back and looked at me as if
I were crazy.

"Okay." I looked around. "Wassup? What is it?"

"Me and you have an argument and instead of continu-
ing to apologize you chillin' with Mrs. Big Drawls and Ru-
Paul?"

"Don't talk about my friends. And anyway, you know
how many times I called you? Please."

"Please what?"

"Excuse *you?*" I said, taken aback. "You thought I was supposed to stay home and cry over you forever? Not."

"You tryna show off?" He pointed in my face.

"You're the one who hasn't been answering your phone!"

"You were on punishment. Don't try and get brand new like you didn't know the drill."

"On punishment? Excuse you. I'm not a kid. I am grown."

"Then act like it. Now, go get your things, we're leaving."

"Boy, please, don't even play yourself. I wish I would leave."

"You're not listening now?" He walked up close to me and I felt like he could swallow every breath I took.

"All I'm saying is that I'm here with Courtney and Asha. I can't just leave like that."

"Oh, so they are more important than me?"

"I didn't say that."

"I see where this is goin'. Ai'ight then," Ameen said.

"Ameen, don't be like that."

"Nah, you don't have to come. It's no thing. I mean, we have a li'l disagreement and now you treat me like this. It's cool. We're done." He walked away.

I caught hold of Ameen's forearm. "Ameen, stop playin'. Just hold it, give me a minute."

"Didn't I just say you didn't have to come with me? I can get me some company if that's what I need to do."

"Don't play with me!" I snapped as I pulled out my phone and texted Asha and Courtney. "Call me later. Ameen needs me."

We stepped into the parking lot and I followed Ameen to a hot-pink Toyota Corolla. "Whose car is that, Ameen?"

"My sister's friend's cousin's car. She let me hold it for a few days."

"Sister's friend who? And why would they let you hold their car?"

"You getting in or not?"

I sighed. I knew this was bananas. "I just don't feel comfortable being in this car," I said.

"Then don't get in." Ameen slid in the car and put the keys in the ignition.

Reluctantly I slid into the car. "Ameen, I hope we don't keep going through these changes."

"Yo, are you gon' nag me? 'Cause if you naggin' you can stay here. But I'm trying to be a man about the situation and show you some attention. I mean, I left my people in there and my food on the table to be able to kick it with you—"

Ameen did have a point. "Ameen, sometimes I just feel . . ."

"Zsa, can we have one conversation where we don't talk about how you feel? I swear, you are so selfish. How about how I feel? I'm over here stressed over you and you out partying with your friends."

"Why are you so extreme?" I said, exhausted.

"Oh, now you usin' big words? Extreme?"

"Ameen, I love you. You know that."

"All I know is what I see. And what I see is that you don't appreciate me. I mean, if you want me to step just say that."

"No." I turned to him. "I don't want you to go any- where."

"Well, show me how much you want me to stay," he said as he pulled into a secluded section of the parking lot. He climbed over the console and pushed my seat all the way back.

"You know I missed you." He started kissing me.

"And I missed you too," I said, feeling my heart become at ease a few seconds later. And we started to kiss and do things that only the night would witness.

5

Ring the alarm, I've been through this too long . . .

—Beyoncé, "Ring the Alarm"

The crisp autumn wind blew through my hair as I drove over to Ameen's house. I turned the radio on and Jay-Z and Young Jeezy were singing about our president being black. I looked in the rearview mirror and I was too cute for words, my heart was at ease, and I felt as if world peace was achievable again.

I placed my car in gear and my cell phone rang. Asha . . . dang, I should've known she was a little too quiet for too long. I hadn't spoken to her since the night we were together at the Chocolate Bar. I started not to answer the phone, but then again I didn't feel like her cussin' my voice mail out. So heck, whatever, she's not my mother and I can take whatever smart thing she has to say.

"You rang?" I flipped my phone open and said as if I didn't have a care in the world.

"You, shiesty bird, how you gon' stand us up?" Asha spat as I started to drive toward Ameen's.

"I didn't stand you up, I texted you."

"You are soooo pathetic. I'll be so glad when you stop lettin' this cat play you. Oh, I can't stand him."

"He is not playin' me, first of all." I waved my index finger as if she could actually see me. "See, this is why I hate telling you anything."

"Whatever. You're the one who told us about how bad he treated you and now you're mad because we're pissed off about it?"

"Well, I'm not mad anymore."

"No, 'cause you too busy wantin' to cupcake with this dude to see that he's doggin' you. You just met him yesterday, dang. I wish you would just dump him."

"Let me shut you down real quick. Ameen and I have been together for six months, that's a long time. And for real, for real, I don't have to explain anything to you. Just because you don't believe in giving your man a second chance and you up and dumped Bryan—"

"Because he cheated on me. I got the hint!" she screamed.

"Well, Ameen is not cheating on me."

"Okay, Zsa-Zsa," she said calmly. "I'm not gon' argue with you. If you like it, I love it. So anyway, Samaad just called and said he and Malachi would be hanging tonight at Club Heated. I borrowed my brother's car, so me and Courtney about to hit the spot. You rollin'?"

"No, I'm about to go and see Ameen."

She didn't even respond, she simply hung up. Whatever, trust me, I know how to keep my man, and if I don't do right by him somebody else will be right there to jock my spot. And believe me, I am *not* the one.

I parked in front of Ameen's building. After I got out of the car I smiled and waved at a few of Ameen's partners and I headed into the lobby. The hallway was dark, and the only light came from a naked and blinking bulb hung over the mailboxes. I walked up the stairs, taking two at a time, and then suddenly I came to an abrupt halt and felt as if I'd hit a brick wall. "Dang." I looked up and realized I'd just bumped into Malachi, and said, "You can't say excuse me?"

"Not when somebody bumps into me," he said as he looked down into my face, and it suddenly occurred to me that he was even finer than the last time I saw him.

Don't ask me why, but I stumbled back to the step below and he grabbed my hand. "Heels too high?" He laughed, stepping onto the same step as me.

"No," I snapped, enjoying our closeness a bit too much for my boyfriend to be two flights up. "What are you doing here?"

"Samaad lives here. What you doing here?"

"My boyfriend lives here."

"Your boyfriend?" He smirked.

"Yeah, my boyfriend. The one that I love and *trust* to never leave me."

"Ma." He gave me a one-sided grin. "You don't even believe that." He placed his hands on my waist and pressed his lips against mine. Oh . . . my . . . God. I couldn't believe this. "What are we doing?" I asked as he slid his luscious tongue into my mouth.

"Exactly what you want me to do," he said as we started to kiss passionately. It felt like the Fourth of July, Christmas, and my birthday all in one.

"I'm ready whenever you are." He gave me one last peck, and afterward he lifted me by my waist, placed me to the side of him, and walked down the stairs. I stood there for a moment and watched him until his presence became a faded blur. I swear I didn't know what to think . . . and then I wondered if that had just happened. *Nah it didn't . . . yes it did, nah . . . wait a minute . . . ummm, can anyone tell me, what just happened here?*

After a few unexpectant minutes of standing in the hallway I headed to Ameen's apartment. I could smell fried chicken cooking, and the music playing inside was so loud that the door shook. The door was unlocked, and after I knocked for a few seconds and no one answered I just walked in. Ameen's mother was sitting on her boyfriend's lap watching TV, while Ameen's sister and her friends were in the kitchen cooking.

"Hello." I waved, no matter what my mother taught me to speak.

"Did Ameen know you were coming over here?" his mother asked me, and I couldn't believe it. She'd never spoken three words to me.

"Yes," I said as I sucked my teeth.

"You better watch your tone," she snapped.

"All I said was yes."

"Is she gettin' smart?" His sister jumped into our conversation.

"Oh . . . kay . . . and all this beef is coming from where? All I wanna know," I said as calmly as possible, "is if Ameen is here?"

"Wait a minute." His mother got off her boyfriend's lap and went to knock on Ameen's door. " 'Cause I ain't up for no nonsense in my house tonight. Anybody get to fightin' up in here goin' to jail." She banged on Ameen's door and he cracked it open. "Did you know this boogzie li'l girl was rollin' over here?"

"Who? Zsa-Zsa?" he said from behind the door.

What does he mean, who, Zsa-Zsa?

"I guess that's her name. She can't have a regular name like Khadejah, Al-Keema, or one of them? A Zsa-Zsa . . . what kinda bull is that?"

"Ai'ight, ma," he said, "just tell her to come in here."

She turned around and snapped toward me, "He said bring ya li'l high sadity behind on."

I hurried and walked past her. I didn't wanna be held accountable for smacking his mama.

"Why was your mother acting like that?" I asked Ameen as he closed the door behind me.

"She didn't know I was having company, that all." He started kissing on me.

"And what did you mean when you said, 'Who, Zsa-Zsa'? You got somebody else coming over here?"

"Don't start, Zsa." He stopped kissing me.

"And what did she mean by, 'if somebody come over here fighting they're going to jail'?" I looked him over and noticed scratches on his neck and shoulder. "And what are those scratches on you? Have you been fighting?"

"Zsa, why are you buggin'?"

"I'm not buggin', why can't you tell me the truth? Was some other chick over here?" My voice trembled.

"Zsa—"

A lump filled my throat. "Know what, I'ma go home." I opened his door and he closed it back.

"What are you doin'?"

"I think you been bringing other girls over here."

He shook his head.

"See"—tears filled my eyes—"I'm out."

"Ai'ight, man, just listen. It wasn't nothin', for real. My son's mother came over here to get some money."

"Your son's mother?" I twisted my lips in disbelief.

"You want me to tell the story or you got it from here?"

"Go 'head." I leaned from one foot to the next.

"She found your picture"—he went in his dresser drawer, pulled a framed picture of me out, and sat it on top—"and she caught a serious attitude."

"Umm-hmm." I folded my arms across my breasts. "Did that really happen?"

"What I'ma lie for, Zsa-Zsa?"

"You tell me."

"I'm not lyin' man, chill. She started buggin' because I told her that I loved you and she started fighting me."

"I told you," I said, "that you needed to tell her about us before."

"Well, she knows now so the rest is on her."

"Ameen, do you really love me, though? Because sometimes I just feel—"

"Look, how many chicks you think I bring around my family? My family now, not my boys. But my moms, my sister, and my niece. Only you and my son's mother. That's it. It's all about you and you know that." He kissed me on my shoulder. "So chill."

"Alright, Ameen," I said, melting into the kisses he was placing on taboo parts of my body.

An hour later after we were done committing our sins and had both showered, I noticed that Ameen was getting fully dressed and had slipped his Tims on. "Where are you going?" I asked him.

He paused and then said, "Umm, I need to run by the church for my mother. Umm, I promised her I would deliver two dinners to the monks there."

"Monks?"

"You know what I mean. What's that they call those people that head the church. The ushers."

"You mean the pastor?"

"Yeah, him. I need to deliver two dinners to the pastor."

"Okay, well, I'm going with you." I reached for my shoes.

"Nah, it won't take me long, I'll be right back."

"How long?"

"An hour."

I hated that I felt like he was lying, but a part of me wanted to believe what he was saying was true. "An hour?" I twisted my lips. "If you say so," I said, not wanting to start another argument.

"An hour, baby, that's it." He kissed me on the neck, picked up my car keys, and walked out the door.

When I knew for certain he was gone I started rummaging through his things. I guess he expected it, because I found nothing. After a while I felt stupid sitting there alone. I thought about leaving, but then again, how would I? Ameen had my ride.

I decided to forget it. I'd wait it out and then when he came back I'd let him know that I didn't appreciate him leaving me here like that. But then again, I really shouldn't have been worried because if he had another chick, how much attention was she really getting when I was in his room alone?

I picked up the remote to his TV and turned it on. Two hours later, I'd had enough of MTV. I turned to look out his window, and out the corner of my eye I noticed my cell phone, which had been on vibrate, blinking. I picked the

phone up and I had three missed calls, all from Asha. As
soon as I decided I'd call her back tomorrow, my cell
phone was ringing again. "What, Asha?" I answered.

"Where are you?" she asked. Her voice sounded as if she
were in a hurry.

"With Ameen."

"You are physically with Ameen?" she asked as if she
didn't believe me.

"Yes," I continued, "we're sitting here watching a movie."

"Well"—I heard her smirk—"this must be what we call
ghetto twins because it's some dude right here in Club
Heated hanging on some busted bitch, feeling all over her
and kissing her on the neck."

I couldn't believe this. My heart started pounding.
"What?"

"It's nothin'," she said. "It's obvious I have the wrong
cat."

"Come get me."

"Come get you?" she screeched. "Then that means I
have to pay twice to get up in here. Hell, no, catch the
bus."

"Asha, now is not the time to be frontin'." My heart was
beating so fast I swore it would fall out my chest. "I'm at
Ameen's. Call me when you're in front of the building."

"You're lucky we're friends," she said, and then hung
up.

Ten minutes later Asha was waiting outside. I stormed
down the stairs and into Asha's car. "Where's Courtney?" I
asked Asha as she pulled off.

"I left him at the club to keep an eye on Black Romeo.
Plus he doesn't really have any money so it didn't make
sense for both of us to pay twice."

Asha kept talking about something but all I could think about was how the lump in my throat was due to explode. Somewhere inside of me I knew that Ameen was cheating. But then again he was with me practically every day, so when did he have time to cheat?

"You know what, Asha," I said as if we were in the midst of a conversation, "if Ameen is cheating on me then why doesn't he just leave me alone?"

"He probably really likes you."

"So then . . . why the other girls?"

"Because he likes them too."

"But Ameen can be honest with me. If he wants to see other people then all he has to do is tell me and I'll leave him alone."

"What?" she said, confused. "Why is everything on his terms? I'm telling you he's doin' him, can't you see that? Just bounce. Be out. You always let him use your car, he's all sleepin' with you whenever the wind blows, and I hope you're using condoms."

"Yes we are—as if that's any of your business."

"Whatever, I'm just sayin', you see what your cousin Toi went through after she had her baby. She practically dropped off the earth; don't let the same thing happen to you."

"You're reachin'."

"All I'm saying is that it's life beyond Ameen. I understand he's your first but you really don't have to be this open. Now, I hope you seeing him in here with this chick teaches you a lesson: That your boo ain't all that." She parked the car. "Now, let's go. And I'm telling you, if you take him back after this don't be in my ear about the mess he's doing to you, 'cause I don't wanna hear it."

"Didn't I tell you I was through with him after this?"

"You said that the other day too."

"This is different."

"I hope so," she said as we exited the car and walked into the club. "But it sure seems to me that your heart got your mind trippin'."

The GS Boyz's "Stanky Leg" was blastin' as we walked into Club Heated. We paid our ten dollars and I could hear the crowd shouting, "Go, Ameen, do the stanky leg!"

Once we were standing next to Courtney, Asha said while pointing to Ameen, "I thought you said this clown was a thug."

"Don't be judging people, Asha, you don't know. He could be a thug," Courtney said and pointed to his chest. "I'ma thug."

This whole conversation was ridiculous. "Shut up," I barked at Courtney, as I attempted to walk up behind Ameen and she pulled me back.

"Hold up," Asha said, "let's see how this plays out for a minute."

"You not gon' tell me to shut up too many more times," Courtney snapped.

"Zsa," Asha said, "if you go over there now, all he gon' say is he was dancing with the chick. No, let's see what he does after the stanky leg."

I couldn't believe my eyes. Ameen was straight clowin'. He would've never danced with me like that, yet he was all over this chick.

Hold it . . . wait . . . I shook my head . . . *hold it, does that chick have on the Gucci boots he bought for me? Oh, my God, he gave her my boots?*

I swear I wanted to drop a river from my eyes, but I

knew if I started crying in here then er'body up in this spot would think my swagger was weak. No way. When I left this place I needed to be known as no joke.

After a few minutes passed I couldn't take it anymore. I felt like Ameen had opened my heart, sliced it down the middle, and pissed on the inside. I walked over to Ameen and pushed him on the shoulder. He was so busy kissing the girl that either he didn't feel my push or he didn't care to turn around.

So instead of pushing him again, I mushed him in the head.

"What the . . ." He spun around and looked dead in my face. He quickly wiped the lipstick from his lips and spat, "What are you doin' here? Didn't I tell you to stay home?" He pointed his fingers like a gun in my face.

"Who is this bitch, Ameen?" I pointed back into his face. "Huh." I pushed him. "I thought you were going to church to deliver some dinners? Huh, I knew you was lyin' from the giddy up!"

"What are you talking about?!" he spat, and it was clear that he was showing off for this bird who looked at me like I was crazy. "Didn't I tell you about stalking me?" he continued. "What are you following me for? How did you get here? You walked over here? Yo, you buggin'."

"I'm buggin'?!" I couldn't believe this. I don't know what hurt more—that he was playin' me in public or that he didn't seem to care how I felt. "You tryna front for this tramp, Ameen? You left me at your house and you driving my whip to come dance like a sissy with this rat."

"I thought that was your sister's cousin's friend's car?" the girl said.

"Sister's cousin's friend?" I couldn't believe this. "That's the same thing he told me when he took me out in some hot-pink Corolla."

"That was my car!" the girl shouted, and pushed Ameen.

I looked at Ameen. "You're nothin'! I swear I should spit in your face!" I raised my hand to slap him and he blocked my hit, causing me to stumble.

I straight blacked on Ameen. I swung on Ameen like crazy, punched him, kicked, and lost control. I heard Courtney and Asha say something about get off of her, get off of me, or something, and then I felt Ameen's fist slam into the side of my face and knock me over the bar stool.

Suddenly, as if a swift wind passed by, Ameen was pulled off of me, Courtney and Asha were hovered over me, and I couldn't see anything but stars.

I thought I heard Malachi's voice say, "You lost your damn mind?! Don't be puttin' your hands on her!" but I wasn't sure if that was him or not.

"You better back up!" I heard Ameen say in return.

"Or what you gon' do?!" That sounded like Samaad.

When I regained my vision and the stars faded away, I saw Malachi right hook Ameen, and it looked as if his fist was going back for more. I ran over and stood between them. "Don't hit him!" I screamed at Malachi.

"What?" he said, stunned.

"You tryna kill him!" I shouted.

Malachi, who was now being pushed back by security, said, "What you say? I could what? Hurt him?"

"Chill." I looked at Malachi. "It's okay. I don't need you to get in it and take up for me, I'm okay!"

"You playin' me in front of everybody, right?" Ameen spat. "I'm done with you, Zsa!" Ameen tossed my keys at me and just missed my face.

"Ameen, wait!" I screamed, as everyone in the club looked at me like I was crazy.

"You know what." Malachi walked over to me with a serious look on his face. "I never expected this from you. You letting him put his hands on you?"

"It's not even like that," I said.

"Yeah, I'm sure your mother used the same excuse."

I couldn't believe he said that. "I didn't ask for your help," I snapped.

"It's cool, ma, 'cause you ain't gettin' it no more." And he left me standing there.

I'm not sure, but I think the world has ended.

"Zsa-Zsa." Courtney called for my attention. "Are you okay?" He ran his hands across my face. "You need to leave him alone. If you have to fight with him you don't need to be together."

Courtney's advice was the last thing I needed. I was more concerned with whether or not the girl Ameen was dancing with left with him.

"Please leave him alone," Asha said.

"Whatever." I walked up the block, found my car, and got in. I placed the keys in the ignition, and as I turned the lights on to drive home, I noticed that one had been smashed in.

By the time I got home I could feel the side of my face swelling. I noticed my mother's car parked outside. *Dang, she would be home.* I sat in my car for a moment, and tried to think of a way to get to my room without my mother noticing. Then I remembered that I hadn't locked my bedroom window and I could climb through.

I crept through the grass, careful not to make too much noise, opened the window, and fell onto the floor.

I dusted myself off, closed my window, and walked over to my mirror. I touched the bruise that shone like a purple crescent moon along the side of my face. Just the mere brush of my fingertip caused me pain. This was crazy.

"Zsa, is that you in there? I didn't know you were home." My mother pounded on my door and simultaneously opened it. "Cousin Shake and Ms. Minnie are here!" she said, excited.

"Ma." I quickly turned away. "Why would you just bust in my room without knocking first?"

"I asked her the same thing about my room," Hadiah said, "and she told me because she pays the bills." Hadiah rolled her eyes so hard they looked as if they were going to fall out. "Leave, please," I said to them. "I'll see Cousin Shake and Ms. Minnie in the morning, my goodness."

My mother took a step back. "I don't have time for your attitude," she snapped.

"You're never home so you don't know anything about my attitude! Just quit busting in my room. Now go!"

Still keeping my face turned the opposite way, I rolled my eyes to the ceiling. When I held my head back down, out the corner of my eye I could see Cousin Shake shaking his chubby body toward my room. He wore too-tight electric blue MC Hammer pants, a clingy royal blue vest that hung open and showed every beady taco-meat-looking chest hair of his, a dookey rope chain with a cross hanging from it, and L.A. Gear high-tops.

Cousin Shake's feet pounded against the floor as he took his Gazelle glasses off and plunked my mother on the side of her head. "What's taking you so long to put down the beat down? These two should be at the hospital gettin' an IV by now, talking to you like they're the mama and you're the bad kid. Don't be embarrassin' me in front of Minnie, I raised you better than that."

"Could you all leave? God!" I raised my hand to cover the swollen part of my face and suddenly Cousin Shake yelled, "Oh, you tryna fight me?! She puttin' the hands up like she wanna throw."

"Fight?!" Ms. Minnie, who looked exactly like a short and fifty-year-old version of New York from the series *I Love New York,* sneered.

I frowned, still holding my face. "Look, I do not have time for this." I turned away from them.

"Now, pardon her back." Hadiah wiggled her neck.

"Ah, hell, nawl!" Cousin Shake spat, and before I knew it he and Ms. Minnie were standing over me and Hadiah with the biggest bottle of blessing oil I'd ever seen. "You better thank God I'ma Christmas!" Cousin Shake said as he lashed that olive oil all over us, causing us both to slip and fall to the floor.

"Oooh, shaka laka bam . . . oooh," Ms. Minnie said as Cousin Shake splashed us. "Shaka laka bam-bam. Please Jesus, Mary, Margret, Raheem, and Joseph, oooh, shaka laka, bam, give Shake the strength not to bust up these two disrespectful asses . . . oooh, shaka laka bam-bam."

Cousin Shake splashed more oil. " 'Cause Shake is home now," Cousin Shake said. "And li'l Zebra and li'l Hawaii gon' have some respect around here!" he carried on. "I don't wanna bust," he started to rap, "I don't bust, ah ah ah, breaka breaka one time. I don't wanna bust . . . I don't wanna bust disrespectfuls asses!"

Cousin Shake grabbed me by the hand and Ms. Minnie grabbed Hadiah's hand and they pulled us from the floor. "Now come out here like you got some damn sense. Acting like you been raised by a pack of wild dogs! If you wanna be in the zoo let me know and I'll put you there. I ain't your mama, I won't miss your monkey asses! 'Cause truth be told I eat kids. Now, unless you wanna be smothered in lard and gravy and socked up with a biscuit you'll do what the hell I just told you to do." They walked to my room's doorway. "Now come out here like we the relatives you ain't seen in a while and you missed us. And do it right, because if not I got something else for you."

I looked toward Ms. Minnie and she had a supersized bottle of blessing oil. I couldn't believe this. My night was worse than horrible, and disastrous couldn't touch it. I'd been beaten twice, once for Ameen making a fool out of me and a second time for acting like a fool. I promise you I couldn't win, and with all of this blessing oil on me I couldn't breathe. Ugh!

"You takin' too long!" Cousin Shake started running in place and his smedium vest started to rise. "Comin' out here actin' like somebody owe y'all money!"

I looked at my mother. "Ma—"

"Don't call her. She's the one got you all messed up." Cousin Shake turned and looked at my mother in disgust. "Told you not to name these chil'ren Zulu and Hanukah!"

"It's Zsa-Zsa," I snapped.

"And Hadiah," my sister stressed.

Cousin Shake frowned. "It could be Halloween and Bronx Zoo, it's still a mess. Shoulda named you Barbara and Jane, you woulda had more sense."

"That's enough, Cousin Shake," my mother said seriously. She was staring at me so hard that I know she noticed the bruise on my face.

"You be quiet," Cousin Shake carried on. "Now, do what I told you to do." He pointed to us.

Hadiah and I looked back at our mother, and she didn't blink an eye. We turned back to Cousin Shake and Ms. Minnie. These two weren't going to stop, so I gave in and Hadiah followed my lead. After the day I just had it was obvious that my life was doomed to fall apart.

So whatever. We walked over to them with our arms wide and said, "Oh, my God! Cousin Shake, Ms. Minnie." Hadiah jumped up and down.

"It's so good to see you!" I said.

"We love you guys so much." We gave them a group hug.

"Hey, babies," Cousin Shake said, "you done got so big. You know Cousin Shake love ya, but he will tap dat. Now, come on and open the presents we brought for you."

"I sure hope you like what Shake got on," Ms. Minnie said, "because we bought you two one each."

" 'Cept y'all vests lights up." Cousin Shake smiled.

I looked at the ceiling and took a deep breath. *Should I ask for somebody to shoot me now or should I wait until things get worse?*

After a few hours passed we convinced Cousin Shake and Ms. Minnie that at three o'clock in the morning me and Hadiah needed to go to sleep. They agreed, and just as I settled into bed, my mother knocked and entered my room at the same time. She flicked the lights on. "We need to talk."

"Can we talk in the morning?" I pulled the covers over my head. I could feel her body heat next to me, and then I quickly decided that if she lost it, I wouldn't see it coming, so I eased the covers down over my eyes and looked at her. "What is it?"

"What is that on your face?"

I was speechless for a moment and couldn't think of what explanation to give fast enough so I said, "I ran into the door."

"The door?" She stared at me as if she could see through me. "You're lying, why?"

"You never listen to anything I tell you. Why do I have to be lying?"

She ignored my question and proceeded on with her own. "How did it get there?"

I could look at my mother's face and tell that she cared, and I thought maybe . . . I should tell her the truth. "Ma, the truth is that I saw Ameen and—"

"You did what?!" she screamed. "I'm so sick of you making stupid decisions. Didn't I tell you to leave that good-for-nothing alone? I'm so sick of you lying!" She continued on. "I'm the mama," she said, not coming up for air, "I'm in charge, and I've already been where you are so I know the outcome! You don't! Did he hit you? Because if he did I'm calling the police right now." She reached for the phone.

I must've been crazy to think that I could share anything with her. It had to be the blessing oil that had me out of my mind.

"I thought you were asking me?" I said.

"What happened to your face, Zsa-Zsa?"

"I tripped out of the elevator on my way to Ameen's apartment."

"I know you're lying."

Sure you do.

"And you may not believe it, but you can tell me any-thing."

I almost choked. Is she serious?

"I'm your mother and I won't judge you—"

Calling me a liar and you're tired of me being stupid is sooooo nonjudgmental.

"I love you, Zsa-Zsa."

Now that I didn't doubt.

"And I just want you to know that I really do under-stand."

Did I miss something or was she a stand-up comedian now? God, I wish she would just leave.

I guess after a few minutes of silence, her running out of words, and me giving her the face that I had stopped listening a long time ago, she got the hint. "Well, good night," she said. "I'm here if you need me."

"Good night." I turned over and buried my head under the covers.

6

You probably say that it was juvenile but I think that I deserve to smile . . .

—JAZMINE SULLIVAN, "BUST YOUR WINDOWS"

I was in hell. I slipped down the slope from being a flygirl to being a desperate one. And what's messed up is that I didn't remember when the transformation took place. All I could see and all I could feel was pain . . . and sorrow . . . revenge . . . and embarrassment. It was like Ameen was proving the point of everyone who said he was worthless and he was making me pay for it.

Sometimes I thought I was waiting for someone to jump out the closet and say, "Psych, chica, this ain't your life. This is an extended episode of Hell date." But no one had jumped out yet.

I eased out the bed, stood at the mirror, and looked at my face. My eye was swollen and red and my face was tri-toned: milk chocolate on one side and black and blue on the other. The bruises on my face felt like aching tears, and there was no way with everybody and their mama in Club Heated last night that I was going to school.

But then again, I had to go, because if I didn't then everyone would think that Ameen and the chick he was with had punked me. I felt bad enough as it was, so there was no way I could go out like that.

Just as I decided that I could wear makeup and my Chanel sunglasses and simply tell my teachers I had pink eye, my phone rang. I looked at the caller ID because there were only a select few that I wanted to talk to. But it was Asha so I picked up.

"Wassup?" I said, attempting to play off the tears trembling my throat. I was so sick and tired of being a crybaby.

"Wassup?" Asha said, taken aback. "We need to talk. I had my brother drop me off. So, I'm outside. Open the door."

I looked at the clock and it was six AM. "You're kidding me, right?" There was no way she could see me like this. "Why are you here this time of the morning anyway?"

"Because I couldn't sleep thinking about you. Now, open the door," she insisted.

"I'm grown. I got this."

"Would you open this door! I already know your eye is black."

"Fine." I hung up and slipped on my robe and slippers. As I tipped to the front door the living room light popped on. "Zulu," Cousin Shake said, "where you goin'? And in ya robe at that?"

Already I was sick of him sweatin' me. I'm not gon' be able to live like this. "I'm not going anywhere, Cousin Shake." I turned around and almost threw up in my mouth. Why was he standing in the doorway of his room with a short waist housecoat on and a tight pair of Speedos? His knees looked as if someone painted them with powder, and someone please tell me why did he have on white sweat socks to the knees with green stripes going around the top and brown corduroy slippers?

I shielded my eyes. "Cousin Shake, please put some clothes on."

"Don't try and get off the subject. I said where are you goin'?"

"Nowhere."

"You coulda fooled me. You ain't walkin' no street corners, is ya? The gold digger in ya comin' out?" He started shaking his shoulders and moving his feet from side to side as if he were doing the crip walk. "I ain't sayin' she a gold diggin'," he rapped, "but she ain't messin' wit' no broke-to broke-to broke figures. . . . That's Shake's remix. Now where ya goin'?" He stopped dancing.

"Cousin Shake, why are you sweatin' me, dang?!"

" 'Cause I'm security. Strollin, bad kids too grown–and ya mama can't control you security. Smell me? Now, where ya goin'?" He picked up his supersized bottle of blessing oil. "Or it's gon' be a problem. And is that a black eye on your face?"

"I have pink eye." I turned my head.

"Eye looks black to me," he said suspiciously.

"Look, my friend is at the door and I need to open it."

"At six o'clock in the morning? What kinda friend is this? She a freak or she owe you money or something?"

I just looked at Cousin Shake, because this grilling was going on too long. Now I knew for sure that I was definitely going to school. There's no way I could swing with this cat at the house all day. Instead of responding I opened the door and Asha walked in. She looked directly at Cousin Shake and for a moment I thought she was going to pass out. "Asha." I grabbed her hand to help her maintain her balance. "He's harmless. Cousin Shake, this is Asha, and Asha, this is Cousin Shake. Now, Asha, just close your eyes and follow me."

"I don't give a damn if you don't like my night gear," Cousin Shake said, "long as you recognize who I am, the house police. I'm gon' police er'thang that go on around here, from the rooter to the tooter. And school is in a couple of hours," he yelled as I closed my door, "so don't make me have to come in there and get you!"

Asha swallowed. "Who is that?"

"'Bout seven I'm gon' be truancy," Cousin Shake screamed through my door. "Don't you worry about who I am. You didn't come to talk about me. You a li'l girl and I already got a wife."

"He sure does!" Ms. Minnie yelled behind him.

I looked at Asha. "Didn't I tell you God hated me?"

Asha laughed. "Oh . . . kay . . . you might want to come and visit me more often. But anyway, I really need to see what's the problem and what is going on with you."

I rolled my eyes to the ceiling. "What are you talking about? And can you talk a little lower? I don't need them in my business."

"You know what I'm talking about," she whispered. "Ameen putting his hands on you."

"I hit him first, Asha. He ain't beatin' on me. Don't get carried away."

"Are you serious, do you even hear yourself? You sound like a health class subject or documentary on abuse. Has he been beating on you?"

"No." I shook my head. "I mean we bang sometimes but it's not abuse, thank you. I am not some kind of victim."

"You shouldn't be bangin' at all."

"Did you come over here to give me a lecture at this time of the morning?"

"No. I came over here because you are my best friend." Her eyes filled with tears. "And I love you."

"Why are you cryin'? Are you buggin' out?" I walked over to my closet and laid my clothing out for that day, including the sunglasses to match.

Asha sat silently as I laid my dark blue skinny leg jeans, sky blue midriff sweater, and accessories on the edge of the bed. I felt like her eyes were burning a hole through me, so I said, "Why are you staring at me like that?"

" 'Cause like, I don't even know what to say or what to do to make you listen."

"Asha, it's nothing. Like, you're making a bigger deal out of it than it is."

"Why don't I believe that?" She shook her head toward the ceiling.

"Well, believe it," I insisted.

"Zsa, do you know how many times I have heard that from you?"

"Could you get out my neck, please?" I said, exhausted.

"Zsa-Zsa." She walked over by my closet and sat on the edge of my desk. "How do you think I lost my mother?"

"You said she died of cancer."

Asha shook her head and wiped her tears. "No, I just told everybody that because I was too embarrassed to say that she was beatin' to death by her boyfriend."

"What?" I turned toward her.

"Yeah, he beat the hell out my mother, and no matter how many times she would say, 'I'm leaving, this is it,' it never was. And if he bought her gifts, then she was all in and back to acting like he was the man of her dreams. And you know what happened in the end?"

While Asha spoke all I could see was my father's face. "What? He died?" I spat out a bit too fast, assigning her the ending of my story.

"No. She died. He slapped her and she hit her head on the bathtub. She died before the ambulance took her out of the house. And I saw the whole thing."

"Oh . . . Asha, I'm so sorry. . . ." I gave her a hug. I didn't know what else to do.

"Don't be sorry." Asha wiped her eyes again. "Just don't let that be your life. I'm telling you, Ameen is trash, dump him and keep it movin'."

I swear I got Asha's point, but it did not apply to my life. "Asha, Ameen doesn't beat me. Besides, I hit him in the club first. And anyway, I'm done with him. He was cheating on me with that busted broad."

"Whatever, Zsa." She shook her head. "Whatever."

"Anyway," I said, "I'ma wear these glasses all day. You think I can get away with it?" I slid them on.

"More than just your eye is bruised," she said as her eyes roamed my face.

"Duh." I rolled my eyes. "I know, but I have concealor for my face, but I can't do anything about my eye swelling."

"Maybe you need to stay home?"

"Not. Then everybody will think that I let Ameen and the chick he was with win."

"Win what?" Asha looked confused.

I ignored her and an hour later I was dressed and my face was made up. I looked at the clock. 7:00 AM. Just as I

went to tell Asha I was ready my door started thumping. I
swear I hated that sound.

Bam! Bam! Bam!

"Zebra, open up!" Cousin Shake screamed.

"Zebra?" Asha covered her mouth and fell out laughing.

Why was he pounding on my door? This man has lost
his mind.

"Minnie," I heard Cousin Shake say through my door,
"you get li'l Hawaii out the bed? She got to be to school
first."

"I don't appreciate y'all bustin' up in my room like
this," I could hear my sister saying.

"Minnie, put the blessing oil in the supersoaker,"
Cousin Shake said. "Let li'l Houston know we ain't the
ones." After a second of silence Cousin Shake started
pounding on my door again. "Zoro!" he said. "Don't make
Cousin Shake come in there after you. 'Cause I'll do it. I
will drag you out that bed and you'll be going to school
lookin' like Amy Winehouse. Don't play with me. You too
busy being grown, but I got somethin' for you. Now try
me." He pounded on my door. "Please try me."

"Get away from my door, now!" I said.

"Oh, hell, no!" Cousin Shake pushed my door open
holding the blessing oil in his hand. "Don't show off
'cause your li'l friend is here. 'Cause she can get it too.
What-what"—he looked at Asha—"you want some, you
tryna do somethin'?"

"No, sir," Asha said.

"I ain't think so. Now come on, and please don't make
me lose my relish on you."

"Relish?" I frowned. "You mean religion?"

"That's what he said." Ms. Minnie butted into our conversation. That's when I realized that these two had on matching outfits: metallic silver MC Hammer pants and matching muscle shirts trimmed in feathers. They looked like one-hit wonders from 1980.

"Okay." I slid my shades on. "I have to go."

"Why you lookin' like somebody slapped you?" Hadiah frowned. "Why do you have those shades on?"

"Could you mind your business?" I snapped.

"Okay, li'l Rihanna." Hadiah rolled her eyes. "Be crazy if you want to."

"Li'l who?" Cousin Shake said as he ushered us into the dining room. "Lawd, y'all got the ugliest names I ever heard. Jazmyn messed y'all up. Anyway, you have to eat breakfast before you go to school."

"That's right," Ms. Minnie said while sitting a bowl of grits in front of Hadiah.

"Now, sit down," Cousin Shake said. "This how Cousin Shake shows you he loves ya. Patrolling you and making sure you eat your breakfast in the morning." He looked at Asha. "That includes you, too. You just a li'l thick so you don't need as much. Next time you come I'll make your grits taste like salad."

I looked at Asha and she had already sat at the dining room table, so, heck, I gave in and sat down too. I picked up my spoon and started eating.

"My Jesus, y'all believe in saying grace?" Ms. Minnie frowned.

"For real," Cousin Shake added. "You eating like a buncha untrained animals. Anybody wanna thank God? 'Cause you could be out in the street eating pissy slop."

He popped Hadiah on the back of her neck. "Halo, say grace."

"I'm shy," Hadiah said. "I don't know what to say." She gave a devilish grin.

I looked at her and practically laughed in her face. My little sister was a lot of things, but shy she was not.

"Okay, well I'm gon' say grace," Cousin Shake said. We all stood up and held hands. "Lawd-Father-Brothah," Cousin Shake hummed, "we come this morning thanking You. Thanking You for Mary, Martin, Luke, and De'Cosey."

"Who is De'Cosey?" Asha whispered.

"He wrote the Ten Commandments," Cousin Shake said, opening one eye. "And we don't talk during prayer time."

"Wasn't that Moses?" Asha whispered.

"That's what I said," Cousin Shake said, tight-lipped. "Now talk again and see don't you get the blessing oil beat down."

"Be quiet, Asha," I said. "Trust me."

Cousin Shake continued on. "So Lawd, we come thanking You for these grits, the butter, the salt, the grains it took to make the grits, and we thank You for the li'l man on the box. He looks like a good family man."

"Oh, my God!" Hadiah said, aggravated. "God has left the building."

Cousin Shake opened his eyes. "You need some oil?"

Hadiah quickly closed her eyes and held her head down. "Thank You, Lord, for this food," she said.

"I thought so," Cousin Shake said. "Now say amen."

"Amen," we all said.

I tried to think of the last time we had breakfast like this . . . and the only thing I could come up with was never. A few minutes passed and we were done and on our way to school. Hadiah walked to school because her school was only around the corner, while mine was downtown Newark and we lived in the Vailsburg section.

Asha and I hopped in my car and I picked up Courtney on our way to school. He walked out his house throwing his pink boa to the back of his shoulders. He slid into the backseat and he handed Asha a CD. "Shut up," he said. "It's Gladys Knight, so just deal with it."

As Gladys Knight sang about a midnight train going to Georgia, I flashed back to what happened last night. I was pissed and hurt all over again. I felt like fire was in my chest as I made a right instead of making a left toward school.

"What are you doing?" Asha asked.

"School isn't this way," Courtney said.

"Relax," I said, "I need to see something."

I drove down a few blocks until I arrived in front of Ameen's building and spotted a hot-pink Toyota Corolla. I don't know what came over me or what took over my body, but if I'd had a gun I would've taken Ameen's whole building out. I thought about running upstairs until Asha said, "I'm not letting you go upstairs."

"You see that car." I pointed. "That's the trick's car from the club last night."

"Touch the hood," Courtney said, "and see if it's cold."

"Why are you encouraging her?" Asha snapped at Courtney.

I double-parked, got out of my car, and touched the hood. "It's cold," I said while looking at Courtney. "Damn near ice cold."

Courtney batted his eyelashes and said, "Dang, homie, two snaps up and a fruit loop, I hate to break it to you but mami spent the night."

"Oh, yeah?" I said to myself more than to him. "Oh . . . okay . . ." I went to my trunk, took out my club, and wrote, "Love Zsa-Zsa" on the handle in permanent marker.

"What are you doing?" Asha said, getting out the car. "Forget Ameen. We're going to get in trouble out here!"

"No, we're not," I said. "We're in the hood and nobody snitches. Plus this gon' be quick." I reared the club back like a bat and rammed it into the windshield. The first hit put a spider's web in the glass, but the next one was a home run and jagged edges of glass rained into the front seat. Then I proceeded with the side windows.

"Would you stop!" Asha screamed. "You could go to jail!"

"You sure *could* go to jail, Zsa," Courtney said as he got out of the car and stood next to me, "but I'm gon' let the air out the tires for you first before we worry about the cops."

I shot Courtney a high five. "This mofo think he can just play me!" I screamed. "Like I'm nothin'. Like he doesn't even care. Like I'm something to play with . . . and all for this trick! Oh . . . okay." I slammed my club into the back windows. "Let's see how they get around now! Since I'ma joke and she's up in his crib, well, take this as a house-warming gift." I tossed the club through the busted wind-shield and said, "Courtesy of Zsa-Zsa."

Courtney shot me another high five.

We piled back in my car and I took off like a bat out of hell. Once we pulled into the school's parking lot Asha was fuming. "What, Asha?!" I snapped. "What?"

"What you just did was so dumb! We could've all gotten locked up and then what? Don't do that anymore! 'Cause bottom line, the girl is still there with Ameen and where are you? Looking like a fool. You my girl, I love you, but you trippin'." She got out the car and walked over to Samaad, who had just pulled up.

"Don't worry, Zsa," Courtney said, "I won't testify against you."

Malachi parked his blue 2000 Xterra. I guess since it was the beginning of October it was too chilly for his motorcycle, but the truck didn't take away from his sex appeal—it actually added to it. He threw his Northface backpack over one shoulder and clicked the alarm to his truck. I knew I owed Malachi an apology but I didn't exactly know what to say or how to approach the situation.

So, I hatched the plan of blocking the school's entrance because then I figured it would force him to say excuse me and then I could rush to apologize. As Malachi approached the door he walked up to me, placed his hands on my waist, moved me out of the way, and continued into the building. I was floored.

Forget it, I'ma say something to him. At first I didn't see him when I entered the building, and then I noticed he was at Staci's locker talking to her. I hesitated at first and then I figured, what the hell ever. I boldly walked over and said, "Excuse me."

Staci looked at me like I was crazy. "I'm getting so tired of you. Why are you always around?" she spat.

For real, for real, I started to give it to this chick. I wanted to say we have a connection that you could only dream of having, but since I wasn't in the mood for another day of unrelenting drama I simply said, "Listen, I just need to speak to Malachi for a moment. You can have him back after that." Before she could respond I continued on, "Malachi." I turned to him. "Can I speak to you for a moment, please?"

He looked at me, and I could tell that he was beyond pissed. "Staci," he said, turning back to her, "I'll catch you at lunch. One." He walked away and left us standing there.

"I need to know this," Staci said. "Are you in love with him or something? Are you two messing around?"

I looked at Staci as if I could've slapped her. "No dis, but not today. Trust me." I walked away and passed by Samaad, who was giving Asha a peck on the lips as I headed to class.

For the next two periods I tried to focus on my schoolwork. I hated that daydreams of Malachi kept invading my mind and confusing me when I should've been thinking of Ameen.

It bugged me how Malachi played me in the hallway. Not that I could blame him. I looked up from my desk and caught a glance of myself in the window. I hated what I saw and I couldn't believe that it was actually me sitting here in sunglasses.

The bell rang. I went to my locker to exchange my books and Malachi walked past me. He didn't even look my way. He just continued on.

I couldn't take it. So I was determined that the next time the bell rang he was going to acknowledge me. Somehow and some way we were going to talk.

I headed to my next class, attempted to focus, and when class ended and the bell rang again, I went looking for Malachi, only to come up with nothing.

As the day went on I didn't see Malachi at his locker for the next couple of periods so I prayed that when lunch came he would be in the cafeteria.

When I walked into the cafeteria I spotted Samaad, Courtney, and Asha sitting at the same table, but I didn't see Malachi anywhere.

"Diva!" Courtney yelled. "Over here!" He motioned for me to come over to the table where they were.

I grabbed a bottle of water and walked over to them. "Hey y'all."

"Wassup, Zsa," Samaad responded.

"Nothin', wassup with you and my girl?" I smiled at Asha, who, although she was mad with me earlier, couldn't help but smile at my question.

"I don't know," Samaad said, "you have to ask her where I stand."

I laughed. "So where does he stand, Asha?"

"Wherever." She blushed. "It's up to him."

"Two snaps up and a fruit loop," Courtney said, aggravated. "Write a damn note or something." He looked at Asha. "Y'all are getting on my nerves. You can't stay away from one another. Every period between classes, you're stealing kisses, and now you're sitting here talking about, 'I don't know. It's up to him and up to her.' You know how many of us want to be in love and you two are acting silly?"

"You feeling some kind of way, Courtney?" I asked.

"Know what," he said, "I'll perform the ceremony. Asha"—he looked at her—"do you take this man as your one and only boo? To love and to cherish and to do boo things with?"

She smiled. "You're so silly, Courtney."

"That's a yes," Courtney said. "Now, handsome, I mean, Samaad, do you take Asha for your wifey, to love and to cherish and to do wifey things with?"

"Word. That's wassup," Samaad said.

"So y'all kiss and make this official. Otherwise I'ma scream."

Samaad looked at Asha. "Wifey?"

She pressed her lips against his. "Yes." She kissed him. "I'm wifey."

I took a shredded napkin and tossed it at them like rice. After a few minutes of well wishes and telling the new couple how cute they were together, I excused myself from the table. I was determined to find Malachi. I walked into the hallway and he was standing at his locker. I walked over and stood in front of him. "Can I speak to you for a moment?" I grabbed his hand. "Please."

He sighed. "What, Zsa?"

I shifted from one foot to the next. "I'm, you know, sorry about what happened at the club—"

"Save it."

"I can't believe you're acting so stank."

"And I can't believe you."

"Believe what? That I won't drop my boyfriend and be with you!"

"You know what?" He took my glasses off and pressed his forehead against mine. "Seeing as though you turned out to be just like your mother, I don't want you."

Immediately tears fell from my eyes.

"I'm sorry," Malachi said quickly. "I love you, you know that."

I snatched my glasses back from him and slid them on. "Zsa," Malachi said as he reached for my hand and his eyes filled with a thousand apologies, "I'm sorry. My fault, I shouldn't have said that."

I snatched my hand back. More tears filled my eyes but I'd had enough of crying. I was not a babbling fool. I was Zsa-Zsa La-Shae Fields, the queen of flyness, and I had been knocked off my hustle for a moment too long. I had cussed Malachi out a thousand times in my mind but for some reason I couldn't get any words to come out of my mouth. So, I gathered the tail end of my heart, rolled my eyes, and as Malachi reached for my hand again I looked at him and said, "Don't."

By the time I got home from school I felt as if I'd been in a war. I parked my car and walked to Ms. Lucinda's to pick up Hadiah, who said she'd rather watch game shows with our neighbor than spend one minute with Cousin Shake and Ms. Minnie alone. I couldn't blame her.

"Thanks, Ms. Lucinda," I said once Hadiah came to the door.

Hadiah waved as we walked away. "I don't think they're home," Hadiah said. "All the lights have been off for about an hour."

"How do you know?" I asked as we stepped onto our porch.

" 'Cause I was watching them. I even threw a couple of rocks at the window hoping they would think it was bullets, say Newark was too wild for them and leave."

"Hadiah." I opened the front door and walked into our pitch-black hallway. "Something tells me they are not going anywhere."

Once we walked into the living room I realized that Hadiah was right. All the lights were out and the house was midnight black.

This was eerie, especially since we always kept at least one light on. As I walked over to the light switch Cousin Shake and Ms. Minnie jumped from behind the couch and said, "Freeze!"

"Ahhhhhhh!!!!!!!!!!!!" Hadiah and I screamed and held our chest. "What the hell are you doing!" I yelled.

"Homework police. So put your book bags down and your pencils up. If you do what we tell you"—Cousin Shake held up the supersoaker filled with blessing oil— "won't nobody get hurt."

The homework police? Are they crazy? "Are you kidding me coming in here like this!" I said. "Attacking us."

"I don't think this is funny," Hadiah whined. "I almost peed on myself."

"Do I look like I'm laughing?" Cousin Shake said. "I want the homework done. Seems to me, being as though your mama go to work and don't come home until she thinks it's a good idea, that you two been running around here a li'l too grown and running your own household. Well, I don't like it. You two need structure, discipline, and somebody here when you come home from school. Children start to feel alone when no adult is around. So ya Cousin Shake and Ms. Minnie is here 'cause we love you.

"But your asses is too grown. Now I want to see the homework, make sure it's right, and then you can do what you want until dinner is done. And you may not know this but Minnie can burn."

"My mother cooks dinner and leaves it for us," I said.

"Shut up, Zero! You 'spose to eat a hot dinner, not no

cold stuff. I got this, and when ya mama get home I'ma handle her too, believe me. Shake is here now and things around here gon' change." He started doing the crip walk. "Shake—shake—shake is home. Yeah, baby! Now do that dang homework."

We sat down at the dining room table and I said to Hadiah, "Just roll with it. Seven and Toi said the way to survive Cousin Shake is to just act as if you are listening to him."

"I'm scared straight," Hadiah said. "I don't know what I did, but I won't be doing it again."

Within the hour we finished our homework and afterward Ms. Minnie dressed the table with roast beef, gravy, rice, collards, fried apples, and biscuits. I felt like I was at Homestyle Buffet. "Dang, Ms. Minnie." I smiled. "This smells delicious."

"Thank you, baby. That's how Ms. Minnie hooked your cousin Shake."

"And you know you got me sprung." Cousin Shake laughed.

Just when I am almost able to tolerate these two they paint me a disturbing visual.

"You ain't the only one sprung, honey." Ms. Minnie laughed.

Is it me or did the visual just get worse?

Cousin Shake said grace and we all sat down to eat. "So what happened to your eye, Zinzalay?" Cousin Shake asked.

"It's Zsa-Zsa, Cousin Shake," I said

"That's what I said. Now what happened to it?"

"Shake, leave the child alone," Ms. Minnie said.

"I'm just asking."

"I walked into the door at school," I said, eating my food.

"You said pink eye this morning," Hadiah whispered.

"Would you shut up?" I whispered back.

"What y'all think we can't hear?" Cousin Shake said. "I just asked a question which apparently the truth is allergic to. All I got to say, Zimbabwe, is don't let me have to hurt nobody 'cause you being a dumb-dumb and got somebody puttin' his hands on you. It's no secret what your mother went through."

"I am not like my mother!" I snapped.

"For your best interest you might wanna bring your tone down," Cousin Shake warned.

"Can we talk about something else?"

"Sure," Cousin Shake said, "tell Cousin Shake some of the things y'all like to do around here. You play the lotto?"

I couldn't help but laugh. Cousin Shake and Ms. Minnie carried on and eventually what I started to realize is that they weren't that bad. They were actually quite funny, at least until they started saying they were going to come out to my school and volunteer.

After we finished dinner, my mother walked in the front door. I looked at the clock and she was surprisingly early, and then I looked back at her and noticed that she was dressed in a cocktail dress and heels. "Where are you coming from?" Cousin Shake asked.

"A date." She smiled.

"You had today off?" he asked her.

"Yes."

"And you didn't think to come home and spend time with these kids?" He frowned. "Oh, hell, nawl." He picked up his bottle of blessing oil. "When you have days off," he lashed her, "you come home and spend time with these children, you hear me?! Here I am bustin' out crazy on them and they're acting like this because of you."

"Don't worry about it, Cousin Shake." I rolled my eyes as me and Hadiah rose from our seats. "It doesn't even matter anymore. That's how we roll around here. We each do our own thing."

I'd had enough for one day. I went to my room and went to bed. I didn't want to think and I didn't want to dream. I just wanted to be still. That's it, simply be still.

7

It ain't where he's at it's where he wanna be . . .

—Keyshia Cole, "Let It Go"

My life was dead. For real, no lie. And I was trying to reincarnate myself by attempting to get in where I fit in all day . . . every day. Mainly because I couldn't remember what life was like before Ameen, the chick he'd cheated on me with, and our breakup came along. My life had been so entrenched in Ameen and the drama he brought that I couldn't remember what I thought was fun and what I liked to do. That's when I realized that everything was about Ameen and nothing was about me. Nothing.

I sat Indian style in the center of my bed with my hair falling over my shoulders wondering what seventeen-year-olds did on Saturdays. I swear I didn't know. Just as I thought that maybe they withered and died after they broke up with their boyfriends my phone rang. I looked at the caller ID and it was Asha.

"You rang?" I answered.

"Hey, girl," she said, a little too damn chipper. "What you doing today?"

Is that a trick question? "I'm waiting for my helicopter to come so I can take a spin around Newark."

"And what? Bust some more windows out?" She laughed. "You ever hear from Ameen about that?"

"No." I sucked my teeth. "He probably bought the girl a new car, since I busted the old one."

"Oh, please, I doubt if he was ballin' like that."

"He was ballin' alright." I shook my head in agony thinking of how much cash Ameen was probably spending on this broad. "You know what, Asha?"

"What's that?"

"Me and Ameen breaking up wouldn't be so hard to accept if I could stay focused on the wrong he did to me instead of imagining that he and this chick were having the time of their lives, not even thinking about me."

"Zsa, believe me, sooner than later that chick will see Ameen for the monster that he is. So stop sweatin' it. Plus you got Malachi wanting you and that mothersucker is ca'yute!"

"Gurl, please, I'm so cold on him, it's a shame."

"Why?"

"We had an argument the other day at school in the hallway. I was trying to apologize for what jumped off with he and Ameen and he played me."

"What did he say?"

"Just a buncha rah-rah."

"Oh . . . kay . . . whatever that means."

I knew I was being evasive, but I didn't have the heart to tell her what he really said to me. "Anyway"—I chuckled—"things have certainly changed since we were twelve and you thought he was the ugliest dude you'd ever saw."

Asha laughed. "Well, he outgrew his ugliness. So anyway, don't try and change the subject, you need to talk to him so y'all can hook up."

"Earth to Asha, let me remind you he has a girl."

"Staci does not count."

"Oh, you wrong for that." I chuckled.

"And anyway, Samaad told me that Malachi broke up with her so the runway is clear, homie. Now what's the deal—you goin' for broke or what?"

"Hell, no, didn't you hear me the first time? I don't want Malachi. I'm sooo not beat."

"You trippin'. Anyway, me and my baby are going to the movies and I want you to come."

"Ill, I am not about to be a desperate third wheel."

"Don't even play me like that. You know it would be fun."

"I'm sure, but no."

"Call Courtney and y'all meet us at Lowes in Mountainside."

"No, Asha."

"Girl, all I know is that you better be there by one." And she hung up before I could protest.

I laid back on my bed, and that's when I could've sworn that I heard Hadiah say, "Cousin Shake, this is how you do the Halle Berry."

I had to see this, so I eased out of my bed, cracked my room door open, looked out into the living room, and oh . . . my . . . Ba'Jesus, Cousin Shake looked as if he was having a seizure. This was too much; now I knew for sure I had to leave. Hadiah seemed to be enjoying the freakish company we had but personally, other than the good food Ms. Minnie cooked, I could've done without them.

I called Courtney and he answered, "Two snaps up and a fruit loop."

"What you doing?" I asked him.

"Wondering if I'm the only one who hears an alarm when Puffy comes on TV."

"What alarm?" I asked, confused.

"The 'how you doin' one," he said, popping a piece of gum in my ear, and all I could imagine was him flinging his wrist.

"Look, I didn't call you for an analysis on Puffy."

"Ill, Diva, what did Puffy do to you?"

"I just don't care if he's sliding off or not."

"How do you know he's the one sliding off?"

"Okay." I laughed—I had to, otherwise I would've screamed. "I'm coming to get you so we can go to the movies."

"You might wanna ask me," Courtney snapped. "I do have a life, thank you." He blew a bubble in my ear and popped it. "I'm tired of you and Asha taking me for granted."

I sighed. He was too temperamental. "Courtney, do you want to go to the movies?"

"Yeah, Diva, God knows I need something to do."

"Alright, I'll see you in a few." I hung up the phone, showered, and dressed in a fitted pair of Juicy Couture jeans, a pink tee with Juicy written in rhinestones across the breasts, a midriff denim jacket, and a pair of pink, sheepskin-trimmed Uggs. I looked at my face in the mirror. The bruises and swelling had disappeared, so I was able to rock my makeup the way it was supposed to be. I decided to wear my hair straight and falling to the small of my back. By the time I stepped out of my room I was too cute for words. The only problem was convincing myself to feel that way.

When I arrived at Courtney's I blew the horn for him to come out and oh . . . my . . . God . . . what a damn sight. Why was everything this fool have on neon yellow? Neon yellow skinny leg jeans, neon yellow button down ruffle shirt, and a neon yellow boa. Hold it, wait a minute, were those three-inch boots sparkling? Yes. They were. I looked at him as he approached the car. "There's a warrant out for your arrest." I leaned out the window.

"What?" he said, shocked.

"Yeah, the You-Look-a-Hot-Mess police are on their way."

Courtney twisted his lips, "Whatever, hater. You know you like this." He threw his boa to the back of his shoulders, placed his hands on his hips, and proceeded to get his top model on in front of the car. "The shirt is Gap," he said as his heels clicked, "the pants are Banana Republic, the shoes are Chanel, and the boa is my own creation."

"Courtney"—I paused—"let's just go."

Courtney got in the car and smiled. "It's so refreshing to be me."

When we arrived at the movies Samaad and Asha were in the lobby waiting for us. Courtney and I walked over to them, and I swear I was getting sick at how they were all over one another. Samaad was standing behind Asha with his fingers locked around her waist, kissing her on the side of her neck, as her head lay against his chest.

"Maybe you two should've opted for a short stay," I snapped. "And got the movie on bootleg."

"I thought we talked about all of this hatin', Diva," Courtney said. "I have love issues too. But don't hate, celebrate."

"Thank you, Courtney." Asha smiled.

"Anyway." I chuckled at the fact that my friends had called me on the carpet. "What are we going to see?" I asked.

"What do you want to see?" I felt the soft tip of a finger slide down the nape of my neck. "You wanna see me?" My heart jumped. I knew from the voice and the heated touch on my neck that it was Malachi. I closed my eyes and said a quick prayer to keep my blushing at bay and my heart from thundering out of my chest.

"Where is your girl?" I snapped. "Shouldn't you be kicking it with her?"

Malachi looked me dead in the eyes. "I'm trying to get with you, and another girl is your concern? Interesting."

"Oh," I said, not knowing what else to say, and that's when it occurred to me that had to be a setup. "Is this a setup? I hope not 'cause if so I'ma be pissed."

"That attitude is not attractive." Asha looked at me and mumbled.

"Let me hollah at you for a second," Malachi said to me as he grabbed my hand and gently pulled me to the side before I could object. "Listen, I'm real sorry about what I said to you the other day."

I hated that my eyes roamed his body, but the bulging

vein on the side of his neck made the tattoo of his name rise. He wore a pair of blue and baggy Ecko jeans, a navy blue hoody with I AM THE AMERICAN DREAM written across it, a blue bubble vest, and a pair of black Tims. His dreads hung loose over his shoulders, and I swear he was too fine for it not to be illegal. I bit the corner of my lip and sighed. "Malachi, I can't deal with that right now. I'm confused enough as it is and you're making it worse."

"But you won't even talk to me. What is going on with you? I feel like I don't even know you anymore."

"You don't," I snapped. "I'm not twelve and I'm not looking for you to save me, okay?"

"What did I do to you, Zsa?" He lifted my chin. "You treat me like trash, for real. I mean, you were happy to see me the first day we saw each other again, but ever since then you've been treating me like I stole your bike. Keep it funky. What's really good with you, ma?"

"Why are you so interested in that?" poured over my shoulder, and when Malachi turned around and I looked up, it was Staci speaking.

I was beyond pissed, and you know what, I'd had it, especially since I thought Asha said he broke up with this chick, yet here she was all in my business. "Look, deal with your girl," I said to Malachi, "because I'm tired of every time I turn around she's popping up like a weed. Let me know when you get a moment and then I can tell you why I don't like to deal with you. Until then, I have a movie to watch." And I left them standing there. I could hear Malachi asking Staci what she was doing there as I walked away.

"Hold up, Diva!" Courtney yelled behind me. "Because I'ma 'bout sick of all of this lovie dovie mess too."

I turned to him as he caught up with me. "I thought you said not to hate."

"I'm not hatin', I'm just statin'."

No matter what, Courtney always had a way of making me laugh. We bought popcorn, and afterward we walked into the theater and took a seat in the back. I could hear a few moans and groans coming from the balcony but I figured it was some young couple kissing so I didn't turn around, especially since I'd had enough of all of these people and their happy relationships.

Once we were settled into our seats Asha and Samaad came and sat next to us. And of course as hell would have it, Malachi and Staci sat directly behind us. I swear I wanted to slap both of them. I could hear Staci whispering to Malachi, "Why do we have to sit here?"

Malachi sighed and then whispered, "Staci, you invited yourself. I told you we were taking a break and you're not giving me any space."

"So what is that supposed to mean, Malachi?" she asked.

"It means you can sit anywhere you want, but I'm not moving."

I could hear the disappointment and pissivity in Staci's sigh. A few minutes later she said, "I'm going to get me some M&M's."

Courtney turned around, "Can you get some Jujubes and some Lemonheads too?" Then he shoved ten dollars into her hand and looked at everyone else in the row. "Anybody else want anything?" Everyone shook their heads no. "Yes, y'all do. Asha, you want some Swedish Fish? You know we houses us some Swedish Fish and purple slushi. Here." He handed Staci another ten dollar bill.

"Bring her back some fish, oh, and some Sno-Caps. And that purple slushi."

Staci stood there and twisted her lips.

"What's taking you so long?" Courtney batted his eyes. "The movie is about to come on."

Staci sucked her teeth as she walked away.

"Samaad," Malachi said from behind me, "when the movie is over I need to kick it with you for a few."

"Ai'ight." Samaad draped his arm around Asha. A few minutes later there was more moaning and groaning coming from the balcony. "You better stop doing that, you know I'm ticklish."

I swear that sounded like Cousin Shake. Dear God . . . please . . . I've been embarrassed enough by them.

I looked at Asha. "That wasn't me," she said.

"Dang," Samaad said, "who are those two old freaks?"

We all turned around and I almost died. It was Cousin Shake and Ms. Minnie, eating the same Twizzler from opposite ends and once their lips met they started kissing. I couldn't believe this. Once they stopped kissing Cousin Shake looked directly at me. I turned around quickly and prayed he didn't recognize me.

"Zimbabwe!"

I froze. *Oh, no.*

"Zimbabwe, is that you?"

I turned back around and attempted to wave on the sly.

"Who is Zimbabwe?" Courtney asked with a mouth full of candy and fruity slob coming out the sides of his mouth.

"Long story," I said, "but that's my cousin Shake and his wife, Ms. Minnie."

"Damn," Malachi said, while massaging the nape of my neck, "must be nice to be in love like that."

My heart fluttered as Malachi ran his hands through my hair and when I felt myself melting, I snapped back to reality and said, "Would you stop?"

"You really want me to stop?" he asked.

"No, she doesn't, but I do." We turned around and Staci was standing there with an arm filled with candy.

I swear I couldn't stand looking at her. "I have to go to the bathroom." I rose from my seat and stormed out of the theater. I just wanted to scream. All I needed was one good day to get me on the right track, but instead drama was unfolding every waking minute.

I walked into the bathroom and for some reason I felt weird as I entered the stalls. But I had enough nonsense going on that week to last me a lifetime and I desperately wanted to pay no mind to the uneasy feeling in my stomach. Needless to say I chopped it up to nerves.

Once I was done using the bathroom I walked out of the stall and suddenly felt as if I'd walked into a brick wall. "Dang! Can you say excuse me!" I said, looking up.

"Shut up!" It was Ameen. My heart raced as I looked toward the exit and noticed that I couldn't get out of there unless I was able to move Ameen out of my way. I looked back into Ameen's face and his eyes were fire red. I needed to get out of there, but I couldn't let Ameen know I was scared because then he would think he had the better of me.

"What the hell is wrong with you?!" I pushed him in his chest, but he didn't budge. "Would you move? What are you doing in here anyway! Following me?"

He yoked me by my collar, and I slapped his hand. "Don't be grabbing on me." I attempted to get away but he pushed me back into the stall.

"You know I owe you one!" He pushed me against the toilet. "You're lucky I didn't catch you when I realized what you did to my girl's car!"

"Your girl?" I said in disbelief, feeling as if he had slashed a knife through my jugular vein.

He pointed his finger in my face. "You know how much money I had to spend behind what you did? Do you know the police towed that car thinking that it was abandoned?"

"Good for the trick!" I practically laughed in his face. I was hoping that he could only see what I was showing on the outside because on the inside I was scared. I knew he could be violent when he got mad, but I'd never seen him like this. This had me shook.

His grip tightened. "You think you're tough. But what you don't know is that I've been watching you. And I could've smacked you up a minute ago and taken you out of here! You think you're so big and bad but you're only what I allow you to be. And if I were you I'd be scared, because if you keep pissing me off I'ma check you!"

"Get off of me, Ameen!" I tussled with him to get away.

"Is everything okay in here?" an elderly voice said from behind us.

"No!" I screamed.

"You're right it's not okay," Ameen said, backing out of the stall as the old woman ran up to him and hit him with her cane. He snatched her cane and threw it on the floor.

"Don't let me catch you, Zsa." He pointed. "Or it's gon' be a problem."

The door slammed behind him as he left. I looked at the old woman who was holding onto the sink. "I'm sorry, ma'am." I handed her her cane. "I'm really sorry."

"I sure hope you are not courting him." She waved her finger as she regained her balance. "Because he is nothing but trouble. Believe me, honey, let sleeping dogs lie."

I was so embarrassed and shaken that I didn't respond. Instead I walked swiftly out of the bathroom and into the theater. I walked over to where my friends were seated and said, "I'm leaving." I looked at Courtney. "You rollin', 'cause I'm gone."

"What?" he said, stuffing a Jujube in his mouth. "You see all this stuff I just bought? Heck, no, I ain't leavin', and what is the matter with you? You need a Midol? I got some in my bag."

I hoped they couldn't see how bad my hands were shaking. "I'm serious. Now either you're staying or you're going."

"Zsa," Malachi said while looking at my trembling hands. "What happened?"

"Nothing, I just don't wanna be here. God!" I looked back at Courtney. "I'm leaving, now either you're coming or not, but I'm going!" And I walked out of the theater doing my best to keep my knees from buckling.

Once I was in the parking lot I heard Malachi calling my name. "Zsa-Zsa." He rushed over to me and cupped my chin. "What happened to you?"

"Nothing."

"Why are you lying?"

"I'm not."

"I can look at you and tell you're scared." He turned his head and looked around the parking lot. "Did somebody run up on you?"

"Nothing happened!" My voice trembled. "I'm just ready to go home."

"You're lying." He looked me dead in the eyes. "Tell me the truth."

"Didn't I say nothing?" I pushed his hands from my face.

"Zsa." Malachi sighed as if he were exhausted. "I'm getting real, real tired of chasing you."

"Then stop."

"I can't. Not when you always have that same look in your eyes that you had when we were kids and you were scared. I feel like you need me."

"I needed you when I was twelve but you packed up and bounced. I'm cool now, I got this, okay?"

Malachi stared at me for a moment and then he said, "So, that's what this is all about? The drama, the attitude, and the treating me like I robbed you for some candy is all because I moved . . . five years ago . . . on a Friday . . . after you probably ate some Chinese food—"

"And the wall jumped." I felt tears coming to my eyes. "And jumped, and jumped, and I went upstairs because I thought you were Superman. But you weren't there. And I cried in the hallway. Begging you to come and take me with you, but you didn't." I sniffed. "And it's cool. Now I have to go."

"Zsa-Zsa, my baby. I was a kid then."

"You could've told me you were moving."

"I didn't know how to."

"And that's cool too. Just let me leave."

"Nah, because something else is haunting you. What is it?"

"Nothing."

"Does it have something to do with Ameen?"

"Not."

"Yes, it does. Now, tell me the truth." He placed his arms around me and pressed his forehead against mine. "I can make it go away," he whispered, "if you would just be honest with me." He kissed me on the lips. "I can make it disappear."

I looked into Malachi's eyes and wondered, were his promises true, could he really make the boogie man disappear? But then I wondered if Ameen was really the boogie man. Was he really that bad or was he hurt . . . and angry . . . and maybe . . . just maybe I'd pushed him away? Certainly I hadn't been the best girlfriend, especially since I'd been distracted by Malachi and my feelings for him. But then again . . . maybe not. . . . I wasn't sure. The only thing I was sure of was that all of my troubles were melting in Malachi's embrace.

"I won't let anything hurt you," Malachi whispered against my lips, "and I promise you I won't leave again. I'ma grown man now." We started to kiss.

"Two snaps up and a fruit loop, excuse you," Courtney shouted as he stomped over to us. "Break it up, 'cause I know you didn't call me out of the theater where I could've gotten my Jujubes on in peace to come outside and cupcake with li'l daddy. Oh, hell, no." Courtney looked at the ring on his index finger that was also a watch. "Since I can't see my movie in peace, then you won't be kissing li'l tender over here. We got about forty minutes before *Tiny and Toya* comes on, and if you interfere with that it's gon' be a sho'nough situation. Now come on."

"Later." Malachi gave me a small peck on the lips.

"Later," I said as Courtney and I got into my car. As I watched Malachi walk back inside the theater, I could see Ameen leaning against the side of the building, smoking a cigarette.

8

When I feel what I feel, sometimes it's hard to tell you so . . .

—AALIYAH, "AT YOUR BEST"

It was a record-breaking seventy degrees outside, which made the classroom in November hot as hell, and me being aggravated and frustrated with my life didn't help any. Everybody and their mama's mama were complaining and wanted to break out. It may have been late fall, but that was no excuse for the project heat that the school officials were killing us with.

"Attention, all juniors," the principal announced over the loudspeaker, interrupting my English teacher's lecture about Shakespeare, "please report to the gymnasium for last period. Again, all juniors report to the gymnasium for the last period." Soon after he finished, the bell rang and all I could hear was spontaneous chatter and binders slamming shut.

"Wassup with that?" I asked Asha and Courtney as we threw our backpacks over one shoulder.

"I don't know." Asha sucked her teeth. "But I was supposed to meet my baby, Samaad, and sneak me a kiss in the hallway."

"Oh, hell, no." Courtney snapped his fingers. "I am not going through the agony of hearing this again." He looked at me. "You can listen to it if you want to, but I've had enough of li'l Nicky Cannon and Mariah."

"I agree." I laughed.

"Haters." Asha snickered. "I want to go to the club this weekend," she said as we walked into the gym, which had been redecorated to look like a day care: filled with small portable cribs, baby bags, bottles, diapers, and Black, White, Asian, and Latino dolls that looked exactly like human babies.

"Two snaps up and a fruit loop." Courtney batted his eyes. "What is this? Why do they have all of these babies stretched out on the table like that? Oh, wait a minute, I'm calling the child protection people, and Asha, call an ambulance."

"For what?" She frowned.

"For me. I'm allergic to babies, I don't like 'em, and I don't want none. And if I'm around 'em too long I'll pass out."

"Would you be quiet?" I said as we took a seat. "They aren't real babies. They're Reborns and they're very popular."

"What?" Courtney's eyes bugged out. "Re-who? Reincarnated babies? Where they get them from? Oh, now, this is a problem."

"They are dolls, fool," I said to Courtney. "Calm down."

"I'm not gon' be too many more fools," he snapped at me.

"Are those real babies?" China, a girl from my home-room class, asked Courtney.

"You lost yo' rabbit-behind mind?" Courtney snapped at China. "Anybody with half a brain knows that those are Reused babies. They're very popular. Matter a fact they are probably made in the country you're named after, China."

"What?" China frowned. "China is not a country, it's a cup," and she stormed away.

As Courtney stood frozen, the gym filled with juniors and everyone was seated by whatever clique they hung with. Samaad winked his eye at Asha, and Malachi walked by and gave me the two-finger peace sign.

"Everyone, please be seated." Ms. Parker walked up to the podium and spoke into the mic. "I want to talk about why we are all here."

Within a matter of minutes the buzzing subsided and the gym was silent.

"Listen up," Ms. Parker continued. "This is National Safe Sex Awareness week, and instead of bringing some-one in to give you a lecture we decided to do something different." She pointed around the room. "We are going to make you all parents for a week."

"Oh, no . . . !" Courtney placed his hand up to his fore-head as if he were going to pass out at any moment, and then he fell into my lap.

"Would you get up?" I said, tight-lipped.

Courtney opened his eyes. "Are you still on birth con-trol? I think I might need one."

"Sit up." I pushed him slightly and he sat up.

"I feel so weak," he said.

"Are you done, Mr. Price?" Ms. Parker said while looking at Courtney. "Can I continue on now?"

"Yes," Courtney said faintly, "go on. Just know that I object. I don't like kids. My eight-year-old brother is enough punishment to last me a lifetime. Believe me, I get the point."

"In any event," Ms. Parker carried on, "as we know, teen pregnancy is on the rise, and the teachers, school officials, and the PTA would like to do all that we can to get you all to take a different route. So, we've decided to pair you off, as many of you as we can, and those who we can't pair off will have the daunting task of being single parents. Those who are single parents will only have to participate in the project for two and a half days. The rest will have five days, and you will have to work out a conducive schedule. A diary is required. You must visit one another and treat this baby as if it is a real baby."

"I object." Courtney stood up. "Somebody could've warned me and I would've stayed home." He started coughing. "Can't you see I'm sick?"

I was beyond embarrassed. "Shut up," I mumbled.

"Mr. Price," Ms. Parker said, "we did not tell you because more times than not teen pregnancy is not planned and it happens just like this, on a whim, unexpected, and the timing is off. So you've learned your first lesson in Parenting 101: expect the unexpected." She returned her attention back to the other students. "You all will have to name your child, and when you turn in your diary, you must have a birth certificate. Are there any questions?"

The room was silent.

"Seeing none, I will call out the couples." Ms. Parker called out a zillion different names, but the only ones that caught my attention were "Samaad Davis and Asha Harris. Malachi Askew and Zsa-Zsa Fields."

My heart dropped. I hoped like heck I wasn't cheesin' too hard. For a moment I felt like I was twelve again, so when I spotted Malachi looking at me I rolled my eyes.

"Staci Jones," Ms. Parker carried on, "and Courtney Price."

"Oh, hell, no." Courtney stood up and said, "Objection, Your Honor, did anyone look at me before they made that decision?"

"Okay," Ms. Parker said, "Staci, you go with Farad Johnson and Mr. Price will be a single parent."

We all laughed at Courtney, who was obviously beyond pissed. "This is some bull." Courtney walked over to the teacher, who was giving out the babies. "Straight-up bull."

"Here you go, Mr. Price," Ms. Parker said, handing him a baby and a baby bag. "Enjoy."

"Hold up," Courtney said, "why is li'l Tink-Tink"—he pointed to the doll in his hand—"Chinese?"

I shook my head. I loved Courtney like a brother, but I absolutely couldn't take his drama king antics anymore. I'd had enough.

"You better not have my baby around some other dude," Malachi whispered in my ear as he pressed his chest up against my back and kissed me slyly on my neck.

"As long as you pay child support, you don't have to worry about me." I laughed as Ms. Parker handed us our baby. "Oh, Zsa," Malachi said, "it's a boy."

For a moment I thought I was giggling too much but I couldn't help it. The butterflies that filled my stomach whenever Malachi was around made me feel silly on the inside. "What's his name?" I asked Malachi, knowing I already had his name picked out.

"What else?" Malachi said. "Malachi the second."

"Hollah." I twisted my neck, allowing the silliness in me to take over. "And you know this. You wanna hold him?" I said, placing the baby bag on my shoulder.

"Yeah, why not?" Malachi said, with confidence. "I'll hold him." And then he proceeded to stuff the baby in his backpack.

"Malachi," I said, slapping him across the arm, "you wanna take the doll from your bag, dang."

"Oh, my fault," Malachi said as the bell rang.

I couldn't believe I was laughing so much. "Why would you do that?" I asked.

"It's you," he said, draping his arm around my shoulder, as I held the baby to my chest. "You make me nervous."

Once I reached my locker, I looked at Malachi and smiled. "You make me nervous too." *Wait a minute, did I just admit that?*

"I do," he said as he pressed his lips against mine, and as soon as we started to kiss this doll baby started crying and screaming. Trust me, that scared the heck out of me, and when I looked at Malachi I realized I wasn't the only one frightened.

Before I could say anything Courtney was storming down the hall. "I'm breaking out into hives already," he said. "Nobody told me this thing was gon' cry. Hush, li'l Tink-Tink." He patted the doll on the back and looked at me. "Let's go. I've had a hard day today and I have got to get home."

I looked at Malachi, and he said to me, "I'll meet you at your house."

"And bring me some tea when you get there," Courtney said.

"Excuse you?" Malachi responded.

"Oh, you're talking to Zsa-Zsa. For a moment I thought you were talking to me."

"You talk too much," I said to Courtney, and then I turned to Malachi. "I'll see you then." I smiled, feeling for the first time in a long while what it meant to be seventeen.

Once I arrived home Malachi was waiting for me. He was leaning against his truck. I swear he was fine. The only problem was allowing myself to chill and be free around him without thinking about Ameen.

"Just so you know and won't be caught off guard, my sixty-two-year-old cousin and his wife are living with us now, and I think they're senile."

"Don't you worry about what we are," Cousin Shake said, snatching the front door open with his security guard uniform on, his flashlight in one hand and his blessing oil in the other. "You just better have a pencil in that book bag." Cousin Shake looked Malachi up and down. "I'm Officer You-Better-Have-That-Damn-Homework and this is my assistant, M.C. Cock Blocker." He pointed to Ms. Minnie. "Who are you?"

"Malachi."

"Who?" Cousin Shake scrunched his eyebrows. "Malachee?"

"No, Mal-la-kai," I corrected Cousin Shake.

"What? Mallory?" Cousin Shake frowned in disgust. "What kinda name is Mallory for a boy? Anywho, before you come in any further, anybody in here under eighteen that walks through the door with a book bag is subject to be searched."

"Hey, Zsa." My mother walked in the door behind me.

"Is this"—she looked at Malachi—"who I think it is?"

Malachi turned around. "How are you, Mrs. Fields?"

"Look at you," my mother said, "as handsome as you wanna be."

"Hold it!" Cousin Shake said. "Don't nobody move." He walked over to me. "Is that . . . a baby? Oh, hell, no. . . ." He placed his hand over his heart. "Oh, hell, to the no-no-no, is that a ba . . . a ba . . . a baby?" he stuttered.

"A baby?" Ms. Minnie said as she looked at my mother. "I hate to leave you like this, Jazmyn. But we gotta go. I'll get the suitcases, Shake. I don't do babies. Li'l Bootsie gave me enough trouble. Seemed like every day of his life I was pushing him out over and over again." She looked around the room. "You feel that, Shake?"

"Feel what, Minnie?" he asked.

"I got pains in my stomach. I think I'm in labor."

"I don't believe this," Cousin Shake said. "We are allergic to babies. I swear to the Ba'Jesus, if you have infected Minnie it's gon' be a situation around here."

"Cousin Shake," I said, exhausted, "it's an experiment—"

As Cousin Shake spoke his stomach shook and the belt underneath his belly rattled. "An experiment in what? The cha-walla-walla bang-bang? The jumpoff? The Hit it and Quit it?"

"Cousin Shake," my mother said, "it's something they do at all the schools."

"You ought to be ashamed of yourself." Cousin Shake looked at my mother as if he was sickened. "Good thing Habitat is over at her friend's house and isn't here to hear her mother and her sister getting their trickin' off. Any other time, Jazmyn, you're complaining about Zorro being too grown"—he pointed at me—"And now you taking up for her? That's what's wrong with parents today, too busy trying to be your child's friend 'cause you scared of being their mama. Here your child is so fresh and so grown that not only is she walking up in here with li'l Denzel on her arm, she comes home with a baby. She's so fast she done skipped pregnancy. Toi wasn't even this bad. At least we had a warning that she was walking the street."

"Cousin Shake," I said firmly, "this is a doll." I shook the baby from side to side.

"Holy hell, you goin' to jail!"

"It's a doll, Cousin Shake," I said as I hit the doll in the head, and wouldn't you know it the doll started crying.

"Don't you hit that baby no more!" Cousin Shake lashed me with blessing oil.

"Oh, my God, Ma." I turned to my mother. "Please explain to your family members that this is a school experiment on parenting. Malachi and I are partners, and at the end of the week the doll is going back."

"I can hear," Cousin Shake said, "I'm not no Mongo."

"What is a mongo?" Malachi asked.

"I don't know." I shook my head. "I tried to warn you."

"So that's really a doll?" Ms. Minnie asked.

"Yes," I said.

"Oh." Cousin Shake snorted. " 'Cause I thought I was gon' have to put on my cape and bust up outta here."

"It's cool, Cousin Shake." Malachi laughed.

"It's Mr. Bruh-man to you, son," Cousin Shake said, "I don't know you."

"Ma." I looked at her, embarrassed.

"Cousin Shake, be for real," my mother said.

"I'm just playin'—I'm just playin." Cousin Shake laughed. "Why don't you stay for dinner, son?"

I gave Malachi half a grin. "I would like that," I said. "I really would."

"Ai'ight." Malachi took off his jacket. "I'll stay then."

After dinner Malachi and I headed to my room for homework, and every five minutes Cousin Shake kept walking by and pointing his flashlight into the crack of my door. I swear I wanted to take that light and knock him upside the head with it.

Malachi had his feet resting on the floor and his back laid across the bottom of my bed. I placed my feet on his chest and began testing him for the chemistry test we had on Friday.

"What chemical—"

"Zsa," he said, cutting me off, "we've studied enough."

"Oh, really?" I closed the book.

"Yeah, talk to me."

"What you wanna talk about?" I put the book on my nightstand.

"Does ol' boy really be puttin' his hands on you?"

"Extra random. Now, where did that come from?" I asked, surprised.

"From me. I wanna know." He sat up. "Does he be hitting on you?"

"No," I said, "and I don't want to talk about Ameen."

"Why do you shut me out?" He looked me in the eyes and brushed my hair behind my ears.

I paused. " 'Cause."

" 'Cause what?"

"The last time I let you in . . . you left me."

"I'm not going anywhere. So how long are you going to make me pay for that?"

"You're not paying for anything."

"Yes, I am."

"How is that?"

" 'Cause another cat in my spot and I want *it* back. I want *you* back. I'm tired of all of this back and forth and guessing. I wanna chill with you. You wanna chill with me?"

Okay, I'ma attempt to play hard to get. "Yes." *Guess my resistance didn't go over too well.*

"And what y'all gon' be doin' while y'all chillin'? Gettin' hot?" Cousin Shake stood in my doorway. "Make a real baby." He looked at Malachi. "I like you, son, but the streetlights are on and around here, that means it's bed-time."

"Get . . . ," I said slowly, "away . . . from . . . my door!"

Malachi laughed. "It's cool. Cousin Shake is my man." Malachi got off the bed. "Plus, Zsa, it is getting late."

"Yeah, I guess."

"I'll keep the baby tonight," Malachi said, "and you keep it tomorrow night."

"Ai'ight," I said, handing him the doll and the bag.

"Thanks for having me, Cousin Shake." Malachi shook his hand, and afterward we walked outside. I walked Malachi across the street to his truck where he placed the doll in the back. Afterward he hopped in the driver's seat. I walked over to the window and leaned through. "Think about me, ma," he said, kissing me on my forehead.

"I will," I said as I watched him pull off. I was grinning from ear to ear as I headed across the street, when a car ran up on me like a Compton drive-by. I didn't know if I was about to get hit or held up at gunpoint. Once the car came to a screeching halt I realized that it was Ameen.

Instantly I froze.

"Can I hollah at you for a minute, Zsa?" Ameen asked.

I slid my trembling hands in my jeans' side pockets. "What?" I tried to seem pissed instead of nervous. "What is it? And what are you doing here?"

"What you showing off 'cause your new man just left?"

I stood still for a moment. Had Ameen been watching me? "Are you stalking me or something?"

"No. I love you, but you be playing too many games."

"Didn't you just run up on me in the bathroom, practically telling me you'll shoot me over some chicken head? And I'm the one playing games?" I looked both ways, hoping there was someone I knew from the block standing around. I spotted a few guys that I knew so I felt a little more relaxed. "Can I go now?" I asked sarcastically.

"Oh, so that's it?" Ameen said. "You don't love me no more? I make one mistake and we're done?"

I practically laughed in his face. "You keep making the same mistake over and over again. I'm tired. Now, if you will excuse me I don't like standing in the middle of the street." I went to walk in front of the car and Ameen pulled up so I couldn't pass.

"Zsa, come on now," he said. "I'm sorry about the way I acted. You know I care about you. You're my heart. Why you think I bought you these boots?" He opened the Gucci shoe box that lay on his passenger seat and practically shoved the boots at me. I held one of the boots in my hand, and I could tell by the scuff marks on the toe and the heel that they'd been worn.

"Are you kidding me? Giving me some used boots."

"She only wore 'em once and then I realized she ain't deserve 'em. You did, so I'm bringing them back."

"Keep 'em." I placed the boot back in his lap. "I'm cold on 'em."

"Oh, it's like that?" It was obvious that that threw him for a loop.

I guess he thought I was about to break down and accept his fake-behind apology. Not. "What you ain't know?" I rolled my eyes. "Now bounce."

Ameen scratched his chin. "Why you keep hanging with this dude that I keep seeing you with?"

I rolled my eyes to the sky. "I'm concerned, why are you following me around? We aren't together anymore, remember that?"

"Nah," he said, "I don't remember that and I suggest you erase it from your memory too, because if I can't have you, nobody will."

"Are you done?"

"The question is, are you done," Ameen said, and then he pulled off. I stood there for a moment. I couldn't believe what had just happened to me. My heart was racing in my chest, but a part of me was happy that I got to play Ameen in his face.

I walked back in the house and headed straight for my room. I flicked my lights off, lay back on the bed, and just as I closed my eyes and started thinking about my day my phone rang. I looked at the caller ID and it was my baby, Malachi. Immediately, I started smiling. "You rang?" I answered my phone while turning my radio on. WBLS's Quiet Storm was playing and Aaliyah's "At Your Best" was on.

"Thinking about me, ma?" Malachi asked. His voice was so soothing that I swear he made all the fear inside of me subside.

"And you know this."

"I know I just left, but I miss you, ma," he said.

"And I miss you too."

Malachi's voice was like sweet heat to my ears and before I knew it, time was flying by and we'd been talking for hours. I looked at the clock and it was four AM.

"Ai'ight, Zsa, I'll get up," Malachi said.

"Okay, talk to you later."

The line went silent. "Malachi?" I said.

"Yeah." He laughed. "I guess we should've hung up."

"Maybe," I said.

"You hang up first," Malachi said.

"No, I can't hang up on you. You hang up."

"Ai'ight, ma. On the count of three we'll both hang up."

"One," we said simultaneously, "two . . . three."

I held onto the phone because I didn't want to be the first one to hang up. "Malachi," I called.

"I'm here." He laughed. "It's obvious that neither one of us wants to hang up, so I tell you what, keep the phone to your ear, lay down, and we'll go to sleep together."

I couldn't stop smiling. "Alright."

I started to close my eyes, and just as I spotted the early morning sun coming up I felt myself drifting into another world.

* * *

I don't remember my sister sneaking in my room to sleep. All I remembered was her taking the phone from my ear, telling me to move over, and the next thing I knew my mother was calling our names. "Zsa-Zsa, Hadiah, time for school."

Don't ask me why, but I rolled my eyes to the ceiling. Why was she acting as if she actually got us ready for school in the morning? This was really over the top.

"Zsa-Zsa," my mother called again while knocking on my door. "Can I come in?" She twisted the knob but the door was locked.

"Say no," Hadiah said, laying across the foot of my bed. "It's too early in the morning to hear her nagging."

"Zsa," my mother called again.

"I can't say no."

"Ignore her, then."

"Be quiet," I snapped at my sister, "and open the door." Reluctantly Hadiah walked over to the door and opened it. "What took y'all so long to open the door?" my mother asked.

"No reason." Hadiah ran out the room. "I have to get ready for school," she yelled behind her.

I could've smacked my sister. She knew exactly what she was doing by leaving me with my mother. Now, she didn't have to deal with her.

"So what's going on?" my mother asked me while sitting on the edge of my bed.

"Oh, nothing." I batted my eyes. "Just work, church, and a few dates that I've been on."

"Are you being smart?"

"Nope, just recapping your life. You seem to be having fun, so I figured like mother like daughter."

"Zsa-Zsa, what is going on that we don't talk anymore?"

"You're not here."

"I am here. But you never want to be bothered. Like yesterday when Malachi came over, why don't you want to talk to me?"

"Ma, not today." I pulled a pair of Deréon jeans from my closet.

"Yes, today," she insisted. "And right now. Tell me, because you are my child and we have to get through this."

"Ever since Daddy died—"

"This is not about your father."

"Why do you always do that?" I frowned.

"Do what?"

"Cut me off"—I chose a pair of stilettos—"when I have something to say about Daddy."

"Because, truthfully, I don't want to hear it."

"I didn't think this was about you. I thought you wanted to hear my side."

"Your side of what? Everything is a problem with you. I want us to be close," she said as her cell phone started to ring.

"Ma—"

"Wait a minute." She smiled, looking at the caller ID. "Let me get this." She rose from my bed and walked out of my room. "Hello?"

I just looked at the door and knew I should've taken my sister's advice. The next time I won't let her in. I finished choosing my outfit and listened to the radio that was still playing from last night. Neyo was singing about being sick. A few minutes later my mother stood in my doorway with her coat on. "After school we'll finish our conversation." And before I could respond she was gone.

I showered, did my hair, fought off thoughts of Ameen, smiled at thoughts of Malachi, and dressed for school. "Bye, Zsa," Hadiah said.

"Bye," I said, walking out of my room and sitting down at the dining room table to eat the breakfast Cousin Shake and Ms. Minnie prepared. Once I was done I kissed them both on the cheeks and headed for the front door. When I opened the door I couldn't believe it, but Malachi was standing there with his hand on the bell.

"Hey." I know I was cheesin' from ear to ear. "What are you doing here?"

"I came to take you to school."

"Are you serious?"

"Yeah, you ready?"

"Of course I'm ready . . . but there's only one thing."

"What's that?"

"We have to pick up Courtney."

"Courtney?" Malachi arched one eyebrow. "Oh, no, baby, you know I don't get down with Courtney like that. He's too . . . too . . . zessy for me. And his clothes be all smedium. I just can't deal with all of that temperament in the morning."

"Boo, he's really a good dude, and in the morning he's really quiet and peaceful."

Malachi stood and stared at me for a moment. "You better be lucky I'm feelin' you."

"Yeah, I am," I said, handing him my backpack.

By the time we got to Courtney's house Courtney was waiting outside on the porch for me. His clothes were tossed on him like a cyclone, the baby was upside down in his backpack, and he had a head full of pink and green sponge rollers.

Malachi looked at me and said, "Yo, ma, dig. No offense and I love you to death but I am not about to ride in the car with no dude and a head full of rollers. That's a li'l far."

"Courtney." I got out the truck and walked over to him. "Why do you have rollers in your hair?"

"Can't you see this is a quick weave gone wrong?!" He twisted his lips. "You see me? I'm sleepy, I'm tired, and I can not do this with this damn recycled doll. Ms. Parker can fail me, kick me out, whatever. But see me and li'l Tink-Tink are done."

"What happened?"

"This thing wouldn't stop crying. I'm tired. I swear I am. So, I talked this over with my mother and I'm staying home today. You take this thing and I don't care what you do with it."

"Courtney—" I called him but he never turned around. Instead he kept going in the house and slammed the door behind him.

I got back in the car with Malachi, and he said, "What happened?"

"I don't know." I hunched my shoulders. "But I think he may have dropped out of high school and now we have twins."

9

To the left, to the left . . .
Keep talking that mess, that's fine
But could you walk and talk at the same time?

—BEYONCÉ, "IRREPLACEABLE"

I had to admit it felt good riding into the school's parking lot being chauffeured by my baby. And believe me, all eyes were on us. Staci and her crew were standing near the school's entrance, and I swore I could see green glob comin' all out of her mouth.

I hated to rejoice at someone else's expense but Ha . . . lle . . . lujah! Hallelujah! Hallelujah! Ha . . . lle . . . lujah! I was his girl now. I promise you I felt like tap dancing. I grabbed the doll out the backseat and patted it on its back. I knew the baby thing was a reach, but it was enough to get Staci to imagine that I wasn't stepping to the left anytime soon.

We parked next to Asha and Samaad, and I could tell by the smile on Asha's face that she couldn't wait to hear what I had to say. "Ai'ight, baby," Malachi said, opening my door and giving me a peck on the lips. "I need to kick it with Samaad for a minute. You got it from here?"

"Yeah. Plus I need to catch up with Asha."

"Ai'ight," he said as he walked over to Samaad and I walked over to Asha.

"Skip all the yadda-yadda and get to the point," Asha said, grinning from ear to ear. "Is it official?"

"Ill." I couldn't stop smiling. "Could you stop sweatin' me?"

Asha batted her extended lashes. "If you don't cough up the business."

"Okay, Asha, it's not exactly official. Like, I just broke up with Ameen."

"So, we're seventeen," she said as we started walking toward the school's entrance, "we don't need that much space between relationships. All we need to do is get the point; which is: Ameen is hot piss and Malachi is a love fest." She snapped her fingers. "Two snaps up and a fruit loop, as Courtney would say. Speaking of which, where is he?"

"Yo." I stopped dead in my tracks. "Courtney was pissed off this morning. I went over there and homie had rollers in his hair."

"Rollers?"

"Rollers. He said it was a quick weave gone bad. For real, for real, I know that's our boy but he was a little extra with the zest this morning. I ain't sayin' but I'm just sayin' I think he's sleeping in fishnets."

Asha laughed. "You stupid." She laughed again. "Anyway, have you heard from Ameen?"

Instantly my heart raced as I shook my head to erase the picture of Ameen from my mind. "Asha, he ran up on me in the middle of the street yesterday."

"He did what?" she asked in disbelief.

"You heard me. Yo, he is really jealous. I was crossing the street after walking Malachi to his car, and as I went to step across the yellow line Ameen pulled up like he was about to do a drive-by. I was like 'do I need to take my jewelry off?' "

"Did you tell your mother and Cousin Shake?"

"So they could overreact?" I waved my hand. "Ameen is retarded but he ain't crazy."

"Yeah, okay." Asha twisted her lips.

"I'm not scared of Ameen, he won't do anything to me."

"Zsa-Zsa, you don't know what he'll do. You didn't think he would cheat on you either, did you? But he did."

"Well—"

"Well nothing. All I'm saying is to be careful. Those type of dudes always get away because we miss the clues."

"Asha, please don't start reciting what you've seen on TV or learned in health class. I'm not a victim, believe me. Ameen wants me when he wants me, and when I don't respond he doesn't know what to do. But I'm done now."

"Are you sure?" She looked at me with one eye open and the other closed.

"Yes, silly. Besides"—I turned around and looked at Malachi, who was still kickin' it with Samaad—"something tells me I have all I ever wanted."

"I'm so glad that's your dude." Asha smiled as we walked into the school and over to our lockers.

"That's my baby, Asha. For real," I said, gleaming. "I love him so much."

"Her baby?" A voice drifted from behind me. "Malachi?" the voice continued. "Is she talking about your man, Staci?"

As soon as I heard that, I rolled my eyes to the ceiling. I was not in the mood to get it poppin' this morning.

I turned around. Staci and her crew were standing at their lockers, and the one spittin' all the ying-yang was named Nyesha.

"We got a problem or something?" Asha rolled her eyes. " 'Cause we don't need the rah-rah, we can get to the heart of the matter."

I waved my hand at Staci and her whack crew. Then I looked them up and down. "Asha, we're not going to even sweat the gutter rats. So, I advise 'the wanna be me's not to let the stilettos fool them. If Staci has something she wants to say to me, then she needs to say it to me. And not wait until she gets around her fake posse and wanna beef. Trust me." I looked Staci in the eyes and then Nyesha. "I am not the one."

"Who is that tramp looking at?" Nyesha spat. "I know not me."

"Who you calling a tramp, skeezer?" I said, looking at Nyesha. "You better get on."

"For real," Asha said. "Come on, Zsa, they don't want it."

"Don't want what?" Nyesha said. "Why would you steal somebody's man? You just a slut."

I spun around so quickly that I think my feet had to catch up with my head. "You a slut, trick." I walked up on Nyesha, and Asha was right by my side. Asha wasn't the one for drama but she always had my back no matter what.

A crowd started to gather around us as I carried on. "Don't let your don't-know-how-to-keep-her-man-happy friend get you a beat down!" I pointed my finger in Nye-sha's face. "You singin' all this rah-rah and she hasn't even opened her mouth. At least I don't need a clique to fight my battles. So yeah, come to think of it I did steal her man, and you know why? 'Cause I wanted to, and at least I had the balls to take him. Now what, what you gon' do?!" We were now chest to chest.

"Nothing," Asha said. "Or it's gon' be on." She started taking her earrings off.

"Yo, chill," Malachi said as he walked in and slid his arm between us, and Samaad grabbed Asha by the hand. "What's up with this?" Malachi looked at me and then to Staci.

"Your ex-girl." I pointed my finger in Staci's face. "You better catch her 'cause I ain't the one." Before I could continue on the bell rang and the crowd dispersed. "You better do something with that thirsty trick before she get a beat down." I looked at Staci, and just to drive the point home, I kissed Malachi on the lips. "Come on, Asha," I said, "you're right, they don't want none." And we walked away, heading to class.

I was pissed for the next two periods, and I don't know what bothered me more—that Staci and her crew ran up on me or that when I walked away from them Malachi didn't run after me. I mean . . . I know he had a different class than me and everything but still, he didn't have to stand there when I walked away as if after I was gone he would be entertaining Staci's sorrows.

I was in calculus, and I couldn't wait for the bell to ring so that I could find Malachi and tell him what was on my mind. Oh, and to also dump this crying-behind doll on

him. Do you know that thing cried every hour on the hour
and the pacifier didn't always work? I know the school
wanted to teach us a lesson, but dang even a real baby
shuts up sometimes.

After the teacher gave us the homework assignment the
bell rang and everybody was up and out of there with the
quickness. I went to my locker to get my book for English
class, but surprisingly I didn't see Malachi anywhere.

I knew I would probably get in trouble, but I left the
doll in my locker, and from the sound of things I wasn't
the only one. I walked away from my locker and I could
swear that I saw Malachi out the corner of my eye as I
passed the study lounge.

"Staci—"

Once I heard that, I knew it was him. Now I was pissed,
and a lump was settling in my throat. I backtracked and
walked over toward them. Malachi was leaning against the
wall and Staci was standing in the doorway of the study
lounge with tears in her eyes. For a moment I felt bad, at
least until I heard her say, "If I catch her, I'ma kill her."

"And who might that be?" I slid in between them. "You
gon' kill who?"

"Zsa," Malachi said, "stop."

"Stop?" I couldn't believe he said that. "She and her
cronies attacked me and you're taking up for her? Is this
your girl?"

"Chill," he said sternly. "For real, fall back."

I looked at him and I felt as if a thousand bullets rang
through my chest. This felt worse than anything with
Ameen. I looked Malachi dead in his eyes and said, "I'll get
up, 'cause I'm 'bout to fall all the way back."

I went to storm away but before I could get far, Malachi

grabbed my hand and turned me around. "I'm so sick of you runnin'. Stand here until I'm done. You tryna be so big and bold but you leaving your man with the very chick you can't stand. Relax."

Damn, did he just call himself my man in front of this chick? I looked at her and smiled. "Checkmate."

"You know what, Malachi"—Staci looked me up and down—"you and this bird deserve one another."

I rolled my eyes to the ceiling. Is that all she could think to say? "At least you get the point!" I yelled behind her.

"What the hell is wrong with you?" Malachi snapped as Staci disappeared from our sight. "I can fight my own battles."

"She and her friends walked up on me."

"Okay, and you checked 'em, it's no need to keep comin' for her throat. She knows how I feel about you, but I didn't want to make her feel like nothing behind it."

"Why do you care how she feels? You know what, I have already been down the road of dealing with other chicks in my relationships, and for real"—I paused—"I would just be more comfortable if you didn't talk to her anymore."

"What?" He looked at me as if I were crazy.

"Like, don't even have no words for her, because I just can't deal with the nonsense."

"Zsa, I'm not doing that."

"What?" I took a step back.

"You know how disrespectful that is? Our families are very close. I can't play her like that."

"You can't play her like that? So it doesn't matter how I feel?"

"Of course it does."

"I can't tell."

"You know what, Zsa," he said as the bell rang, "it's a wrap talking about this." He placed his hands on my waist and moved in for a kiss. I nicely backed out of his embrace, turned my back, hit him with a two-finger peace sign, and with every ounce of motion in my ocean I sashay away.

"It's cool, ma," Malachi said from behind me, "I like that view too."

It was last period, and just to keep it one hundred with you I was really pissed off with Malachi. I mean, I guess I could understand where he was coming from, but still I felt really insecure with him talking to this chick. . . . I felt like . . . like something she'd said or did would make him change his mind about me and reconsider her. And then where would I be? I was just starting to feel normal again and not have to think about having a boyfriend who cheated on me every five minutes, but now I had to deal with this.

I tore a piece of loose-leaf paper from my binder and started writing Asha a note:

I'm stressed as hell. And I'm not beat for this Staci nonsense. Do you know I saw him chillin' with her in the hallway a few periods ago?

After I finished writing the note, I dropped it on the floor and kicked it slyly with the tip of my stiletto over to Asha. She picked it up, started to read, and then re-sponded. A few minutes later she passed the note back the same way I had given it to her.

The note read,

Chillin' with her how, Zsa? You know you can be a li'l extra at times. No diss.

That pissed me off. I was a lot of things but I was not extra. Now Courtney, he was extra.

I'm not being extra. I saw them near the study lounge, not sure what they were saying, but she had tears in her eyes. He called me his girl in front of her, she got mad and stormed away.

I passed the note back.

A few seconds later the note was given back to me.

And your point to being pissed is what? Be pissed if they were kissing or he was feeling on her.

After reading Asha's response I couldn't respond fast enough.

If they were doing that I would've stole on both of 'em. I'm pissed because he was talking to her in the first place. What about him asking me what happened before he spoke to her? I told him I didn't want him speaking to her ever again and he said "no," he couldn't play her like that.

I had to hold the note for a second before I passed it back because my health teacher was looking toward the back of the classroom. A few minutes later the teacher turned around and I quickly slid the note to Asha.

I could tell by the frown on Asha's face that she was writing something that I wouldn't like, and once I got the note back, my gut instinct was correct.

Are we seventeen? Or seven? So what if he was talking to her? Stop taking out on him what applies to Ameen. Bottom line you don't know what they were talking about. Everybody can see that he loves you. You said he called you his girl and she was in tears, so chop that conversation up to be Staci's loss. Not yours. And yes, it is ridiculous to ask him not to ever

speak to her again. Their families are close and as
long as Malachi is respecting you—you need to chill.
Don't be mad either because I didn't tell you what you
wanted to hear. But I like Malachi and you need to
relax.

I sucked my teeth.

Thank you, Mother-Love. And do not write back.
And yes, that is a diss.

I wanted to fling this note at her head, but I didn't.
When Asha received the note back and read it, she looked
at me and smiled. I hated having such an honest best
friend. I gave her the gas face and she started laughing,
which caused me to laugh. But don't get it twisted, I was
still pissed.

When the bell rang I hit Asha with a peace sign and
walked out the door. I had to think about whether I
wanted to ride back home with Malachi or if I wanted to
make him sweat. I pulled the drawstring tight on my fitted
goose down jacket. My legs were cold although I had on
striped tights underneath my Deréon miniskirt, and my
backpack was so full from stuffing the doll inside that my
shoulder ached. I walked out the school's entrance and
Malachi was standing there. Instead of walking over to
him I decided I would make him sweat it out a little bit, so
I headed toward the curb, and that's when I realized that
Ameen was standing there leaning against the passenger
door of an olive green Mercedes with dice swinging in the
window. He smiled at me and said, "What's good?"

"I was about to ask the same thing," Malachi said from
behind me.

"I don't know what's good." I turned around and said
to Malachi, "But seems I better find out."

"So you gon' talk to that cat right in my face?" Malachi asked in shock.

"What's the problem, sweetie. Neither one of us can play our exes like that. I'm sure you understand." And I walked away leaving him standing there. I walked over toward Ameen and said, "Yeah?"

"Oh, you wanna front on me?" he whispered.

"No, honey," I said, loud enough for Malachi to hear, "I'm just wondering what you're doing here."

"I wanted you to see my new ride so I came to pick you up from school. Plus, I noticed you had a ride this morning so I wanted to make sure you had a ride this afternoon."

For a moment I felt creepy. Why was he watching me? I started to ask him did I need to call the cops on his stalkin' behind, but seeing that Malachi's eyes were green and red at the same time, I played along with it. "Oh, that was sweet, boo," I said to Ameen.

"And, wait, that ain't it," Ameen said as he reached in his car and pulled out an oversized green and white wreath of evergreen leaves and carnation flowers, with a white nylon ribbon going across it that read I MISS YOU.

Oh, hell, no. "Ameen"—I looked at him as if he were crazy—"are those funeral flowers?"

"It doesn't matter where I got 'em from. What matters is how much I was thinking about you. What, you don't like 'em?"

"Umm, I ain't say that," I said, mindful that I was still trying to make Malachi jealous. "They alright."

"Alright?" Ameen said, pissed. "You just ungrateful. Do you know how long I spent looking at these trying to figure out which one to bring home for you?"

"Ameen, you don't need to get so upset."

"You just be pissing me off, man. I don't even know why I came here. Here I am trying to show you how much I care and you acting like this." He looked me up and down. "You don't know how to act." He pointed toward the sky. "Every time I try to show you I'm a better man and what they taught me at Sunday school you take me outta my zone. Is this how it's gon' be, Zsa? Me loving you and you treating me like subway trash? Them some beautiful flowers." He pointed to the wreath. "My mama said them flowers was off the hook. They got a stand and everything. I ain't even have to buy no card. They said exactly what I mean. Get it, A-meen."

I swear I couldn't move. Was he always this ignorant or did he just get this way? "Ameen, just relax, okay?"

"I just wanna talk to you, Zsa."

"Okay, we can talk."

"Oh, now you wanna be nice, but any other time, you nasty to me. Always so angry."

"I'm not angry."

"Yes, you are. Zsa-Zsa, anger is not good for anybody. It just makes you rotten inside. You need to pray about that."

"Oh . . . kay." I looked from side to side, not knowing what to say next, and then I said, "Umm, just give me a second."

I walked over to Malachi and said, "I'll catch you later. I have a ride." And I walked back over to Ameen swiftly before Malachi could say anything smart to me.

I slid into Ameen's Mercedes and turned around toward Malachi, who was now sitting in his truck. Malachi held two fingers up, and just when I thought I'd got him back and he was good and pissed, he pointed to the flowers that were still on the sidewalk and blew me a kiss. Whatever.

Once he disappeared down the block, I turned to Ameen.

"Zsa, I know I messed up, but you shouldn't be out here talking to some random dude because you know I would never let you go. So I'll forgive you this time but don't let it happen again. Feel me?"

"Yeah, I feel you."

"So do you think we can be together again?"

"You wanna know what I think?" I arched my eyebrows.

"Yeah."

"Okay." I swallowed. "I think you a whack excuse for a man. You think you can run up on me like you some jake and I should what? Run into your arms? Hell, no. I'm done. Tired. So you can take your fake, dingy funeral flowers and kiss," I said slowly, "my . . ."

"Kiss your what?" he asked in disbelief.

"You know."

"I hope you don't think you gettin' a ride home after your li'l outburst. And leave my flowers right where they're standing on the sidewalk."

I held my fingers out as if I was counting on them. "Forget you, them whack flowers, and this stupid car that probably ain't even yours." I got out, slammed the door, and kicked the flowers down.

"Oh, hell, no, Zsa."

"Shut up!" I screamed.

"You know you got to pay for that, right. This ain't over!"

"Ameen."

"What?"

"Lose yourself." I spotted a bus across the street and boldly crossed in front of Ameen's car, leaving him and his funeral wreath sitting there.

I rode the bus home, and once I stepped off I noticed Malachi sitting on my porch in the rocking chair. He was so cute that I couldn't stand it. I have to admit that I was happy with my fit because my baby was right where I wanted him to be.

I walked over to him. "How often does a girl get two stalkers in one day?"

"Let me set the record straight." He eased up and looked dead into my eyes. " 'Cause you seem to either think the stunt you pulled was cute or that I'ma fool."

"I didn't say that."

"I'm talking, don't cut me off again. Understand this: I'm not the one, Zsa. For real, don't even do it to yourself. I don't chase and I'm not gon' sweat you. I'm feeling you, I'm feeling the hell outta you, otherwise I wouldn't be sittin' here, but I will leave you alone so fast you'll wonder if I was ever real."

"You were all in Staci's face. What did you expect me to do!"

"Did you ever think to ask me why? Did you ever think that she stopped me? I'm her ex-boyfriend, she was hurt, and she felt like she had some things she wanted to get off her chest. Is that a crime? What you should've done was asked me if you could hollah at me and I would've explained, but no, you assumed you had the answers from beginning to end." He stood up. "I'm not that cat who smacked you in the club, I'm not no cheating and disrespectful dude. My mother and my father both raised me to love and respect women. Therefore I know I'ma good man, so I have a choice and I don't tolerate childishness. Now either you wanna be a kid or you wanna be the grown woman you claim to be and chill with me."

Did he just read me? I started to say something smart but judging by the look on his face I decided against it. "You know I wanna be with you—"

"Then don't pull a stunt like that again."

My ego and pride wanted to be like "I'm not sweatin' you either, so you can step." But that's not what my heart wanted . . . so I gave in to my heart and said, "My fault. But he didn't bring me home, you saw me getting off the bus."

"Umm-hmm." I could tell he was fighting his smile.

"My baby was jealous?" I locked the tips of my fingers around his neck. He was too tall for me to cross my arms. "I cussed that cat out as soon as you pulled off. He was all in my grill like, 'yo', what you just say?' "

"Stop testing fate and leave that cat to himself, ai'ight?" Malachi said, more as a warning than a statement. "The next time just tell him to get ghost. Don't even play with him like that."

"You're right." I kissed him. "It won't happen again."

Malachi stroked my hair and looked down into my eyes. "I love you, Zsa."

"And I love you."

"Tell me, how long have you been in love with me?" He pressed his lips against mine.

"Since I was twelve." I responded to his kisses. "And it won't go away."

"It better not either."

After we kissed, I laid my head against Malachi's chest and I could feel his heart beat. "Can you stay for a while?"

"If Ms. Minnie cooked, I'm all in."

"What, you don't trust my cooking? I can burn." I put my keys in the door.

"Yeah, baby, I'm sure you can burn."

I opened the door, and to my surprise balloons and streamers were everywhere. There was light jazz playing in the background and my mother was prancing nervously around the dining room table and dressing it with her best china.

"Hi, Malachi," Hadiah said, and then turned to me. "Jazmyn Fields left out of here this morning and Glenda the Good Witch came back. Yo, she is being real nice, dancing, singing, and straight buggin'."

"Ma," I said, watching her place the silver cutlery on the right and then on the left of the plate, "what's going on?"

"I have a surprise." She smiled at Malachi. "Hi, sweetie. I'm glad you're here. How's your mom and dad?"

"They're fine. My mother said to tell you hello."

"Tell Karen I said to call me, we need to catch up."

"So what's the surprise, Ma?" I asked, and that's when it clicked. My brother might be coming home. "Ma, is Derrick coming home?" I jumped up in glee. I couldn't wait to see my brother.

"Derrick?" she said, surprised. Before she could go on, Cousin Shake walked into the room.

"Zoom-Zoom, are you looking for the homework police?"

"Not really."

"Well we're right here," Cousin Shake said. "I know you missed us. Hey there, Moses." He waved at Malachi as he stepped into the living room, and I swear I almost lost a week's worth of lunch looking at him. Cousin Shake wore a three-piece, clear plastic suit, trimmed in tiny green bulbs that lit up his lapel like a Christmas ornament. On the back of his jacket was a blinking flamingo, and written across the butt of his pants was, STRAIGHT CHILLIN'. His knotty chest hair was smashed against the smedium vest he had on, and his tiger-print, booty-chokin' briefs could be seen straight through his pants, yet he thought he was sharp. "I see you lookin', Zebra. I see you, Hollyhood. Milky Way," he said to Malachi, "you seem to be a nice li'l dude so I'ma let you in on my dressing secret. The reason why you don't see no sweat coming from this suit is because I put holes right here." Cousin Shake bent over and pointed to his butt. "See, nobody will ever know they're there."

We were all silent, except for my mother, who was too busy to notice. And just when I thought Cousin Shake was bad, his wife stepped into the room. "Here come Minnie," Cousin Shake rapped, "lookin' like good and plenty. She got nothin' but love, lookin' sharp like a tree shrub."

Ms. Minnie danced around in her blond Afro wig and plastic minidress with her neon pink underwear and Vickie Secret bra to match. "And you know this," she said.

I turned to Malachi. "I'm sorry. I know your appetite must be ruined."

"Nah." He did all he could not to fall out laughing. "I'm straight. This is funny to me."

"That's 'cause you don't live here," I said, tight-lipped.

"My brother is gon' trip when he comes home to this." I couldn't stop smiling. I hadn't been this excited in a long time. I turned to Malachi. "I can't wait to see my brother."

"Okay," my mother said, as if she'd just returned to the same planet we were on, "how does everything look?"

"Ma, can you just tell us, is it my brother?" I asked again. "Please."

"I asked her the same thing, Zimbabwe, but all your mama would tell me is that she wanted us to get dressed because she had a surprise," Cousin Shake said.

"So here us is," Ms. Minnie said. "We so sharp it don't make sense."

"It don't make no sense," Hadiah said. "Not even a little bit."

"Behave, Hadiah," my mother said as the bell rang. "Okay, okay." She took a series of deep breaths. "How do I look?"

She wore a fitted red and black kimono dress with rhinestone accessories. Her hair was pulled back behind her ears, and her makeup was flawless. "You look fine." I hurried to the door. I couldn't wait any longer for her to primp, I had to see my brother now. I snatched the door open, and instead of Derrick standing there it was a six foot tall, caramel-colored man with sprinkles of premature gray in his short hair and beard. He was dressed in a two-piece Armani suit with black wing tip shoes.

I looked at my mother. "Who is this?" I turned back to the man. "Who are you? You're not my brother."

"You must be Zsa-Zsa," he said. "I'm Kenneth."

"Who?" I looked him over, and that's when I noticed that he held two plastic bags filled with Chinese food cartons in his hands. Don't ask me why, but my eyes looked at the calendar and noticed that it was Friday. I felt like bells were going off in my head as I saw flashes of my father's face.

"Everyone"—my mother walked over and grabbed his hand—"this is Kenneth and Kenneth, this is my family." She pointed around the room and introduced us by name. "Family"—she took a deep breath—"this is my fiancé. We're getting married."

"What?" I was in shock and felt frozen in my spot. My mother had officially lost her mind. She was never home, never had time for us, acted as if my brother and father didn't exist, and somehow in the midst of all of this, she managed to date a man long enough to agree to become his wife. Oh, hell, no. "Are you serious?" I blinked my eyes in disbelief.

"Chill, Zsa," Malachi mumbled to me.

"Jazmyn," Cousin Shake said, "I need to speak to you."

"After dinner." My mother arched her eyebrows.

"All right," Cousin Shake said, "I'ma give you that, a li'l later."

"How's everyone?" Kenneth said, extending his hand to the men. Malachi and Cousin Shake shook his hand. He turned to me and Hadiah. "I've heard a lot about you two."

Hadiah walked over to me and grabbed my hand the same way she used to when she was little. "Me and my sister were fine," she said. "At least until the bell rang."

My mother shot her a look and instantly she was quiet.

"Well," Kenneth said, clearly uncomfortable, "I hope every one likes egg foo young. I brought plenty, especially since your mother said it was your favorite."

I looked at my mother as if she had really gone bonkers. I couldn't believe she told him that. She of all people should have known that I hate Chinese food.

"They love it," my mother said. "Everyone have a seat."

"Stay cool, Zsa," Malachi whispered from behind me.

I watched my mother fix us plates of egg foo young while I did all I could to fight off memories of my daddy. Malachi squeezed my hand underneath the table, while Hadiah held the other one.

"Can you say grace, Cousin Shake?" my mother asked, fostering a smile.

"I sho' can."

We all stood up, held hands around the table, and bowed our heads. "Father and Brother man God, what's crackin'? We come before You askin' You for strength. Strength that I don't take my grown niece and put her over my knee for being selfish. Strength that I don't bust her up for thinking that she can just walk up in here, announce that she is about to be a Mrs., and she hasn't even taken the time out to be a mama. Strength, dear Jonathan, that I don't lose my relish, be less than a Christmas, and bust me up some thangs up in here. Dear Father, I need patience, and give li'l Zulu some strength 'cause she look like she about to bust a cap at any minute. Oh, and bless this food, 'cause we don't know this man and don't know where he got this food from. Now, say Amen."

"Amen," everyone responded.

For the first few minutes everyone was silent, and Kenneth and my mother were the only ones eating. "You want something to drink, sweetie?" my mother asked Kenneth, while doing her best to ignore us.

"Sure," he said, obviously uptight.

My mother went quickly into the kitchen and then returned with a beer and a shot of Hennessy. "A Coke would've been fine, sweetie," Kenneth said. "I don't really drink alcohol much."

"Oh." My mother blinked as if she just realized what she'd done.

True story, I was outdone. I felt like I was in the Twilight Zone as flashbacks of my past kept running through my mind. After a few more minutes I absolutely couldn't take it anymore so I said, "So, Kenneth, tell me since you like Chinese food so much"—I pointed to his empty plate—"do you kick your women's asses in the morning, at night, or only on Fridays?"

"Zsa-Zsa!" my mother said. "You better shut up!"

"Really, I better shut up?" I sat up straight in my seat. "Did you tell him about us? Or are we just as mysterious to him as he is to us?"

"Zsa, chill," Malachi mumbled to me.

"No, I'm not chillin', I'ma say what I have to say. Tell me, Kenneth, did my mother ever tell you how she used to get her butt kicked? How she used to drag us behind her to press charges on my father, who she likes to pretend didn't exist? Did she tell you that I hate Chinese food"—I pushed my full plate away from me—"and I hate it because it's the same thing she used to make us eat before she got bust in her head? Did she tell you that?"

"Shut up!" my mother yelled.

I ignored her. "Did she tell you that I have a brother, who I was hoping was the one really at the door and not you? Don't let this big house fool you. But it's cool, 'cause when I turn eighteen, I'm bouncin' and I'm takin' my little sister with me, so you two can have these four walls all to yourself."

"You better shut the hell up!" My mother rose from her seat.

"Or what? You gon' hit me? You gon' finally recognize me? You gon' finally see that I'm here and that I didn't disappear. What, what are you going to do?"

My mother looked too shocked to respond.

"Exactly what I thought," I continued. I shook my head and could feel years of tears filling my throat and eyes. "I'm out of here."

"You better sit down!" my mother screamed.

"Let her go," Cousin Shake said. "I can understand the child needs some air. Because finally I see what the problem is." He looked at my mother. "It's you."

"How could you say something like that to me!" my mother screamed.

Cousin Shake continued on. "Jazmyn, right now you just the woman who had three kids. Not a mama. See, when you called down to Atlanta, I thought me and Minnie were coming up here to get them in check, but you need to be in check. You wanna be the mama when it suits you. Even I noticed that you don't have one picture of Zach up in the house."

"Zach beat on me!" my mother screamed. "I don't have to celebrate that!"

"No, but you have to deal with these kids." Cousin Shake turned to Kenneth. "I'm sure you are a nice man, and this is no reflection on you, but Shake-a-Deen Green is gon' say what's on his mind."

"And while you do that, Cousin Shake, I'ma bounce," I said, standing up. "I'm out of here."

"Zsa." Malachi grabbed my hand, and I snatched it away. "You don't understand, I need to leave." As I ran outside I could hear Cousin Shake telling my mother, "You need to be ashamed of yourself!"

I got in my car and put my keys in the ignition, and before I took off Malachi slid in the passenger seat. "Where are you going?"

"I'm leaving!" I took off and headed down the street.

"Ai'ight," Malachi said. "Can you let me close the door first?" I stopped for a moment so that he could close the door and then I took off again. "So where are we going?"

"Far away from here."

"Okay, but when we come back you know you'll still have to face this, right?"

"I'm not dealing with that nonsense." Tears rolled down my cheeks.

"Pull over in the park." Malachi pointed.

"I don't wanna go to the park!"

"Would you just pull over and stop for a moment. Just stop."

Reluctantly, I pulled into the park. The gravel made music beneath the tires as I parked by the lake, where the moon made a shadow on the water. I got out and Malachi followed me. I sat on the hood of my car and he sat beside me. Rain had started drizzling from the sky, but I was too mad to care.

"You can't run away, Zsa," Malachi said, wiping tears from my face.

"Yes, I can. My mother doesn't give a damn. The only

one who'll look for me is Hadiah and maybe Cousin Shake and Ms. Minnie."

"And what I'ma do?"

"Come with me."

"I don't run away from problems. I deal with them." He stroked my cheek.

"It's just that she acts like our life and my daddy, and my brother, and everything we had was nothing. I'm sorry my daddy was like he was. I am, but I didn't know how to change him." I cried. "No matter what I tried, he was the same and then he died. He died!"

"Zsa," Malachi said, "you gotta let some of that pain go. Your father being the way he was was not your fault. There was nothing you could do. But running away from your mother is not going to change anything."

"I can't stay here with her." I wiped my eyes.

"Ai'ight," he said, "so you run away and what changes? Your mother tried to run away from everything. And what happened tonight? It slapped her right in the face."

"I wanna slap her in the face." I cried and laughed at the same time.

"Look, that's your moms, no matter what. She's doing her best. Just talk to her. But don't run away, it'll only make things worse."

"I just feel like I need to leave and go somewhere far away."

"Listen, we could always run, but I promise you your life is going to still be the same. Just chill, baby. For real, I promise you it'll get better."

I looked into Malachi's eyes and for some reason, at that moment, if at no other moment, I believed him. I did. We started to kiss and this time, with so much pain and hurt that had filled my chest, I didn't want the way he was making me feel to end. "Let's stop here."

"But I want to," I said, kissing him again.

"No, you want a distraction. Getting back to your family and working things out with them is more important than this. No matter how bad we really want to, we can't. Not now."

I hated that he was right, but I had to accept it. "Thank you," I said to him.

"Why are you thanking me?"

"For loving me, flaws and all."

"You know you my dude." He playfully gave me a pound and before long we were laughing, dreaming, and talking the night away. By the time I got back home the moon had completed its dance, the rain had stopped, and the sun had come out to play in the sky.

10

Hopped up out the bed, turn my swag on . . .

—SOULJAH BOY, "TURN MY SWAG ON"

A week had passed since our family blowup and the house had been quiet ever since. Well, not exactly quiet, more like a loud silence where we could each hear one another's thoughts of why our lives had to be like this, were they ever going to change, and when would somebody—anybody—whomever was really in charge bring this to an end?

My mother had been hanging around all week a little more than usual and I could tell that she wanted us to make up. We were not the type of family who apologized to one another or talked about our problems, we just woke up one morning, pretended our differences didn't exist, and went on about our business.

"Hey, Zsa." My mother knocked on my door. "Can I come in?"

"Yeah," I said, lining my lips.

"Your mail came." She handed me the monthly check I

got from my father's death benefits. "Are you getting ready
to go somewhere?"

"Not now, maybe later when Malachi gets off of work."

"Where does Malachi work?"

"With his dad. Construction."

"Oh, that's nice."

I could tell she was stalling so I took the bait. "Why,
Ma?"

"I was just wondering—if you wanted to go to the mall.
Thought maybe we could catch up."

"About what? Kenneth? I'm soooo not doing him." I
gave a disapproving laugh.

"No," she said quickly, "we don't have to talk about
Kenneth. I just wanted to spend some time with you."

I rolled my eyes to the ceiling; my mother and I were
like oil and water inside of the house so God only knew
how we would be gettin' it poppin' in the street. Before I
could say no, my mother said, "Come on, it'll be fun."

I could look at her and I could tell that she was as nervous about this outing as I was, but I could also tell that
she really wanted it to happen. "Where's Hadiah? Is she
coming?"

"No, she's gone with Cousin Shake and Ms. Minnie."

"So just me and you are going to the mall?"

"Yeah, I think that would be cool."

"I don't have any gas in my car."

"Do you ever?" She laughed. "I'm going to grab my
purse. Meet me outside, we'll take my car."

Before I left I dialed Asha's number and when I couldn't
get her I called Courtney. "Two snaps up and a fruit loop,"
Courtney said with a drag.

"Ill, what's wrong with you?"

"Nothing really," he said, "just that time of the month. I'm drinking some hot tea with my pinky sticking out now. Wassup with you?"

"I'm going to the mall with my mother."

"Oh . . . my . . . Gawd, Diva. Did somebody die?"

"No. She just wants to spend time together."

"Okay, so what you want me to do?"

"Call me in an hour, scream on the phone, and act as if it's an emergency. This way I'll have an excuse to leave and come to your crib."

"Okay, Diva. Now I have to go, I have cramps."

All I could do was laugh at Courtney. I swear he was a trip. Not long after I hung up with Courtney did my cell phone ring. It was my baby. "Hi, sweetie."

"Wassup, ma?"

"Nothing. You on break?"

"Yeah, for a minute. I just called to tell you I was thinking about you."

"I love you."

"You better love me. I'll see you when I get off." And he hung up. Every time I heard Malachi's voice, butterflies filled my stomach. I never imagined anything would be like this. My only regret was that Ameen wouldn't leave me alone. He hadn't done any drive-bys lately but he kept calling me constantly.

I walked outside and got in my mother's red Explorer. The entire car ride was in silence and the only thing that filled the air was the music playing. Once we arrived we parked in front of H&M's entrance, went inside, and started combing the aisles.

"So, Zsa," my mother said, "how's school?"

I stared at her for a moment. I knew that's not what she really wanted to ask me so I said, "I was failing, so I dropped out. Who needs school?" I picked up a sweater, looked it over, and put it back. "All I need really," I said, picking up a blouse, "is a good man to take care of me."

My mother squinted her eyes. "You want me to pop you now or when I get a better angle?"

"Whatever suits you, I've taken a lot worse . . . from you."

My mother rubbed her temples, "You really hate me, don't you? Nothing I say, do, or even think is good enough for you."

I sighed. "Ma, I don't hate you, I just wish things were different."

"I'm trying, Zsa-Zsa. You have to give me credit for something here."

Don't ask me why but I felt bad. "Ma, it's cool. Let's just enjoy our time here. I don't see anything in this store and I'm kinda hungry. You wanna go to the food court?"

"Yeah." She smiled. "I would like that."

As we walked toward the food court, I caught a few glances of my mother in the stores' windows and realized how much we resembled. I wondered if she thought the same thing. "You know," she said, as we walked into Applebee's, "you look just like me."

"I know." I gave her a dimpled smile. "I was just thinking the same thing."

She laughed. "See, if we spend enough time together I'll be able to read your thoughts all the time."

"Umm-hmm." I laughed. "So what am I thinking now?"

"That that boy over there is cute." She pointed. "I wonder if he has a daddy."

I cracked up. I couldn't help it. "Ma, stop playing," I said as the hostess walked over and showed us to our booth. The waitress came quickly, we ordered our food, and soon after it arrived.

My mother took a bite of her cheeseburger. "So, Zsa, what's up with you and Malachi?"

There's no way anyone could mention Malachi's name without my smiling or feeling butterflies in my belly. "It's cool," I said as calmly as possible, without blushing too much.

"Cool?" My mother frowned. "Zsa, he's at the house almost every day. You light up when he's around and it's simply cool?"

"Alright, Ma," I said cautiously, "I'm crazy about him. He's kind, he's smart, and I love him."

"He doesn't put his hands on you, does he?"

"No." I frowned.

"You would tell me if he did?"

"Ma, he doesn't, okay?"

"Okay. Now, do we need to have the discussion about safe sex, or better yet abstinence?"

"Ma, would you chill? I got this."

"So"—my mother paused—"when would be a good time to talk about Kenneth?"

"Never. He doesn't exist to me." I started eating my salad.

"What about me?" She pointed to her chest.

"See him on the creep, but he can't live with us."

"Maybe we should change the subject," she said, and before I could respond she continued on. "Guess who called me last night?"

"Who?"

"Aunt Nona and Uncle Easy. They said they wanted to come up for Thanksgiving."

"Thanksgiving? Ma, please." I folded my hands in prayer position. "I can't take those people. The last time they were here all they did was argue."

"But they're family, and when my mother passed they raised my brothers and sister as if we were their own. We wanted for nothing, so I can't tell them no. Plus they are fun to be around."

"But Ma, the last Thanksgiving they were here, Cousin Shake and Uncle Easy were riding up and down the block on a two-seater bike."

"So?"

"Ma"—I snapped my fingers—"two grown men on a bike and in the cold. Don't that seem a little suspect to you?"

She laughed. "Zsa-Zsa, behave."

"And you know Uncle Easy's kids are not right in the head. Something is very wrong with them."

My mother cracked up. "They are normal children and your cousins."

I laughed so loud I screamed. "Outside of Seven, Toi, and Man-Man, oh and the homework police, I don't have any cousins."

"You are a pure mess." My mother laughed so hard she cried.

Before long, hours had passed and we were having a blast. By the time we got back home it was evening. "Ma," I said before I got out of her car.

"Yes."

"You kinda cool."

"Oh, really?"

"Yeah," I said as my phone rang. "You ai'ight. . . . Hello," I answered without looking at the caller ID.

"Deeeeeeeeeeeee-vaaaaaaaaaaa!!!!!!!!!!!!!!!!!" Courtney screamed. "Help me! I need you to leave the mall from being with your mama and come help a queen, I mean a king, out."

My ear had a headache. I could get no words to come out of my mouth.

"Is everything okay?" my mother asked, concerned.

"Yeah, Ma." I kissed her on the cheek as I got out the car and hung up on a screaming Courtney. "Everything is fine."

11

Will this last for one night or do I have you for a lifetime?

—Xscape, "Am I Dreamin'"

"Zsa," Ameen screamed into my voice mail as I listened to my phone messages. I was preparing to go to Malachi's house, so I stood in front of the mirror and entertained myself by listening to Ameen's begging. "You're really playing me, huh?"

"Yup," I said as if he could hear me and I were not listening to a prerecorded message. "You got it."

"Ai'ight, when I see you I'ma mess you up," the message continued.

"Whatever."

"Zsa." Ameen called my name as if I were really going to answer. This cat had to be crazy; surely he knew he was talking to a machine. "Ai'ight, I see what I'ma have to do for you," he carried on.

"What?" I said to Ameen's message. "Get lost?"

"Don't worry, I'll be seeing about you again."

"I'm sure, Ameen." And the machine moved on to the next crazy message he'd left me. I had at least three more all saying the same thing and the last one saying he just wanted to talk to me because he loved me.

I rolled my eyes to the ceiling. Ameen didn't appreciate me when he had me, so there was no need for him to try to cupcake with me now. Anywho, I decided that I didn't like the way my lavender sweater was fitting me so I changed into my pink V-neck long-sleeve T-shirt with NAME BRAND PRINCESS written in rhinestones across the breasts. And then I looked at my Ck jeans and felt like they were played so I changed into a pair of Deréon jeans, and Coach boots. I slid on my rhinestone jewelry, made sure the ring I wore on the necklace around my neck was in place, and was now satisfied that I was beyond cute.

I cut my voice mail off, tossed my phone in my pink Coach bag, picked up my keys, and was on my way to see my baby.

"Where are you going, looking all cute?" my mother asked me as she and Hadiah sat in the living room watching a movie.

"To see Malachi," Hadiah said. "Tell his brother, Matthew, I said hi."

"Hadiah, please."

"See you later, Zsa." My mother laughed.

"Okay," Cousin Shake said, "I like Malory, but don't let me have to come and get you, 'cause I will come and drag you out of that house if you're not home before the street-lights come on."

I didn't even dignify that with a response, especially since it was already five o'clock in the evening and the street-lights were already on. I simply waved and continued on about my business. Once I got in the car I peeked in the mirror and checked my makeup one last time. I put on a little more gloss and then I pulled off down the street.

Malachi didn't live too far from me, so I was at his house in no time. For some reason I was nervous. I mean, I knew his parents and they knew me, but still I didn't know how they would receive me, being as they were all so close to Staci. I rang the bell and tapped the heels of my boots nervously. A few minutes later Malachi was opening the door.

"Damn, girl." He looked me over. "You got a man? 'Cause I'm sayin' you just my type."

Why the heck am I cheesin' so hard? "What does my man have to do with me and you?"

"That's what I'm sayin'." Malachi's ten-year-old brother Matthew came to the door and said, "What's good with you?"

"Back up, Matt," Malachi said.

"I'm sayin' is this your girl or can I get up on her?"

I had to laugh. This was too much. Matthew was the spitting image of Malachi when he was his age. "Little boy," I said, "please."

"So wassup with your sister, then?" Matthew said, giving up.

"Ma," Malachi said as we walked in the house, "get your son."

"He's just admiring a beautiful woman," said Malachi's dad, who was just as handsome as his sons.

"Senior," Malachi's mother, Ms. Karen who resembled Angela Bassett, said, "stop embarrassing the girl. Come here, Zsa-Zsa, and give me a hug. I haven't seen you since you were a little girl."

I walked over to Ms. Karen and gave her a hug. "You are really a beautiful young woman." She looked at Malachi. "Did you ever tell Jazmyn I said hello?"

"Yeah, Ma."

"You better. Now, Zsa-Zsa, how is my son treating you? Do you know he never stopped talking about you over the years?"

"Ai'ight, Ma," Malachi said.

"I swear I was so glad Senior wanted to relocate back up this way I didn't know what to do."

"Ma, don't you all have a weekend retreat you're going on?" Malachi looked at his watch. "You're going to be late."

"Junior," Ms. Karen said, calling Malachi by the nickname he only allowed her to call him. "Just wait a minute. I need to take a picture of you two before we go. I still have one when you two were little. I need another one."

"Ma." Malachi sighed.

"Boy," she said, "what did I tell you?"

"Ai'ight, Ma." He walked over to me, placed his arms around my waist, and we posed for the photo.

"Nice," Ms. Karen said in approval. "Very nice. Okay we have to go now. You know my rules, Malachi. I don't mind Zsa-Zsa but no one else and no overnight guests."

"Bye, Ma. See y'all later," Malachi said, grabbing me by my hand.

"Okay, okay." She smiled at me. "It's really nice seeing you again, Zsa-Zsa."

"You too, Ms. Karen. You too."

"Your mother is really sweet." I smiled at my baby as we entered his room. Malachi's room was in the basement of his house. It was a typical male's room, a full-size black wooden platform bed, basketball posters on the wall, *Sports Illustrated* models on the back of his door, and a pipe running through the middle of the floor from the ceiling.

I was so nervous that I kept playing with the pole in the middle of his room.

"You like the pole?" he asked, reaching for the stereo remote, and a few seconds later an old Luther Vandross classic filled the room.

I laughed. "Funny."

"Come over here."

"In a minute," I said, walking around his room and poking through some of his things.

"What are you doing?" he asked.

I couldn't say "trying not to be nervous," so I said, "Just looking around." I took the top off of a shoe box on his dresser.

"Leave that alone." He rose from his bed.

"What?" I gave him a one-sided smile. "What, you wanna do something?"

"All I know is that if you open that box it's gon' be a misunderstanding."

"What, you got some nasty pictures in here of some chicks? Don't let me run across Staci in here naked." I started combing through the box and found a crumpled and old piece of paper. I pulled the paper from the box and began to unfold it.

"Zsa." He laughed, reaching for the paper. "Stop playing. Now give it here." He reached for the paper again.

I was laughing so hard that I swear slob was due to fall out of my mouth. "I'm not giving it to you."

He reached for it again. "Give it here," he said playfully.

I quickly stuffed it down my shirt and in my bra. "Now you're really not getting it."

Malachi looked at me like I had lost my mind. "I hadn't planned on going in there this early in the evening but I will." He gave me a devilish grin.

"Don't be fresh. Now let me read it. Unless, of course we're keeping secrets."

"Ai'ight." He laid back on the bed. "Go 'head, read it. But remember that the next time we're in your room."

"Don't even try the reverse psych on me. Not falling for it." I pulled the note from my shirt and began to read it. "You wanna be my girl? Circle yes or no." Immediately I stopped laughing and tears filled my eyes. "You still have this?"

"Yeah," he said, looking at me as tears slid down my cheeks. I was so stupid, why was I crying? I crawled on his bed and sat next to him. "I don't believe you still have this."

"It's corny, I know. But it means something to me." He kissed the tears on my cheeks. "Don't cry, ma. 'Cause when I ask you to marry me, I'ma write that note on the back of this one."

"And I'ma circle no."

Malachi turned over and started kissing me. "You gon' circle no?" He looked me dead in the eyes. "Huh?"

I wished I could lie, but I couldn't. "I could never tell you no."

"I didn't think so," he said as we kissed again, and just as I wrapped my arms around his neck my phone started ringing. "Don't answer that," he said.

"It could be my mother or my sister, though." I rose from the bed and pulled my phone from my purse. It was

Ameen, so I sent him to voice mail. No sooner than I tossed the phone back into my purse did the phone ring again. "Damn." It was Ameen again. I sent him to voice mail, and the phone started ringing all over again. This time I cut the phone off.

"Who was that?" Malachi looked at me suspiciously.

"Asha," I said quickly.

"You lying to me now?"

"Alright, it was Ameen."

"Ameen?" He paused. "He's still calling you?"

"Yeah."

"Now, you know if that was Staci calling me you would be having a fit."

"I'm not telling him to call me."

"Well, tell him to stop calling you."

"Okay, Malachi, I will." I walked over to his TV and picked up the dice on top. "You play craps?"

"Craps." Malachi laughed. "What, you looking to get spanked? Sent home crying?"

I placed my hands on my hips. "Boy, please, this is not hopscotch. I will house you in some dice."

Malachi cracked up. "Baby, don't even do it to yourself. Please. Now if you want, I'll let you beat me at the Wii boxing game, but you will never house me in dice."

"A hundred dollars says I will."

"Oh, my baby talking big bucks?"

"You gon' put up or shut up?" I rolled the dice around in my hand.

"Ai'ight." He hopped off the bed. "Ladies first."

"But of course." I juggled the dice in my hand and then said to him, "Blow on these for me?"

"Yeah, ai'ight." He laughed.

"Haters never win," I said as I rolled the dice and popped them against the wall. "Seven!" I jumped up and down. "And you know this."

"Whatever, that was luck," Malachi said as I rolled again.

"You can't beat me." I started talking smack. "You think you so big and bad, but what, what you got?"

"I got a turn," he said, pointing to the dice.

I sucked my teeth as they came up snake eyes. "Whatever. You put that bad luck in the universe."

Malachi laughed. "That ain't all I'ma put out in the universe." He tapped me on the butt and then rolled the dice.

"Snake eyes, buddy," I said. "Give it here, give it here." I popped the dice against the wall and voilà, I was kicking Malachi's you know what. By the time we were done, I'd won three hundred dollars from him and he was staring at me saying, "You think I can borrow a few dollars?"

"Maybe." I started to dance as a Michael Jackson throwback came on. "Dance with me."

"Did you forget that I wasn't your boy Courtney? I'm not dancing to no Michael Jackson."

"Men dance," I said, moving from side to side.

"Not this one. Now chill and come here." He sat on the edge of the bed.

"What?" I smiled and stood before him.

"You know I love you, right?" He placed his hands on my hips.

"Yes."

"And you know I would never hurt you intentionally, right?"

Suddenly my heart started skipping beats. "I know."

"Good." He snatched the cash from my hands. " 'Cause you being jacked. I want my money back."

"Oh, no, you didn't!" I playfully jumped on top of him, lightly punching him on the arm and tickling him in his hard belly. "Give me my money!" I couldn't stop laughing, and being that I was acting so silly and Malachi was now tickling me, I was unable to keep a steady hand and money was flying all over the place. Yet, in the midst of all of this somehow and some way we started to kiss passionately, as if we'd been desiring this kiss all of our lives.

Just when I thought sparks were about to jump off, Malachi said, "Zsa, we gotta slow down."

I sighed. "Why?"

"Because"—he paused—"not only do I not have any condoms, the timing is not right."

"So you don't want none? You must be the only seventeen-year-old in America not trying to get down."

"Don't try and act like I'm some corny li'l dude. I'm just trying not to get you strung out."

I laughed. "Yeah, right."

"Nah, listen." He looked me dead in the eyes. "I can't even lie to you and front like I'ma virgin or when I see you I don't want none, because I do." He paused and looked me over. "I want some bad. But you got a lot going on right now and the last thing we need is an unexpected baby, or to be chasing a late period. I am not beat for that. Plus, I'm not messing with you until I know that you and Ameen are completely through."

"Ameen? I'm not messing him."

"All I'm saying is that for right now, we gon' lay here, watch some TV, and chill."

"Chill?"

"Chill. You ai'ight with that? I mean, let me know, you want to be wifey or you want to be a jump off."

"You know what I want."

"Then relax. I love you. I'm not going anywhere, but there's a lot more going on with you right now that's more important than taking our relationship to a sexin' level. When the time is right it'll happen."

"So what do we do in the meantime?"

"Chill." He kissed me.

"Okay, we can chill." I laughed. "But you still ain't getting that money back."

12

You the best,
Best I ever had . . .
We can do it real big,
Bigger than you ever done it . . .

—DRAKE, "BEST I EVER HAD"

Today was me and my baby's anniversary and I wasn't sure what he had planned. I knew I needed a break, though, so I was hoping it involved a faraway day trip, especially since my midterms had kicked my butt. Don't worry, I passed all of them. But it was not without my share of migraines or the itch to write the answers on my hand or put them up my sleeve and cheat. But I didn't. I studied, and judging by my grade point average so far, it had paid off.

It was the day before Thanksgiving and my mother wanted me to stay home with her and prepare for our family coming to visit. . . . Not.

I dressed in a pair of skinny-leg Bebe jeans, stiletto riding boots, and a tangerine hooded sweater to wear to the mysterious place Malachi was taking me to. A few minutes later, my phone rang. It was Courtney. "You rang?" I answered.

"Hey, Diva, what are you doing?"

"Getting ready for my anniversary celebration with my boo."

"Oh, wow," Courtney said, "and how corny are you?"

"Ill, don't be hatin' on me and my man."

"I'm not. I'm just saying that y'all are corny. You have only been together two days? My Jesus."

"Shut up." I laughed. "It's been longer than that."

"Whew, somebody ring the alarm," he said, and I could imagine him arching his eyebrows and flinging his wrist.

"Anyway," I said, "I've been wanting to get your opinion about something."

"What? And please don't ask me if I like turkey."

What is he talking about?

"'Cause the answer is no," he rambled on. "Stuffing does not melt in my mouth, I hate that lumpy gravy you be making, Mama! And please don't nobody in their right mind use Jell-O as a replacement for cranberry sauce. Stop being so cheap!"

"Ahh, Courtney," I said, completely put off, "what are you talking about?"

"I'm sorry, Diva, I just had to vent. Every Thanksgiving my mother insists on making this mess of a meal instead of letting us go out to my grandmother's. I swear I just can't take it anymore so I had to get that off my chest. My fault for blacking out, now, what do you wanna ask me?"

"Never mind, I'm scared now."

"Diva, just ask me and stop playing."

"Okay, and you better not tell anybody, not even Asha."

"Oh, this must be good. You stole your mama's credit card? Girl, I did that one time and my mama chewed me out. Don't sign your real name 'cause that's how I got caught."

"Oh, my God, T.T.M.I. Totally too much information. Is that why you called me crying and screaming from the police station last year?"

"Yeah, she called herself teaching me a lesson."

"You needed to learn one. You don't steal your mother's credit card, are you kidding me?"

"You can calm down, it was only QVC. You act like it was Ashley Stewart or something."

"Oh, my God." I shook my head. "Oh-my-God—why can't I hold a conversation without it being all about you? Why?"

"Hello?" Courtney started banging on the phone. "Hello?"

I rolled my eyes to the ceiling. "Yes, Courtney, I'm here. Why do you keep saying, 'hello'?"

" 'Cause I wanna know who are you talking to? Two snaps up and a fruit loop, certainly you aren't talking to me."

"Okay, you know what, never mind. I don't need to ask you anything."

"Diva, don't be like that. You know I have to live vicariously through your love life being that it's so hot and all. Tell me, what's the problem?"

I sighed. "It's about Malachi."

"What about him?"

"We haven't, you know . . ."

"Know what?"

"Slept together."

"Like gettin' it in?"

"Yeah." I sat down on the edge of my bed. "Exactly."

"So?"

"What do you mean, so?"

"What, you got a disease you trying to give away? Here, Malachi," he said mockingly, "here's herpes on me."

"Shut up! I don't have herpes, or anything else for that matter."

"Exactly, so relax."

"All I'm saying is that I never ran across a dude like Malachi. I mean, we kiss and it gets serious, but he always says the time is not right. Sometimes I wonder if he's a virgin and he's hiding it. I mean, he could just tell me."

Courtney yawned. "You done?"

"Ill, that was rude."

"I just want you to hurry up so I can tell you off. 'Cause I need to borrow some money and I want to be sure to ask you before we get off the phone."

"What do you mean, 'tell me off'? Why?"

"Allow me to grace you with jump-off therapy. Earth to Zsa-Zsa." I could hear him snapping his fingers. "Allow a man to treat you like a lady. Sex too soon can cloud your judgment, and the next thing you know you'll be thinking a man like Ameen is king, but then again he is king, king of the retards."

"What does Ameen have to do with this?"

"Because you expect Malachi to want the same things out of you that Ameen did. No, he's a different type of dude. He's respectful, he loves you, and he cares. But if you keep acting as if your body is for sale he's gon' start questioning your wifey status. You better get you a Rita's Water Ice and cool off. I know you don't think sex is love."

"No," I said, although I was questioning that myself.

"Okay, then fall back. Keep your panties on and be a

lady. And anyway, even if he was a virgin, which my alarm tells me he is not, but even if he was it's nothing wrong with that, 'cause we need love too. Now, do you have twenty dollars until next week? I need my nails and feet done. Can you say crusty?"

"Yeah, Courtney. I'll text Asha to swing by and bring it to you because I won't be home and I know she and Samaad will be out."

"Okay, cool. Call me if you need anything, I have to go and take a nap. I can smell my mother cooking and I'm getting a headache."

Conversations with Courtney drained me, I swear. "Bye, Courtney."

"Bye, Diva."

I texted Asha for Courtney and a few seconds later, Cousin Shake pounded on my bedroom door. "Zingaling, Malory is out here to see you."

I'm so tired of this man messing up my name, and who the heck is Malory? Oh, my God. "It's Malachi!" I snatched my bedroom door open.

"What? You tryna raise up?" Cousin Shake started jogging in place. "Huh?" He lunged his chest toward me and then pretended to be holding himself back. "I ain't think you wanted none. Now get on out here and get where you goin', 'cause if them streetlights come on and you not back in this house by then I'ma start bustin' my guns."

"And you don't want that," Ms. Minnie said, "'Cause then I'll have to spray air freshener for days." She shook her head. "Sometimes I sit and wonder, 'did somebody die up in Shake?'"

"Ain't nobody die, Minnie." Cousin Shake rubbed his belly. "That's just all that pinned up love I have for you."

"Awwl, Shake." She started to blush and I was utterly embarrassed. "You sooo sweet."

"And nasty all at the same time." I frowned.

"Get yo' li'l behind outta here." Cousin Shake growled at me. "Malory, I wish you luck."

"I know." Malachi laughed. "Pray for me."

Oh, God, why did he say that?

"Pray?" Cousin Shake said. "You need prayer? Well, you've come to the right place. Welcome to the Church of Shake, where layin' a prayer down is my thang."

"I didn't mean right at this second, Cousin Shake. I was using that as an expression," Malachi said.

"You know you meant that for right at this moment. Don't front," Cousin Shake insisted. "Now, come on, I'll make it quick. Everybody hold hands."

I looked at Malachi and rolled my eyes. I swear if he wasn't so big and fine I would've probably punched him right in the face.

We held hands and Cousin Shake began to pray. "Bruh Man, Jesus and Papa John—oh, wait." Cousin Shake shook his head. "That's the pizza parlor. Minnie, remind me to order a pizza pie when I finish praying."

"Okay, baby," she said. "With olives?"

"Yeah, and eggs. I like eggs on my pizza."

"Shake, you know eggs give you gas."

"I know, but I been taking that Zantac."

"What are you two doing?!" I asked in a pissed disbelief. "Is this a prayer or you placing an order? Please, can we get on with it?"

"Our Father." Cousin Shake bowed his head. "Please bless Zingaling so that she don't catch a beat down. Amen. Now get outta here!"

Cousin Shake couldn't have said it fast enough. I was out the door in a flash.

By the time Malachi got to his truck he was cracking up. "Yo"—he opened the passenger door for me—"Cousin Shake is funny."

"Glad you think so," I said as he slid in the car and turned the key in the ignition. "Let's see how funny you think he is when the rest of his clan gets here."

"There's more?" Malachi said as we headed for the highway.

"Hmph, you just don't know."

"Dang, baby, well at least the kids will have my relatives to give them a mentally sane balance."

I playfully punched him on the arm. "Alright now."

"I'm just playing." He laughed. "I'm just playing."

"Now, where are we going?"

"Just ride and see."

Malachi and I rode for at least an hour and we talked about everything under the sun. I swear I'd never laughed so much. By the time we arrived at the restaurant, which was on the beach and overlooking the water, the sun had settled for the night and the moon was dancing in the sky. It was so romantic, and just when I thought it couldn't get any better the hostess showed us to a secluded booth with burgundy velvet drapes that hung around the space. It was as if we were in our own world with a perfect few of the ocean. I promise you, and I'm not sure who else I would outright say this to, but Malachi had me open. I never dreamed I would have someone so perfect, which is why I placed my phone on vibrate. I didn't want him to know that Ameen had been calling me nonstop since we left my house.

Shortly after we took our seats the waitress came, took our order, and quickly delivered our food.

"Malachi"—I ate a piece of my salmon—"this place is beautiful. And this view is breathtaking. How did you find this place?"

"Don't be all jockin' my pimpin', girl," he said jokingly while eating his steak. "And the next thing I know, Samaad and Asha will be frequenting my spot."

"I don't believe you said that." I laughed.

"Nah, I'm just playing." He sipped his soda. "But don't worry about how I found it, just know that your man has class."

I smiled. I loved the sound of him saying "my man." "You know"—I paused—"when we were kids and you moved away I thought I would never see you again."

"How'd that make you feel?"

"Scared. Nervous, and like every time I loved someone they were going to leave me."

"Is that how you felt about your dad?"

Instantly I felt my heart sink in the center. "Kind of. When I think about my dad, I get confused."

"Why?"

"How can you love someone and hate someone at the same time?"

"I don't have an answer for you, Zsa."

"Exactly." I arched my eyebrows. "No one does. So I really don't want to talk about my dad."

"Ai'ight, well . . . let me share this with you; when I left I couldn't stop talking about you. And for real as time went on I thought my feelings for you would somehow disappear, because like, when you're twelve who thinks the love you feel for a girl is real? But when I turned thirteen, and fourteen, and fifteen, and sixteen, and seventeen, and I was still feeling you, I knew I had to get back to you. I had to at least see what we could be together. So, I talked my father into moving back to Jersey."

"Really?"

"Yeah, I told him Jersey was a better state for his business and that Newark wasn't the place everybody wanted to make it out to be."

"And he went for it?"

"We're here."

"All of that for me? You sure not Staci?"

"Don't start. 'Cause I haven't asked you once why does your phone keep vibrating."

My mouth fell open. "How did you know that?"

"Because I can hear it. You have to put it on silent for the phone not to make a sound, Zsa."

Dang he is right.

"I know I'm right," he said as if he'd read my mind. "Now, what's good with that? You gon' see Ameen about leaving you alone or am I gon' have to do that? 'Cause for real, this cat is irking me."

"Ameen is harmless. His feelings are just hurt."

"He seems a li'l more than hurt. I'm wondering if you need a restraining order."

"Extra random, Malory. Too far to the left."

Malachi laughed. "I got your Malory. Anyway, have you started thinking about colleges?"

"Yeah, I think I may want to go to Morgan State. It's far enough from home where I can bounce in peace, but it's close enough for me to get to my little sister."

"Morgan is cool. I thought about Howard."

"Awwl, my baby want to be next to me?"

"I'm on it, Zsa, but not like that."

"Did you just diss me?"

"Did I?" he said, getting up from his seat and sliding next to me. "I wouldn't diss my baby." He kissed me.

"Yeah, right. You're lucky I think you're hot."

He gave me half a grin. "And what makes me hot?"

I pressed my forehead against his and sang softly, "'Cause you're a matter of extreme importance, my first teenage love affair. . . ."

After dinner, we walked along the shore behind the restaurant. Although it was cold outside, something about the chill in the air and the crisp breeze made it romantic. I walked in front of Malachi with his chest pressed into my back and his arms around my waist. "I wish I could stay here forever," I said.

"I bet you do, but we have to get back home, because your country crew is coming."

I laughed. "Don't be talking about my family."

"I'm buggin'. Hey," he said, filled with surprise, "do you know how to ride go-carts?"

"What, boy, I will tear you up in a go-cart."

"Is that a yes or a no?"

I stepped out of his embrace and turned around to face him. "Is that a challenge?"

"It could never be a challenge because in go-carts you could never house me."

"Okay, well, let's go somewhere and see."

"Bet, we're going to Ray's a few minutes from here and when I spank you, don't get upset."

"Yeah, okay, let's not forget dice."

"I let you win."

I fell out laughing. "You are such a liar."

"Well, do something about it then." And he took off running. "See, look at you." He turned around. "I'm Superman, girl, you can't even catch me." And he turned back around, giving me a two-finger peace sign over his shoulder.

I tried to run as softly and as swiftly as I could, and when I got close to him I jumped on his back, wrapping my arms around his neck. "I thought I couldn't catch you."

"Ai'ight." He laughed as he carried me on his back. "You got me."

A few minutes later we were on the highway and shortly after arrived at Ray's. It was an indoor/outdoor amusement park, and it seemed that everybody and their mother had packed the place. Every game, ride, and everything else you could think of was in this place. Malachi and I immediately walked over to the go-carts.

My car was hot pink, and of course Mr. Man had to have a black one. "I hope you're ready for the challenge," he said.

"Boy, this chick can handle anything," I responded.

"Yeah, that's what they all say."

We each got in our cars and on the count of three we took off. I was in the lead so I shouted at Malachi, "What, you scared? I thought you were going to beat me, huh? What, you don't have anything to say?"

"Yeah"—he gave a devilish laugh—"I have something to say."

"What?"

"You lost." He took off and passed me like a swift wind. I was pissed and couldn't believe he'd beaten me. We rode the track about three more times and each time he was hard to catch. Whatever, at least I beat him at dice.

"You cheated," I said once we were out of the cars.

"Say whatever you will, just know that Malachi housed you."

"I bet you can't beat me at Pac-Man."

"Is that another challenge?"

"It sure is," I said as we headed to the arcade section. I held up two tokens. "On me."

"You know you cheated, right?" Malachi said once the game was over. "You gave me a defective token."

"Yeah, okay." I laughed.

We were having a blast, and I couldn't remember the last time I felt so free and at ease. Before we knew anything it was two AM and the place was closing.

"I had so much fun," I said to Malachi on our drive home.

"Me too," he said. "We'll have to come down here again."

"Yeah, we have to."

"Happy anniversary, baby," Malachi said.

"Yeah." I held his free hand. "Happy anniversary."

By the time we got to my house and I saw my mother's car parked and the living room light on, I knew I would have some explaining to do. But tonight was worth being grilled about.

We kissed and afterward I stepped out of the car. As soon as I placed my key in the door and Malachi had taken off I heard George Clinton's Atomic Dog blasting into the street. I turned around and oh . . . my . . . God, Cousin Shake's crew had arrived. Uncle Easy, the only man in America who still rocked a Jheri curl, was driving his entire family in a tricked-out yellow school bus. Not the short one, but the long one. I swear I was stuck in my spot. All six wheels had gold spinners and hanging around the mirror was five pairs of baby sneakers, one for each of his children. There were crushed red velvet seats, and along with the luggage strapped to the roof were two 72-inch speakers and a turntable. You heard me right. A turntable, not CDs but records.

"Zeke," my uncle Easy said, "is that you, Zeke?"

"No," I said, "no Zekes live here." As soon as I said that I felt oil running down the back of my neck.

"What you lyin' for?" Cousin Shake walked around me with his supersoaker in his hand.

"My name is Zsa-Zsa."

"That's what he said," Cousin Shake growled. "Now get in the house. You have enough explaining to do."

"Shake!" Uncle Easy screamed. "Is that you?"

"Yeah, baby!"

"Us is here, Shake! Easy Belvadeen Green has entered the building." And he pulled up that nasty-behind bus, parked right behind Cousin Shake's hearse and in front of our house.

Just when I thought life had punished me enough, here came a new chapter.

13

"Zsa." Hadiah called my name and shook my hips as I laid in the bed between sleep and wake. "Zsa-Zsa, wake up. It's an emergency!"

"What?" I turned over and peeled one eye open. "What emergency?"

"We've been attacked!"

I sat up and said in a panic, "Attacked? What are you talking about?"

Hadiah swallowed and wiped her glassy eyes. "All I know is that when I woke up this morning and headed for the bathroom there were a bunch of people in our living room who looked like they hadn't changed clothes in about ten years. It's 1999 in the flesh."

I frowned and rolled my eyes. "You mean 1989. That's Uncle Easy and his crew."

"Uncle Easy? I don't remember him or them."

"You met them when you were little. They live outside

of Atlanta, in Manchester, I think. Anyway, it's been on and country ever since."

"Well"—she twisted her lips—"that explains why they're having a break dancing contest in our living room."

I stood to the floor. "A what?"

"You heard me. Cousin Shake is spinning on his head."

"Oh, no!" I grabbed my housecoat, wrapped the belt around my waist, and hurried into our living room, where it looked as if two old men had reincarnated themselves into a bad mix of Run-DMC, Whoodi, and the Jungle Brothers. LL Cool J's throwback "Radio" was blasting and for real—true story Hadiah hadn't lied. Everybody in there was caught in a time warp. Uncle Easy, his wife, Aunt Easter, and their children: Ho-Shay; the triplets, Li'l Boy, Li'l Girl, Li'l Buddy; and the youngest, Big Baby. Oh and Aunt Nona, Uncle Easy's sister, who was always dressed for a funeral.

"You can't touch this!" Cousin Shake shouted as Ms. Minnie turned him around by his shins so that he could spin on his head, and the faster he spun around the more his wedgie filled the crack of his butt. Uncle Easy was spread out on the floor, looking like Jesus on the cross trying to do the worm, but the only things moving were his ankles and his shoulders. And all of this was going on while Aunt Easter and their children were screaming, "Go Daddy, it's your birthday!"

"Now, why y'all got to act like fried monkeys?" Aunt Nona placed her hands on her hips and admonished them. She stood next to my mother, who was obviously in as much shock as we were. Aunt Nona continued, "Jazmyn don't want this nonsense in her house. You need to getcha old asses off that floor and do something positive with yourselves."

Hadiah tapped me on the arm. "What's a fried monkey?" she whispered.

"I don't know."

"Y'all just acting like a buncha raggedy cat-lovin' dogs. I swear!" Aunt Nona carried on. "Mornin', babies," she said as she spotted me and Hadiah standing in the doorway. She walked over and gave us a hug and a kiss. "Aunt Nona missed y'all. I'ma make sure we spend some time together while we're here. I have a few funerals I need to attend but after that, we gon' have us a good time."

Cousin Shake, who was no longer spinning on his head but was now walking tilted to the side, said, "Nona, er'-body that you know is already dead and buried. So don't start with your mental illness."

"You mentally ill, Shake-a-Dean." She placed her hands on her hips.

"Who died, Nona?" he pressed.

"Johnny Vasquez."

"Who the hell is that?" Uncle Easy frowned. "He sound like he lives in Mexico. Don't tell me, Nona, you been messing around in Mexico? Are you the real cause of the swine flu? Went down there and ate like a pig, passed gas, and now you done infected everybody."

"Shut up, Easy! Johnny was a good friend of mine!" Aunt Nona wiggled her neck as she spoke.

"Stop lyin'," Uncle Easy said. "I think you get your freak off by looking at dead bodies."

"And how you get your freak off?!" Aunt Nona squinted her eyes. "By running through the park naked?"

"That ain't right," Ho-Shay said. "You shouldn't have said that, Aunt Nona."

"And your mama and daddy shouldn't have named you Ho-Shay. Now stay your child's place!"

"Don't be cussin' in front of these kids!" Cousin Shake said.

"If they living with you they have heard a lot worse than that."

"Okay, everyone," my mother interjected, "we are here to have a good time and enjoy ourselves, not argue and fall out with one another."

"Yeah, you're right," Cousin Shake agreed. "I'm glad to see y'all."

"And we glad to see you too, Shake." Aunt Nona hugged him.

"Yeah, I missed ya, Shake." Uncle Easy smiled, showing off his mouth full of gold and diamond-encrusted teeth.

"Easy," Cousin Shake said, "remember you used to try to rap and would sound a hot mess?"

"What?" Uncle Easy gave Cousin Shake a nasty look. "Are you challenging me, Shake?"

"Can't be a challenge," Cousin Shake said, "'cause when it comes to rappin' you can't touch me."

"I will bury you."

"You gon' have to, 'cause when I get through with you, Nona gon' be goin' to your funeral."

"Leave me out of it," Aunt Nona snapped.

"Ai'ight, Shake." Uncle Easy waved his hands in the air. "Let's drop the science one time."

"Word to your mother-son, cousin, we can do this." Cousin Shake started doing a profile of jailhouse poses.

"Okay, okay," Uncle Easy started to rap, "they call me Mike and Ike 'cause I get down on the mic and I can ride a bike, and I can drop it cold . . . on a stove . . . and the ladies call me Low-Low, hooo!"

"You killed that, Easy," Aunt Easter said. "You straight broke that rhyme all the way down."

"Yeah, you got that off, Daddy!" Ho-Shay clapped.

"Oh, it's like that?" Cousin Shake said.

"Sock it to 'em, Shake," Ms. Minnie said. "Drop it down on 'em!"

"Ai'ight, ai'ight." Cousin Shake started moving his shoulders. "They call me Hot Tamale, 'cause I'm so jolly, and I got a wife named Minnie who got plenty of love, like a dove. We got a lot of oil which we will put right on your neck, and have you soak and wet. Hey'yay!"

"Oh, my Father." Aunt Nona held her chest. "I feel violated."

"Ai'ight, Shake," Uncle Easy said, "you got that off."

Cousin Shake nodded. "Yeah, well, hey, but don't sweat me now. You on the come up yourself, Easy. Maybe we should put our group back together."

"You had a group, Daddy?" Ho-Shay asked.

"Yup."

"What was it called?"

"Over Fifty-five Percent," Uncle Easy said with confidence.

"Those were the days," Cousin Shake said. "Now, Easy, come on so we can go outside and you can show me what's going on with that tricked-out school bus. Man, that thing is fly."

"Shake, you got to see it. The top drops down and

er'thang. We got a pool in it, black carpet on the floor, and red bulbs in the ceiling."

"That ain't nothin', man," Cousin Shake said as they walked toward the front door. "I got leopard seats."

"I bet you don't have no hydraulics."

"I betchu I do."

"I betchu it don't bump like mine, though," Uncle Easy insisted.

"I betchu it don't either." Cousin Shake twisted his lips. "I betchu it bump better."

"Ain't nothin' but a word, Shake," Uncle Easy said, twirling his keys around his fingers. "We can handle this right now. Race down the street, pop a couple of wheelies and what?"

"Let's do this, then."

"Let's."

They walked out the door, and the next thing I knew they were taking off down the street and their hydraulics had the block sounding as if the entire world had had an accident.

"They will never change," my mother said as she and my two aunties went into the kitchen, which left me and Hadiah all by ourselves staring at our cousins, who looked fifty years older than we were. "So, Ho-Shay," I said, "wassup with you? Do you graduate from high school this year?"

"Yop, sho'ly do and it's a good thang too," Ho-Shay said with a southern twang, " 'cause there's no way I could see myself turning twenty-two and still be in high school."

I'm speechless.

"So when y'all leaving?" Hadiah asked Li'l Buddy.

He hunched his shoulders and started talking baby gib-
berish.

"Okay," Hadiah said, "who else is confused?"

"The triplets don't talk that much," Ho-Shay said. "They
just three years old."

"They look ten!" Hadiah screamed. "Are they drinking
horse's milk?"

"Would you shut up?" I gave her the evil eye.

"You know they look strange. Hands and feet bigger
than mine." Hadiah hunched her shoulders as the doorbell rang.

"Don't say another word," I said as I walked over to the
door and opened it.

"Zsa-Zsa!" my cousin Seven screamed from the porch. I
couldn't believe it, it was Seven; my aunty Grier, Seven's
mother; Toi, Seven's twin; Man-Man, their brother; and
two-year-old Noah, Toi's son. I picked Noah up and started
dancing around with him. "Oh, my God! I'm so happy to
see you!"

"What's cracka-lackin', Hadiah?" Man-Man walked into
the living room and gave her a high five. "We missed y'all."

"Aunty Grier, did my mother know that you were coming?" I asked.

"No, she didn't."

"Zsa." My mother walked into the living room. "Who
was that—" She stopped herself midsentence when she
saw her sister, her nieces, and nephews. "Grier!" Tears filled
her eyes. "Oh, I'm so happy to see you. I missed you so
much!"

"I missed you too. I told Khalil that I really wanted to
see my sister and my favorite nieces."

"Khalil?" My mother blushed. "And what does Khalil have to do with this?"

Aunty Grier held out her left hand and her index finger rocked a diamond wedding band.

"Where is he?" My mother ran to the door.

"He couldn't come. He had to work."

"I can't believe you two," my mother carried on.

"It was nothing big," Aunty Grier said, "just something small with the kids. I wanted to surprise you."

"Well, we have some catching up to do," my mother said.

Aunty Grier smiled and said, "We certainly do. How's Kenneth?"

I looked at my mother as if she had lost her mind. Even my aunt from Georgia knew about this man?

"Not now, Grier," my mother said, taking Aunty Grier by the hand and leading her into the kitchen.

"Not ever," I mumbled, as I turned to my cousins. "Come in my room so we can kick it for a minute."

"Ho-Shay," Seven said to her, "where are you going? Don't you want to go in the room with us?"

"Heck, nawl! And Li'l Boy, Li'l Girl, Li'l Buddy, and Big Baby aren't going, either." She placed her hands on her hips.

"Why not?" I frowned.

" 'Cause everybody in the family know y'all too grown. And anyway, we will not be getting in trouble kickin' it in the house. Suppose something breaks?"

We all stood silent for a moment and then I said, "You know what? I get it now. You're right, Ho-Shay. Let's go." I waved at my cousins, as Uncle Easy's clan marched into the kitchen. "Forgive us for asking."

"Come on, Man-Man," Hadiah said. "Let's play the Wii game."

Noah ran over to Man-Man and said, "Me go too." Man-Man picked him up and they walked into Hadiah's room.

"Okay," I said as we sat on my bed. "Wassup with Harlem and Josiah? And don't spare the details."

Seven blushed. "Josiah's still playing ball. He's thinking about entering the draft."

"Really? So wassup with that?" I asked her. "Him being away so much, is that cool with you?"

"Yeah," she said dryly. "I guess. I mean I love him and everything, but it gets difficult being with a dude that is so popular."

Toi rolled her eyes to the ceiling. "He only has eyes for this chick and she is acting like he is Kobe Bryant or something. Look just roll with it."

"So what's good with you and Harlem?" I asked Toi.

"Oh, that's my boo." Toi grinned from ear to ear. "I am not complaining."

"I hope you come to Spelman for college," Seven said to me, "so we can have a ball together in school."

"I might. But I've been thinking about Morgan State. Malachi may go to Howard and I don't wanna be too far."

"And who is Malachi? What happen to Ameen?" Seven asked.

"Can you say loser?" I frowned. "He calls like every day though." I picked up my cell phone and showed them the fifty missed calls I had since this morning, all from Ameen.

"Is he a stalker?" Seven asked.

"No, he's only stupid," I said, and we fell out laughing.

"Anyway," Toi said, "back to Malachi."

"That's my sweetie." I was blushing so hard that my cheeks hurt.

"Is this the same Malachi that you used to go to school with?" Toi asked.

"Yeah, that's him."

"I thought he moved," Toi said.

"They moved back this year."

"And y'all started kicking it again?" Seven asked. "When?"

"We just celebrated our two-month anniversary yesterday."

"Oh." Seven held her chest. "How romantic."

"I know," I said, picking up my ringing cell phone. "Malachi is romantic."

"Who's on your phone?" Toi asked.

"This fool, Ameen." I twisted my lips.

"Let me answer it." Toi took the phone from my hand and pressed the intercom button. "Hello, stalkers anonymous, may I help you?"

"Yeah," Ameen said, "I'm looking for this chick named Zsa-Zsa."

We started laughing so hard Toi couldn't even respond to that. "Zsa," Ameen screamed on the phone, "is that you? Are you laughing at me?"

We were still laughing.

"Oh, you think I'ma joke?" Ameen said, and I could tell by the sound of his voice that he was furious. "When I catch you, I'ma smack you again! Trick wanna play Ameen?"

Instantly we stopped laughing, and for some reason I felt like I was back in the club and he was cussing me out in front of his random chick again. "You don't be calling her no damn trick," Toi spat. "You the trick, bum-wanna-be-down-stalking behind. Your boys know you over here chasing? And I wish you would put your hands on her and see what the hell you get!" She hung up, threw the phone across the bed, and within a matter of seconds it had rung again.

"Don't talk to him." Seven reached for the phone and cut it off. "He's crazy."

"For real," Toi said. "I thought he was just an ordinary nut but I don't like that slickness he was talking, and what does he mean slap you again?"

"He's crazy," I said. "We had it out one time and now all of a sudden he's threatening me. It's nothing. You know I fight back."

"But you cannot beat a man," Seven said sternly. "Zsa, you know how you felt when we were little and your mother and father used to bump—"

"Do we have to go there?"

"Alright," Seven said, "I'm just saying."

"Umm-hmm, well, I'm going to take me a shower, I'll catch you in a minute." I grabbed my clothes and went into the bathroom.

By the time I was out of the bathroom and was fully dressed, Cousin Shake and Uncle Easy were back home, looking as if they had been to war.

"Let's go hook up the grill," Cousin Shake said to Uncle Easy.

"The grill?" I frowned. "For what?"

"For what?" Cousin Shake squinted his eyes. "Don't you go embarrassing me. Seven, Toi, you better tell her how Cousin Shake do it."

"He likes to cook his Thanksgiving dinner on the grill," Toi said.

"He would roast a pig with an apple in his mouth if he could," Seven said.

"Don't test me, Fat Mama," Cousin Shake warned Seven, "'cause you know I will put it down on you."

"And where are we going to eat?" I frowned.

"Outside. Where the hell else do you eat barbeque?" Cousin Shake snapped and Uncle Easy laughed.

"Oh, no, I'm not eating my Thanksgiving dinner off no nasty-behind grill or outside in nobody's yard," Aunt Nona said. "Heck, no."

"Well, don't eat then." Uncle Easy looked Aunt Nona up and down. "You could stand to ignore a few calls to dinner."

"You don't talk to me like that!" Aunt Nona snapped.

"And you just don't talk to me. Keep messin' with me, you'll be running down the highway to Georgia."

"I don't need you!"

"You need somebody," Cousin Shake said, " 'cause you ain't got to go home but come tomorrow morning you got to get the hell outta here."

"Okay, everyone," my mother interjected, "I have already prepared most of the meal so why don't you put a few steaks on the grill if you want, and afterward we bring it inside and eat it with the rest of the dinner I cooked, at the dining room table."

"Exactly," Aunt Nona said, "have some class for once. Instead of acting like the wet side of a pigeon's behind."

"I'm 'bout sick of you, Nona." Uncle Easy frowned.

"Join the club, fishy drawls!" Aunt Nona snarled.

"His drawls are not fishy," Aunt Easter said.

"Ain't nobody talking to you, Memorial Day!"

"You don't talk to my wife like that!"

"I don't give a hoot about your wife or your five over-grown chil'ren."

My mother walked over to me and said, "You, Seven, and Toi go and set the table and leave these four to themselves."

"Now you see what I put up with," Aunty Grier said to my mother. "They'll be like that until we leave in the morning."

"Cousin Shake," my mother said, handing him a pack of steaks, "you need to go and grill these now because dinner will be served shortly."

While we set the table, me and my cousins kicked it about everything from boys, to love, to college, to what we liked and didn't like. I really missed them being in Jersey. I looked at the clock and realized I hadn't spoken to my baby all day, so I excused myself into the other room and called him.

"Hey, sweetie," I said as he answered the phone, sounding sexy as ever.

"Wassup, ma?"

"Are you coming over?"

"Nah," he said, "not today."

Instantly my heart sank. "I thought you would stop by for a minute."

"Oh, look at you missing me."

"I want to see you," I whined.

"Really?"

"Yes," I admitted.

"Well, then open the door, I'm outside."

"I don't believe you!" I said while hanging up the

phone. I ran to the front door, opened it, and there was my boo. "Don't be playing with me like that," I said, giving him a hug.

"I can't stay long." He kissed me on my forehead. "But I wanted to stop by to see you and to bring your mother this cake my mother baked." He looked around my living room. "Where's your mother?"

"In the kitchen, follow me."

Once we were in the kitchen I introduced Malachi to my aunts and cousins. "Ma," I said, "Ms. Karen sent you a cake for Thanksgiving."

My mother smiled. "Tell her I said thank you, Malachi. Karen knows she can bake some cakes. Are you staying for dinner?"

"No," Malachi said, "I just stopped by to see Zsa and to bring you this."

"Nice to meet you, young man," Aunt Nona said, "and if you have any uncles let an old bird know."

"You more than a bird," Uncle Easy said as he and Cousin Shake returned from outside. "You mo' like a vulture. A flying creature that can't nobody recognize."

"And what are you," she said, "a walking piece of Viagra?"

"Okay." I ushered Malachi out of the kitchen. "Don't you need to get going?"

"Nah, baby, this is funny."

"Malachi," I said.

"Ai'ight." He waved at everyone, but they were so entrenched in their argument they didn't pay him any attention. He kissed me before he left and already I missed him.

"Dang, he was cute," Seven said.

"He sure was," Toi followed up.

"Fall back now," I joked. "Fall all the way back."

"Whatever." Toi laughed as we headed into the dining room, and my mother walked over to Aunt Nona, Uncle Easy, and Cousin Shake who were still exchanging words.

"Can we please stop arguing," my mother said, "long enough to eat dinner?"

"Sure, we can." Cousin Shake nodded. "Y'all be quiet and let's go in the dining room."

"You don't tell me what to do, Shake," Aunt Nona said as she grabbed the bowl of cranberry sauce. "Don't get it confused. I ain't Minnie."

"Oh, you don't want none of me," Ms. Minnie said. "Take Minnie's name outcha mouth."

We all took our seats. "Hold it," Cousin Shake said. "Did anybody forget that we need to pray?"

"If anybody forgot," Aunt Nona said, "it would be you, Shake."

"I'm just gon' ignore you, Nona."

"Yeah, you do that."

"Let's just pray," Cousin Shake said, as we stood around the table and held hands. "Dear Bruh-Man Father."

"Hmm, tell it!" Aunt Nona said.

"We come before You thanking You for this day."

"Thank ya!" Aunt Nona followed up.

"Thanking You for a day we've never seen before—"

"Never seen," Aunt Nona said, "never seen."

"And day we'll never see again—"

" 'Cause we all gon' be dead one day and it'll be a lot of funerals to attend."

"You gon' lose all control then," Uncle Easy said. "It'll be more dead people than you can stand."

"Help him, Lawd," Aunt Nona said. "Continue on, Shake."

"Lawd, I just wanna thank You for Margarite's baby, Julio."

"What are you talking about Shake?" Aunt Nona interrupted. "Margarite was the prostitute that used to live down the street from us. She had that baby and didn't know who the daddy was. Was that your baby, Shake?"

"Baby?" Ms. Minnie said, opening her eyes. "Who the hell is Margarite, and since we're on this, who is this Julio you keep calling on every time you say a prayer? You been cheating on me, Shake?"

"Heck, no, Minnie. You know I love you. Don't listen to Nona."

"Don't listen to me," Aunt Nona said. "You're the one who brought up Margarite."

Cousin shake twisted his lips. "I was talkin' about Jesus' mama."

"Oh, you mean Saint Millie?" Aunt Nona asked for clarification.

"Yeah," Cousin Shake said. "Mildred, that's her."

"That's who it better be to, Shake," Ms. Minnie said. "'Cause I don't play that. Now say Amen and let's end this prayer. It's gone on long enough."

"Amen," everyone said in unison.

As the night went on we ate, laughed, and recapped memories. By the time we woke up the next morning came and I hated to see my family go.

"Oh, sweetie," my aunty Grier said to me, "you have to come down and stay with us for a few weeks this summer."

"Yeah," Seven said. "We miss you."

"I miss you too."

"I love you." Aunty Grier hugged my mother. "Call me."

"I will."

"Well, Shake, it was good seeing you," Uncle Easy said. "Maybe next time you come down to Manchester and we play some dominos."

"You mean have me beat you at dominos." Cousin Shake grinned.

"You can't beat me at dominos, Shake."

"There y'all go," Aunt Nona said. "Acting like a gorilla's rotten teeth."

"You ought to know about rotten teeth," Uncle Easy said as he walked outside toward the bus.

"Oh, it's on now," Aunt Nona said as she boarded the bus behind Uncle Easy and his family.

We watched them from the door and within a matter of minutes they were all gone. "I don't know about you," I said to my mother, "but I'm tired."

"And I'm sore," Cousin Shake complained. "Minnie, I need you to come and rub me down in some Bengay. Jazmyn." He turned to my mother. "Next Thanksgiving, they can't come back."

14

. . . .now you have no interest in anything that I have to say . . .
Does she want you with the pain that I do
I smell you in my dreams . . .

       —MESHELL NDEGEOCELLO, "FOOL OF ME"

For two hours Ameen had been calling my phone like crazy, and all I could do was lay in the center of my bed and wonder what it was going to take to make him stop. Ignoring him hadn't worked, cussing him out at my school a month ago only seemed to rev him up even more, so I didn't know what to do, what to think, or where I needed to go from here.

All I knew is that I needed this cat to bug off, yet no matter what I tried he was not falling back.

I looked at my ringing phone and could only imagine the message he was about to leave.

"Zsa," he began into my answering machine, "you mean to tell me you hate me so much that you can't even talk to me for two minutes?" He sounded so pathetic. "I know I wasn't the perfect boyfriend."

Wait a minute, is he crying?

"And maybe I didn't do everything right." He sniffed.

This fool is really in tears.

"But you of all people know that I was going through some things."

What "things" was he going through?

"I was going through changes with my son's mother and everything. You know people always trying to kick my back in and I thought, if nobody else, even if we weren't together, I would always be able to kick it with you."

The machine cut his message off but of course he gave me the courtesy of calling right back to finish. "It's cool, Zsa. You hate me. Everybody hates me. Maybe I should just kill myself since I'm so evil. I don't believe this cat got you so sewed up that you can't even give me five minutes of your time for me to apologize to you. Ai'ight, I'm out, and if you don't hear from me again, just know that I probably put a gun to my head."

Suddenly I felt guilty. Not about our relationship being over but about leaving Ameen hanging like this. He had been there for me . . . sometimes . . . and I didn't exactly hate him. I just didn't want to be with him anymore.

I wondered if I needed to call Ameen back and hear his gripes for no longer than a minute or if I needed to continue ignoring him. But—then—what if he actually killed himself simply because I wouldn't talk to him? Then I would feel guilty forever.

I thought about calling Malachi but I knew he would flip if he thought I was going anywhere near Ameen. And then I thought about calling Asha but quickly changed my mind, I could do without the preaching. And Courtney's advice was not even an option.

Heck with it. I quickly dialed Ameen's number. He didn't

answer so I figured forget it, I'd done my charitable duty for the day. I walked over to my television, turned it on, and the phone rang. I looked at the caller ID. Ameen.

"Hello?" I said in a serious tone.

"Speak to Zsa-Zsa?"

"Wassup, Ameen?"

"You. Like damn, you hate me so much you can't even accept my calls?"

"I never said I hated you. It's just that I think we don't—"

"Zsa, listen," he cut me off, "can I see you?"

"No," I said. "You can't."

"So you mean to tell me that what we had was nothing? Even if we don't have it anymore, what we had doesn't mean a thing to you now?"

"I never said that."

"So what you saying?"

"I'm saying that I don't want to see you."

"How could you be so cold? What do I have to do, jump off a bridge, die or something to get your attention?"

"Why are you so dramatic?"

"Because I love you."

"I'm sorry that you love me but I'm—"

"Zsa," he interrupted me again, "five minutes of your time, that's it. Five minutes. Just swing by, let me come see you, something."

"I'm not coming to your house and you're not coming here," I said.

"Can you meet me somewhere? How about the park? Drive over there and I'll meet you in the parking lot. I just want to see you for a minute. That's it. Please."

I sighed. I knew that Ameen had turned out to be a pest,

but he wasn't always like that. He had some good things about him. He was just . . . just . . . misunderstood. It's not as if he had the easiest life, which is how we related to each other in the beginning. He understood where I was coming from with my mom and my home life. I mean, he didn't know about my dad or anything, but he did understand me. Maybe we're meant to be . . . and maybe I did owe him five minutes. Right? Right? Yeah, I did. "Five minutes and that's it." I hung up.

I got in my car and it took me less than ten minutes to drive to the park. "Five minutes," I said to myself while parking near the entrance. "And I'll set my cell phone alarm to make sure that I don't stay any longer than that." I reached in my purse for the phone and I couldn't find it. I don't believe this. I shook my bag and nothing. Dang, I must've left it at home.

Bang!

My heart jumped. I looked up and saw that it was Ameen pounding on my window. He scared the mess out of me. Ameen stood there smiling and looked as if he hadn't shaved or maybe even bathed in days.

"You think we could pull over there?" He pointed to a more secluded section of the park. "I don't want everybody in the park in our business."

"Ameen," I said, "it's cold outside. It's nobody even in the park."

"I just didn't want to be sitting right here in the entrance. I mean, you could park your car here and ride with me over there."

I sighed. "Alright, but I'll drive over there."

We both drove our own cars to the secluded area and

parked them next to each other. Ameen got out of his car and walked over toward me. "Can you step out?" he asked me.

I shook my head no.

"Why are you acting like this?"

I knew I should've stayed in the car, but I went against my better judgment, got out, and leaned against the door. Ameen leaned in for a kiss and I turned my head. "No."

He stepped back and I turned my head back toward him. I couldn't believe my eyes. Ameen had never looked that bad. He had bags under his bloodshot eyes, his clothes were dirty and disheveled, and he smelled of alcohol and weed. "Are you high?" I asked him.

"Man"—he snorted—"I'm some of everything. I've been stressing like crazy. You won't talk to me. And no matter what I try it doesn't seem to work. Look at you, Zsa, you're looking at me like I just disgust you." Tears filled his eyes. "Tell me, please, what is it going to take for me to make this right? I need you and I need for us to be back together again."

"Ameen," I said, getting more and more turned off by the moment, "we can be friends. But I don't want to be with you again."

"Friends?" He frowned. "What, you wanna be my boy now? Is that what you and that ugly motherfucker that you hang with are? Friends?" He flung the ring on my necklace around my neck with the tip of his finger.

"Don't call him names." I snatched my ring back in place.

"Now you protecting this dude?" The vein on the side of Ameen's neck jumped. "You don't even care that I love you?"

"You love me?" I swear I almost laughed in his face. "Ameen, when you had me, you dogged me. Like for real, I got tired of that. You ran up on me in the bathroom talking about your girl this and that. So I bounced and gave you what you kept asking for, space."

"I never asked you for space. And I know I was wrong, and I admit that . . . but that chick wouldn't leave me alone. She kept calling me, coming to see me, and everything. You know I'm weak sometimes when it comes to women and that chick kept pushing up. Yo, my head was all confused, so yeah, I made bad choices. And when I ran up on you in the bathroom it was because I felt bad for her. That girl didn't have any money to fix her car. And you know you shouldn't have done that, Zsa. I mean . . . I'll admit, I went overboard. But I'm sorry and you gotta forgive me. You have to. And plus you all rockin' it with some other dude. How you think that makes me feel?"

"Ameen, me not being with you is not about you or him, it's about me."

"How can you say something selfish like that?" He looked at me with fire in his eyes. "As much as I love you and you gon' come out of your face like that?"

"Ameen, maybe—you know—this wasn't a good idea."

"Oh, now this wasn't a good idea?" He stood in front of me and placed his hands on both sides of me. "So what you really sayin'!" He mushed me and I slapped his hand.

"Don't put your hands on me!" I pushed him in his chest. "I'm done. Don't call me no more. We're through. And if you call me I'm changing my number and you won't know how to reach me. You are the worst thing that ever happened to me. My new boo"—I toyed with my necklace—"is the best. Now take that and step to the left."

Ameen snatched my necklace off of my neck and tossed it into the air. "Who you talking to, Zsa?"

I pushed him in his chest. "You better find my damn necklace!"

"I ain't finding it! And don't push me again!"

"This is exactly why I'm done with you! You better find my damn ring!"

"Or what?" He gave a sinister laugh. "What you gon' do?"

WHAPPPP!!!!!!!! I slapped him so hard that spit flew out the side of his mouth. Ameen turned around and before I could even think about how I shouldn't have done that, Ameen made me feel like fire was crawling up my face. "You think he's better than me, Zsa?" He yoked me by my collar and pushed his face into mine. "ANSWER ME!" he screamed.

"No, Ameen, I don't—"

"You know what?" His breath was hot against my face. "As much as I've done for you, this is what you're doing to me?!"

"I'm sorry."

"You're not sorry! But you will be!"

Ameen's blows felt like they were landing all at the same time.

This must've been how my mother felt when my father was beating her up. This must've been what all the warnings were about . . .

I knew my mother was nowhere around, but the memory of her screaming invaded my ears and I could hear my father saying, "Shut up!" and I could hear Hadiah crying.

I tried to fight back, but I was no match for Ameen. I felt like giving up. Suddenly, everything for me went black, and the last thing I remembered was Ameen's car engine revving and me falling to the ground.

15

Don't you be ashamed to say he hurt you . . .

—DESTINY'S CHILD, "GIRL"

I remember blaring sirens, someone asking my name, and someone else taking my pulse. But I don't remember how I got to the hospital.

My eyes were puffy and swollen painful slits. From where I lay in the hospital bed, all I could see were clean white walls, the doctor, my mother, and Malachi.

"Hey, baby," my mother said while patting my hand.

I don't know why but I wasn't at ease when I heard my mother's voice. I was tense. I was looking at her and I knew that I was me and she was her, but for some reason I felt like her reflection and I couldn't stand it. Somehow, I had to get out of there.

My mouth was parched as I looked at Malachi and tried to smile. He smiled back, but I could tell that he felt sorry for me.

"How do you feel?" My mother held a cup of water to my mouth and I sipped.

"Sore and tired," I said.

"Well," the doctor said, "you took a pretty bad bruising, young lady. You'll be sore for a couple of days but nothing is broken and you will heal. Once everyone is done here, I would like for you to participate in a domestic violence group we have here at the hospital for victims. I'm recommending you attend, prior to discharge." The doctor stepped to the doorway and said, "Call me if you need anything, but I'll be back in a while to check on you."

Counselor? Group? Victim? Tears rolled down my cheeks. I felt dumb, like why did I let this happen to me? Why was I laying here with them thinking I was some kind of victim? I didn't exactly mind labels, but I was not going to own that one. "I'm not a victim and I feel fine," I said, despite the tears burning from my eyes. "I don't need to see any counselor or attend any group."

"I'll go with you, Zsa," my mother insisted.

"Zsa." Malachi walked over to the side of my bed and wiped my tears. "It wouldn't hurt for you to go."

"Don't." I shook my head, ignoring the pain in my neck and back. "You of all people know how I feel. Don't insist that I do that."

I looked at my mother and her face was wet with tears. "Not my child," she mumbled under her breath. "Excuse me for a moment," she said, walking out of the room.

"Malachi," I said, feeling him caress my hand. "I'm not weak or anything like that."

"Zsa, you don't have to talk about this right now."

"But I want to. I went to see Ameen."

"Ameen?" Malachi blinked. "Ameen did this to you?"

I broke down and started crying. "I only went there to tell him to leave me alone, but when he snatched my ring off I lost it and I smacked him. I probably should've just stayed home or maybe kept my mouth shut and things wouldn't have gotten out of control."

"Ameen did this to you?" Malachi said again. "Ai'ight." He nodded. "Straight," he said as if he were confirming a conversation he was having in his head.

"And things just got out of control," I continued on.

"Zsa." Malachi kissed me softly on my forehead and then wiped my eyes with the soft tips of his thumbs. "You didn't do anything wrong."

"But I did. I should've stayed home or not have gotten smart with Ameen."

"It didn't give him a reason to put his hands on you!" my mother said, startling me and charging back into the room, followed by a police officer. "You hear me?" She walked over to my bedside. "Don't you ever let me hear you say that again! The police are here to get a statement from you, and Ameen's going to jail. Right now, today! Now tell the police what happened."

I was in shock, like I couldn't move and I couldn't erase the flashback of my mother carting me and my sister in and out of the police precinct to press charges on my father. I swallowed. I had to bring myself back to the present and erase the past from dancing before my eyes.

I shook my head no, and I knew at that moment I wasn't telling the police a thing. It's not that I was hung up on not being a snitch or anything stupid like that. I just couldn't bring myself to be like my mother, to warp into her or be some type of victim. No. Not now, not ever. Having to call the fight between me and Ameen "domestic violence" was a stretch for me. I knew boys weren't supposed to hit girls, but girls shouldn't hit boys either and I did slap him.

I mean, I wasn't not saying that he should've beat me

like that, but still . . . still . . . it was only a fight. Nothing more—nothing less. And if I could just stay away from Ameen then he'd go away. Right?

"No," I said, looking at my mother and then to the officers. "I'm not doing it."

"Malachi, officers"—my mother turned to them—"can you excuse us for a moment?"

"No problem," Malachi said as he squeezed my hand before he and the officers walked out of the room.

My mother exploded once they were gone. "What the hell do you mean 'no'?! Are you serious? I know you don't think Ameen loves you."

"I'm not even with him!" I screamed back. "I love Malachi and you know that!"

"You need to love yourself," she spat back. "Now, I like Malachi and he is a good catch and all of those things, but you need to deal with you and why you allowed Ameen to put his hands on you! I swear"—she shook her head—"I'ma beat him. I told you to leave that loser alone, but did you listen? No," she said, answering her own question. "Instead you lied to me!"

"You were never home long enough to know anything about me. Don't start acting like you are mother of the year because you're trying to butter me up so I will one day accept Kenneth."

"This isn't about Kenneth!"

"And it isn't about you, either," I snapped. "You think Ameen is Daddy? No, he's not, he's Ameen and I'm not you. I left my abuser. I didn't need to wait for him to die. Now, if you have unresolved issues with Daddy then take them up with the grave. Not me."

My mother stood silent for a moment and then she said, "I don't care what you say, I'm pressing charges. You are a minor and I'm in charge!"

"I said no!"

"Is everything okay in here?" Malachi peeked in. "Kinda loud down the hall."

"Everything is fine," I said.

My mother looked back at me and shook her head.

"You guys can come back in," I said.

"Are you sure?" Malachi said to me but looked at my mother.

"Yes," I said sternly. *"I'm sure."*

"Ai'ight," he said, "well, everybody's out here waiting to see you, Zsa."

"They can come in." My mother wiped her eyes. "And ask the officers to come in as well."

I don't believe she's doing this.

"Diva!" Courtney walked into my hospital room with Asha and Samaad following close behind him. "The nurses at the station said we could all come in for a few minutes."

"Yeah, Zontoe," Cousin Shake said, walking in with Ms. Minnie behind him, "I told them we needed to see you now or I was gon' turn the E.R. out."

I mustered up a smile and a small wave. Hadiah walked over to me and started crying.

"Hadiah, it's okay." I rubbed her head. "I'm okay."

"I was so scared when the police came to the house and said someone found you on the ground and you were at the hospital. I thought someone killed you."

"Shh," I said. "Don't cry."

Ms. Minnie hugged Hadiah. "Let's go and get something

to drink. Your sister is fine, okay? And you heard the doctor tell us in the lobby that she'll be home by morning."

"Yes, I remember him saying that." Hadiah sniffed.

"Okay, so let's go." Ms. Minnie held Hadiah's hand and they walked out of the room.

"Here." Courtney placed a purple boa around my neck. "I made this for you."

"Oh, hell, no," Cousin Shake said, placing his hands on the wall and spreading his legs. "I swear I was gon' pay them tickets," he said, looking at the officers.

"Cousin Shake," my mother said, tight-lipped, "get off the wall. They are not here for you."

I looked at my mother and whispered, "Please don't embarrass me. I can't deal with this right now."

"We will deal with this. I will not let Zach—Ameen," she stuttered, "get away with this."

"Please, make them leave. They can come back later. I'll talk to them then."

"Okay, but if they leave now you have to promise to go to that group and not try to get out of it."

I quickly nodded in agreement.

"Officers," my mother said, "can I speak to you in the hallway for a moment?"

They followed behind her and Cousin Shake said, "Zoo, let me tell you something. If somebody you know did this to you, all you have to do is say the word and I'll have er' cousin you got from the state of Georgia and North Carolina come up here to turn it out. All you got to do is say the word and tell me the deal." He flipped his cell phone open and quickly dialed a number. "Sha'Pookie," he spoke into his phone, "get your manz and them on standby. We may have an emergency."

"Cousin Shake," Malachi said, looking at me, "tell 'em it's cool. This one's on me."

"Malachi." I shook my head no.

He ignored me and turned to Samaad. "You ready to roll?"

"Ain't nothin' but a word, son." Samaad nodded.

I looked at Asha. "Don't let them go."

"I'm sorry, Zsa, but Ameen needs his behind beaten," she said as Malachi and Samaad left the room with Cousin Shake running behind them. "Don't leave an old man hanging!" Cousin Shake screamed. "I know how to put in work."

"Asha," I said, "that's not funny."

"No, it's not."

"Suppose they kill him?"

"Suppose he had killed you?"

Silence.

"Zsa." My mother walked back into the room. "The police are gone. But you have to speak with them at least by tomorrow. Ameen cannot get away with this!"

"I don't want to talk about this now, Ma."

"Then when?"

I closed my eyes. I couldn't do this right now. I didn't want to think, I just wanted to be still and maybe sleep. Yeah, that's it. Sleep. I turned over on my side, left Asha and my mother in this world, and drifted, at least for a few hours, into my own, where there was no pain, no police, and no Ameen.

16

Don't be a hard rock, when you really are a gem . . .
Respect is just the minimum . . .

—LAURYN HILL, "DOO WOP"

Have you ever been in a rush for life to speed up so you can get to the good parts again? Well, that's where I was at. I couldn't take another minute of thinking about Ameen, and abuse, and I hated the damn memories and dreams that had haunted me since I'd been in the hospital for two days.

I was due to go home, and I prayed like heck that I could leave everything that I brought there—pain, misery, and embarrassment—on the hospital's white sheets, between their walls, and on their floors. There was no way I could travel with that ache hovering over me. I needed it gone, out of my emotional pockets, and dumped in the gutter where all the nonsense belonged.

My mother sat on the edge of the hospital bed and asked me, "Zsa, are you sure you don't want to press charges?"

"Why are you doing this to me? Huh?" I snapped. "You can't bully me into doing something you never had the courage to follow up on. So get off my neck, please. I just want to go to this stupid meeting and be done with it."

"I really think we need counseling."

"Well, you go for the two of us, because I'm not getting involved." I sucked my teeth. "And I'm only going to this meeting so that I can be discharged from this hospital."

"It's girls your age, Zsa."

"Who I have nothing in common with."

"You're in denial."

"Then I guess it's hereditary."

"Okay," my mother snapped, "I think I've had enough of your smart mouth. You're pushing your luck."

I didn't even respond to that. I'd learned that sometimes it was better to have your parents think they'd shut you down, when in reality you were just ignoring them.

We waited for the nurse and I wondered why there would be a group that celebrated your problems. That was so crazy to me. I mean, why would there be a teen domestic violence group? Why would teens want to meet every week to share stories and talk about their problems as if they were badges of honor?

That's how I knew that this group thing wasn't for me and I wouldn't relate to any of these chicks. I'd rather not deal with my problems than to be standing before a crowd acting as if I collected issues for sport. Not.

"Good morning, ladies." The nurse walked into my hospital room with a goofy smile on her face. "The meeting will be held in room 411. The counselor's name is Jona. She's really nice, so be sure to introduce yourselves to her."

"Thank you, nurse," my mother said as I sat there un-fazed.

"Take care," the nurse said before turning to walk out of the room.

The meeting room was only an elevator ride up to the next level.

When my mom and I walked in the room, everyone smiled at us and said, "Welcome." There were about two or three women who looked to be my mom's age, and they were holding teenage girls' hands. I assumed the pairs were mothers and daughters. The girls were every color and creed you could imagine—White, Black, Latin, and Asian.

My mother's face lit up like Christmas as we took our seats. I gave a small wave to everyone and my mother said, "Hello. I'm Jazmyn and this is Zsa-Zsa."

"Thanks for coming," the counselor said as she intro-duced herself. "I'm Jona and I represent every girl and every woman in the world who wants to say 'no more' to domestic violence. We are a weekly group, and you can choose to share or not to share. We don't push you to do anything"—Jona looked at me—"so you speak when you are ready to."

Don't ask me why but tears filled my eyes. I did my best not to cry.

"Okay, ladies, let's begin with our opening prayer."

For a moment I laughed to myself, wondering if she would be thanking Jesus or Julio, like Cousin Shake had.

Everyone stood up and held hands.

"Let's bow our heads," Jona said. "Father on high," she began, "we thank You for blessing each and every girl here with the will and the strength to say no more. We thank You for their courage and we ask You to bless us to continue to touch the lives of those who need to hear our stories and know they are not alone. We ask this as we ask all continued blessings in Your son Jesus' name, Amen."

We all took our seats, which were placed in a circle. "Who would like to begin?" Jona asked.

"I would." A blond-haired, blue-eyed girl raised her hand.

Jona nodded and the girl began to speak. "Hello, my name is Susan. I'm sixteen, and I represent every girl in the world who has to take a stand and say no to domestic violence."

Tears rolled down Susan's face. "I never thought of myself as a victim—"

Then why are you here? I shook my head and then looked her over. She looked like your average, everyday Valley Girl. Something I was not and could not relate to, leaving me certain that nothing she said or did would have an effect on me.

"But then I realized that I was a victim," Susan continued. "I ran away from home a few months back because I thought I found the man of my dreams. He was twenty-five and I was only sixteen. Past the age of consent so no one could do anything about it. Not even my parents. And I was happy, in love, and free . . . so I thought.

"My love was charming and he filled a part of me that had been empty. All of my life I didn't feel good enough. I mean, my sister was smart. And I thought she was prettier. She was always rewarded for doing well in school. While I was just . . . just . . . here. I was Susan. Average student, nothing to write home about, nothing to miss. Just there like a bump on a log.

"So I attached myself to the first man that made me feel worthy. I did whatever he wanted me to do, and there was nothing my parents could do or say to me. He had the control. And when the first slap came because I didn't know how to cook his favorite dinner the way he liked I accepted it—and tried to forget it. Especially since he apologized and swore he would never do it again. He was stressed, you know"—she hunched her shoulders and pushed her hair behind her ears—"and I knew I couldn't stand to be without him and I didn't want him to leave me. But that didn't stop the next slap, or the next punch, kick . . . or rape. Me being silent only made things worse, and not until I said 'no more,' you will not do this to me anymore, was I able to call my parents and confess to them what was going on. I just wanted a way out. They came and got me. But he still haunted me, stalked me, and called me nonstop. I took out a restraining order, but that didn't stop him. He caught me one night hanging out with my friends at a local club, and he dragged me from the club to his car, beating me all the way. I don't remember what happened after that. All I know is that he's in jail for a long time and I can't walk now." She lifted the blanket from her lap and revealed the wheelchair she sat in.

"So I'm here to talk about how it feels to be saddled with this for the rest of my life. If I could just change one girl's life by telling her to listen to her parents, to her friends, just listen when they say something is not right. Hear them when they tell you they only want the best for you, because they mean it. Thank you for listening to my story."

I thought for sure she was going to fall apart, because I knew that my heart ached for her. *The difference between us, though, is that I broke up with Ameen on my own and when he hit me, I hit him back.*

The group clapped for Susan, and then Jona said, "Who would like to share their story next?"

A short and petite Asian girl raised her hand. It was obvious that someone had beaten her up pretty bad because her left eye was swollen shut. I thought for a moment that we had nothing in common . . . but then I remembered what my face looked like. So me and this girl must've resembled to everyone else in here.

"Hello, my name is Kai-Ming, I'm seventeen, and I represent every girl in the world who has to take a stand and say no to domestic violence."

Everyone clapped and said, "Welcome, Kai-Ming."

"A lot of people think leaving is such a simple choice and that we can walk away one day and not look back, but it's not true." She shook her head. "I grew up with my mother being beaten by my father. Day after day after day, and night after night after night, he beat her. And if me or my brother got involved he would beat us." She closed her eyes as if she were fighting off a bad memory. "We would beg my mom to leave my dad, but she never did and she never expressed a desire to. I felt so alone. I had no self-esteem, and because we lived in Franklin Lakes, New Jersey, we appeared perfect on the outside, but inside of our house was hell.

"So when the first guy who promised to love me forever came along, I believed him. He was thirty and I was fourteen. He had his own place. He was always there when I needed him. I never had to call—he was always calling me. Shortly after we hooked up I was pregnant with my son. He promised to take care of me, and he said that he wanted to raise our son differently than I had been raised. So I ran away from home with a baby and a pocket full of dreams. My mother didn't care and my father didn't look for me. So when my boyfriend moved us hours away from everyone and everything and said he wanted me all to himself, I thought that was cool. He wouldn't allow me to get a job, and when I told him that I couldn't take it anymore and wanted to leave, he slapped me and I took it. I felt that if he hit me, then he had to love me, because hitting was the only type of love I knew.

"By the time I was pregnant again, I was sixteen. My boyfriend beat me all through my pregnancy, and shortly after I had our daughter, the beatings got worse. But what made me leave was my son. He was three, and every time he got mad with me he would jump on me to fight me. And he would say to call him Daddy. I knew I had to go then. But I didn't know if there was any place for teens. Because everybody thinks you have to be old, like in your thirties or something, to be beaten by your boyfriend. But it's not true.

"I saw the number for this program in the phone book. So I called and they came and got me when my boyfriend was at work, fleeing with nothing but my children and our lives. I went to a shelter that night and have been there ever since. He doesn't know where we are, and I plan on moving far away so that he can't ever get to us again. And I hope that wherever I go or wherever I land that I am able to change someone's life by telling them you are beautiful, you are special, and you don't deserve his hands on you."

Why is a river of tears running down my face? I had to get out of there, and when I looked at my mother to tell her we needed to be ghost, she was holding and hugging the Chinese girl, thanking her for her story.

"Anyone else?" the counselor asked.

"Yes." A Latino girl with thick, black curly hair stood up. "I would like to share. First, I want to begin by saying my name is Consuelo, I'm seventeen, and I represent every girl in the world who has to take a stand and say no to domestic violence. I hear a lot of people and girls, you know"—she hunched her shoulders—"speak about their boyfriends hitting them, and their boyfriends are like these old dudes. Or the girls say they ran away from home and lived with these men. So I never thought that this"—she pointed around the room—"was me or could be me. My boyfriend was seventeen, like me. A basketball star. We went to school together, but we didn't live together. He started out perfect. We met in the hall every day for a quick kiss. We spent all of our free time together, and his parents gave him a lot of freedom. I was able to chill in his house and everything, no questions asked. I could even stay over some nights if I wanted to. He always had money and bought me anything I wanted. I accepted a lot of non-sense from him. He cheated on me, talked down to me and everything, but I thought I could love him enough to change him."

Consuelo twisted her lips as tears rolled down her face. "But that was such a joke. He started out grabbing me by my collar when he would get mad or I didn't answer my phone. Then the grabbing went to pushing me, and then the pushing went to slapping, and slapping turned into getting beat down on the regular. I would always lie to my parents or people who asked and tell them that I was jumped, or in an accident at school. I would never tell the truth, because I loved him and he was always *soooo* sorry.

"Eventually though I got tired and couldn't take it anymore so I broke up with him. I thought it would be simple. Leave him and he would be free to cheat and do his thing. But he started stalking me, and calling me all the time. Things got worse after we broke up and one day he cornered me on my way home, and he beat me so bad that I woke up in the hospital with no memory of how I got there. He was arrested and went to jail, where he is now.

"But I feel guilty, like I brought this on myself, and my mind keeps playing the what-if game—what if this, what if that. I don't know. All I know is that I'm here and I'ma keep coming back until I get it. Until I understand what made me take the abuse. And once I know what is it, I'ma deal with it, and then maybe I'll be able to feel like myself again."

My heart sank in the middle of my chest. These stories were driving me crazy. I wanted to feel like none of these stories reminded me of my life or the choices I'd made, but they did.

I couldn't stand it. I didn't want to be one and the same as these girls because then what would that say about me? What would that say?

I was not this weak. No. I shook my head. I looked at my mother and said, "I'm done. The doctor can decide he doesn't want to give me my discharge papers, but I'm leaving."

I got up from my seat and hurried into the hall. I could

hear my mother on my heels. "Zsa," she called, but I was trying to get away. I wanted to be far away from that place.

My mother ran over to me and blocked my path. "Stop." She placed her hands on my shoulders. "Where are you going?"

I started to tell her to hell but I couldn't get any words to form. Then I started to tell her that those girls weren't me although it felt like it, but that wouldn't come out either. I didn't know what I could say. All I knew is that this had to end, and it had to end that day.

"Ma, please," I managed to get out of my mouth while wiping my tears away. "I just want this all to go away. Just let me make it go away."

"Zsa-Zsa, it doesn't happen like that."

"But it can for me. I can't do this right now. Please."

My mother stared at me and I begged her again. "Please."

"I only want the best for you, Zsa. You didn't deserve what Ameen did to you."

"Ma, I can't wallow in that. At least not right now. I'm begging you. Please, I don't want to talk about this anymore. I just want to go on. There's no more me and Ameen, I won't even let him speak to me. He can't come around. I won't take any of his calls. I will act as if he doesn't exist. But allow me to do that. That group"—I pointed toward the room—"is not for me. Those are not my stories."

"Okay." My mother nodded reluctantly in agreement. "If this is how you need to handle things, I'll respect that."

"Thank you, now can we leave?"

"Yes, yes we can," she said with no sincerity. We went back to the hospital room, where the doctor was waiting for us.

"How'd it go?" he asked.

Neither one of us answered, so the doctor continued on with signing my discharge forms. "Within a week you should be back to yourself."

Thank God, finally a date when I will be better.

"Take care of yourself," the doctor said as I walked into the hall with my mother behind me.

17

Me, myself and I . . . gon' be my own best friend . . .

—BEYONCÉ, "ME, MYSELF AND I"

It had been a week since everything had jumped off with Ameen, and I felt like . . . like I'd lost myself. Everywhere I looked for myself there was no Zsa-Zsa. Instead there was this girl dealing with a buncha bullshit that belonged to other people—my father, my mother, Ameen, the girls at Say No More—but had been dumped on my doorstep. I was tired of being this person that I'd warped into. Although the bruises were mostly healed and by the next week I'd be back in school, I didn't feel like myself. Instead I felt like someone who'd gone to space, gotten lost, and happen to stumble across home again.

I was also upset that my mother didn't keep her promise and ended up giving the police Ameen's information.

"Zsa." My mother called my name and knocked on my bedroom door at the same time. "I'm on my way to work." She cracked the door open before I could say "come in." "Cousin Shake and Ms. Minnie went to visit with some of

Ms. Minnie's relatives in upstate New York. And Hadiah is having a sleepover with her friend, so you'll be here by yourself for a while."

"You're working late?" I asked.

"Yeah, we need the money so I may pull a double."

"Oh." I frowned. *I'm sure I'll be great company for myself.*

"Are you still upset?" my mother asked me, opening my door completely. "I had to tell the police something, Zsa. I know you may not understand it now, but when you become a mother I promise you will."

"As long as you know I'm not getting involved with anything. I don't want to press charges and I'm tired of talking about it—"

"No, you'd rather run from it. But you know what? Like Kenneth said, I need to give you enough space to be yourself."

"Kenneth? Why are you still seeing this man? You really don't get it, do you? We don't like him, we will never accept him. And don't talk about my business with him! What's next? You coming home to announce that he's your husband?"

"Look," my mother said sternly, "I will not have you speaking to me like this. All of that energy you need to save for Ameen."

"Oh, that's great advice." I rolled my eyes to the ceiling. "How understanding of you."

"Zsa"—my mother gave a heavy sigh—"I can't continue to do this with you. You are old enough to understand that I am a woman as well as your mother. I'm sorry about the way I brought Kenneth into your life. That's why I didn't invite him back over here. So for the introduction I will apologize for the way I did that. But for wanting someone in my life, for wanting Kenneth in my life, I will not apologize for that."

"Whatever, Ma, I'm not beat for it. I'm cold on it anyway. Do you."

"I don't know what any of that means." She arched her eyebrows to let me know she wasn't asking for a translation. "But I think if you stopped being so resistant and started going to counseling with me—"

"You go to counseling now?" I couldn't believe it.

"Yes. After that meeting I realized that I needed to deal with some things. And hopefully it will help you too."

"Please. Me and counseling. Not. I am not crazy."

"I didn't say that."

"Well, I don't want to discuss it, and please don't bring up that sad behind and pathetic group again."

"Okay, that's enough," she snapped. "This conversation is finished. I have to go. Love you and goodbye." She walked away from my doorway and a few seconds later I heard the front door close behind her.

Heck with it. I walked over to the mirror, and as I looked at the fading bruises on my face the doorbell rang.

"Ma," I said, walking toward the front door, "you forgot your keys?"

"I am nobody's mama!" That was Courtney, and he was screaming from behind the door like a fool. I opened the door and Courtney continued, "Just because I wanna be a Dallas Cowboys cheerleader when I grow up doesn't make me somebody's mother."

"Courtney, please," Asha said as she and Samaad walked

behind Courtney. They carried three Pathmark bags and balloons.

"What's in the bags?" I said smiling, happy to see my friends. "And what's with the balloons?"

"Food," Samaad said as if he were exhausted.

"And streamers." Courtney smacked his lips. "And let's not forget the sparkling cider, girlfriend." Courtney swung his hot pink boa to the back of his shoulder with one hand and swung the bottle with the other. "We need to celebrate."

"What are we celebrating?" I asked, confused.

"You," Asha said. "We love you."

"We sure do."

Courtney smacked his lips. "And we noticed that you hadn't been yourself since all of this stuff jumped off. So we decided to throw a party." Courtney sang, "This way we can blame it on the trone that got you in a zone and not Ameen like to beat womeen—Oh, wait," Courtney said, as if he had just realized what he was singing. "I was just trying to rhyme. My fault. Bad Courtney." He slapped himself in the mouth. "Bad—bad—Courtney."

"That's enough." Asha gave Courtney the evil eye as she began to take the food from the bag.

"You don't have to be lookin' at nobody like that," Courtney said, rolling his eyes. "Don't make me go Ameen slash Chris Brown on you, Asha. This boa might be pink but I am a man." He placed his hands on his hips and sucked his teeth.

"It's cool, Courtney," I said, hoping to end their inevitable argument before it started. "I would only allow *you* to get away with saying that."

"Thank you, my sistah," Courtney said, as the doorbell rang again.

"I'll get it." I laughed. I walked over and opened the door. It was my baby standing there. "Malachi." I hugged him tightly. "I missed you."

"Of course you did." He laughed and kissed me on the lips. "Because I missed you."

"Oh," Courtney said dramatically, "how lovely. Y'all got that . . . that . . . *Love Jones* kinda love. Feel me? I swear that a beautiful thing. Beautiful thing." He snapped his fingers and moved his shoulders from side to side. "Get it, y'all."

"Could you calm all that zest down?" Samaad asked Courtney. "Like for real."

"Or what?" Courtney placed one hand on his hip and pointed the other like a gun. "What you gon' do, Maad? Huh? You can't even handle Asha, now you gon' get with me and my zestful quality?"

"We gon' ignore you," Asha said. "Anyway"—she turned to me—"we're having a party. I cooked chicken, greens, mac and cheese, cornbread—"

"We get the picture, Oprah." Courtney waved her off. "You like to eat. Well, Diva, I got the drinks and the music. Hey 'yay!" He slid in a Patti LaBelle CD and started singing, "Somewhere over the rainbow . . ."

"Oh, no," Malachi said, "I'm 'bout to roll."

"Malachi, don't be like that," I said, tight-lipped.

"Zsa"—he pointed at Courtney—"look at him." I turned to look at Courtney, who was singing at the top of his lungs and slow dancing with himself. His arms were crossed over his chest and his hand rested on his shoulders. "Don't no grown man have any business watching that."

Before I could say anything Asha hit Courtney in the back of his neck. "Stop it."

"Oh, damn," Courtney said, as if he'd been in a trance, "I almost forgot where I was at. Good thing I didn't take my shirt off."

"So anyway, Zsa," Asha said. "Come help me set this food up in the dining room."

"Yeah." I shook my head at Courtney. "That sounds like a good idea."

"Y'all do that," Courtney yelled behind us, "and I'ma switch to some Elton John."

"I got the music man," Samaad said. "I got a mixed CD, 'cause this is some nonsense you playing."

"For real," Malachi agreed.

"Don't y'all be ganging up on me!" Courtney shouted as we headed into the adjourning dining room.

"I'm glad y'all came over," I said to Asha, handing her a pack of paper plates.

"I missed you," she said. "*We* missed you."

"Awwl, boo-boo. I missed you too." I gave her a hug.

"Now look," she whispered as we resumed to setting the table, "you know Samaad and Malachi caught Ameen."

"What?" I blinked in disbelief and whispered back, "When I didn't hear anything I thought they didn't do that. I was hoping they didn't even get involved."

"Well, they did."

"How do you know?"

"Samaad told me. He asked me not to say anything so don't open your mouth."

"I won't. And for real I don't even want to know the details."

"Cool, then I'll end the conversation right there. Let's call the boys in here to eat."

I walked into the living room. "The food is ready," I said to them, and they followed me into the dining room. We sat at the table and started to eat, and I couldn't believe how good the food was. "Asha, this food is slamming!" I said.

"And you know this." She laughed.

"My baby be putting it down," Samaad said.

"Now I don't have an appetite." Courtney sucked his teeth. "Samaad, why must we hear the details of your sex life? I mean, really."

"You need to get your head out of the gutter," I said. "He was talking about the food, fool."

"You got one more time to call another fool," Courtney snapped, "and it's gon' be a situation."

"Anyway," Asha said, "we should go play paintball next weekend."

"Maybe," I said. "That sounds like fun."

"Straight." Asha smiled.

Courtney sucked his teeth. "I'm not playing paintball. Mess my face all up. Not."

"Ill, and what crawled up your butt?" I asked.

"Time out," Malachi said. "Hold it." He looked at me. "Don't be asking him no questions like that. I don't wanna hear his answer to that."

"I'm just gon' ignore you, Ma-Mal." Courtney sucked his teeth, rose from the table, and started dancing. "This disco throwback is my jam. Come on, girls, let's bust us a soul train line. Come on, Divas." He started rocking his hips from side to side. "Stand on the side, so I can dance down the middle."

I cracked up laughing. Even when we were little, Courtney knew how to be the life of the party. Me and Asha stood up, walked to the living room, stood across from one another, and started moving from side to side. A Gwen Guthrie throwback about padlocking your heart that had to be as old as Jesus was playing on this mixed CD. The beat was tight though and of course Courtney knew every word.

Courtney worked the middle of the floor with a vogue and then he ended it with some of the moves from Beyoncé's "Single Ladies."

"Come on, Samaad and Malachi," Asha and I insisted, and waved our hands at them to join us. "It'll be fun," I said, giving Malachi the puppy face.

"I'm not doing that." Malachi waved me off.

"Yes, you are." I walked over to him while Asha walked over to Samaad, and we pulled them to the floor. "I promise you," I said. "You two will still be men when you finish dancing. Now come on." I grabbed Malachi's hand and proceeded to work the middle of the floor.

I moved my hips from side to side and bounced up and down on my knees while Malachi stood behind me nodding his head.

"Can't neither one of y'all get with this," Asha said as she and Samaad started to do an old school dance called da whop.

"Samaad." Malachi laughed. "Tell me you didn't, man. You didn't let her break your resistance down."

Samaad laughed. "Happy wife, happy life." He twirled Asha around and dipped her back.

"Oh, ai'ight," Malachi said, "you can't touch me and my girl. . . ."

We started working the floor like nobody's business, and eventually we were having too much fun to even explain. Courtney was on the floor doing a spin when the front door slammed and caused us to jump. I looked up and it was Cousin Shake and Ms. Minnie. "You scared the mess outta me," I said, holding my chest.

Cousin Shake looked around the room at the decorations, balloons, and food. "You're having a party and nobody invited us?"

"It was a surprise, Cousin Shake," Asha said.

"Oh, hey, Salad." Cousin Shake nodded at Asha. "It's cool," he said, "now where were you? 'Cause me and Minnie got a Pop-Lock-and-Drop-It that's gon' put all y'all to sleep."

I cracked up as Cousin Shake started to dance, and before I knew anything the entire living room had turned into a dance floor. The music was bumpin', the dancing was going, and I felt like . . . like, I could do this. I could really somehow do this thing called life and get back to being Zsa-Zsa.

After a few hours passed, we started to wind down and I said to Asha, "Thank you."

"For what?"

"For being my friend."

"You know how we do it." Courtney snapped his fingers. "Now come on, Asha, I need to be dropped off right away. *Bridezilla* is about to come on, and if I miss it, it's gon' be on and crackin'."

"And I don't wanna see you crackin' nothin', Cora," Cousin Shake said to Courtney. "Come on, Minnie, I'm going to bed."

"Bye, Zsa," Asha said, kissing me on the cheek, as she, Samaad, and Courtney left.

Once they had all left, Malachi and I began cleaning up.

"I'm so happy you guys came over," I said.

"You feel any better?" Malachi asked.

"Yeah, I don't think this night could've ended any better."

He gave me a great big ol' Kool-Aid smile. "Not even a li'l bit better?"

"No." I gave him the same Kool-Aid smile back. "Why?"

"Well"—he playfully hunched his shoulders—"I guess it doesn't matter why if you're saying the night couldn't have been any better. I wouldn't—you know—want to ruin the great time you had." He reached in the pocket of his carpenter jeans. "So I'm just"—he pulled out a red ring box with a white bow on top—"take this back to the store."

My eyes lit up with delight. "Stop playing, what is that?"

"Nah," he said, putting it back in his pocket, "nothing."

I stood on the chair and playfully grabbed him around the back of his neck. "Don't make me take you down."

Malachi fell out laughing. "Imagine that."

"Then tell me what it is."

"Ai'ight, get down first."

I stepped to the floor and Malachi pulled the ring box from his pocket. "I know you felt bad about no longer having the first one I gave you." He popped the box open and revealed a gold ring with *wifey* written in white gold script across it. "I thought the magic marker might've been played out a li'l bit." He gave me a half a grin.

"This is beautiful," I said in awe.

"You like?" He smiled.

"I love it." I hugged him tight. "And I love you."

"You wanna be my girl?" He whispered against my lips. "Circle yes or no."

"I circled yes." We started to kiss. "And I'ma always circle yes."

18

There's something you do
That got me walkin' on the moon . . .

—THE-DREAM, "WALKING ON THE MOON"

Let me put you down on this real quick: Love is a drug. Word. I'm so serious. Once you have a man like Malachi, who loves you, treats you right, and is kind and sensitive yet still able to put down his thug thizzle when needed, you will forever be addicted to being treated like a princess. When my baby calls me his girl or his wifey it actually means something. It just doesn't sound good, it feels good. . . . It is good. So why I was trippin' over telling him that Ameen had been back to calling me a hundred times a day was beyond me.

Honestly . . . I think . . . that maybe . . . I just didn't want the hassle. I didn't want to deal with the nonsense again. I'd already gotten the hint. Ameen liked to beat on women. But I couldn't deal with Malachi exploding, going out into the street, and beating Ameen down again. Malachi had too much to lose.

So I dealt with Ameen's calling like I dealt with everything else that bothered me. I ignored it.

Me and Malachi were chillin' in my room. I lay across the foot of my bed looking at Courtney's Facebook page on my laptop. "Come look at this," I said to Malachi, who was sitting on my floor watching a football game.

"Run the ball!" Malachi screamed at the television.

"Would you pay attention to me?"

"Ai'ight, Zsa, ai'ight," he said to me but continued to look at the TV. "Wassup?"

"Look at this." I cracked up. I was laughing so hard that tears were falling from my eyes.

Malachi walked over to the bed and sat beside me. He looked at the computer and said, "Who is that?"

"Courtney."

"Courtney?" Malachi said, surprised. "Why does he have his robe hanging off his shoulders and a cherry tattoo on his chest?"

I was laughing so hard I couldn't respond. Apparently Courtney had lost his mind.

"Yo," Malachi said, "don't call me over here to look at another man with a dang cherry on his chest. I'll never be able to eat cherries again."

"Awwl, my baby's upset? Me sorry." I started kissing him all over his face until he started laughing and tickling me in my belly. "Zsa," he said, sitting up. "I want to ask you something?"

"What?" I laid my head in his lap.

"When are you going to cut your mother some slack about Kenneth?"

"What?" I sat up and looked at him like he'd lost his

mind. "Where did that come from? Did my mother tell you to talk to me about Kenneth?" I stood up.

"You a little amped, don't you think?" He arched his brow. "Sit down."

I sat down reluctantly. "I don't want to talk about this."

"Would you stop that? Why do you run away from everything?"

"It's easier that way."

"Some things have to be faced and your mother having a boyfriend is one of them."

"Why are we talking about this? I mean, really."

"Because when I came here earlier, I saw him talking to your mother on the porch as if he couldn't come in."

"He can't come in *here*."

"Do you pay the bills?"

"No, but so."

"Look, I'm not trying to start an argument," Malachi insisted.

"I can't tell."

"All I'm saying is that at some point you have to stop interfering with your mother's life and allow her to chill like you wanna chill."

"Boy, please, what are you, a documentary? Both your parents are together, so that's easy for you to say."

"You are so hardheaded." He laughed.

"And you love it."

"Yeah, too much of it," he said. "But you better learn to listen and start dealing with your problems, or one day they will blow up in your face if you don't."

"Whatever, Malachi," I said as my cell phone started ringing and I tried to ignore it.

"You gon' answer your phone?" Malachi asked me.

"Nah," I said, returning my attention back to Facebook. "I'll call whomever back later."

"Well, they must want to speak to you," he said, "because your phone stopped ringing and now it's ringing again."

Malachi looked at me like I was nuts. I reached for the phone and the number was restricted. I started not to answer but the cell phone numbers of a lot of people I know also comes up restricted, so I took a deep breath and took the chance.

"Hello?"

"Zsa, please don't hang up." It was Ameen.

I started to hang up but I didn't. "Yeah, what?"

"I've been calling you like crazy to say that I'm sorry." He spat out superfast as if he were scared that I was going to hang up at any moment.

I rolled my eyes to the ceiling, but still I didn't respond.

"I know," Ameen continued on, "that you probably feel like you've heard this a thousand times, but I'm really serious this time. And I'm not calling you to ask you to be my girl again. I know that you've moved on and I'm happy for you. But I couldn't let another day go by without me saying that I was scum for putting my hands on you. No woman deserves that. And especially not you. So, that's all I wanted to say. I won't be bothering you again."

When I didn't respond, he said, "Ai'ight. One." And he hung up.

Malachi looked at me while I held the phone to my cheek replaying the conversation in my mind, and said, "Who was that, Zsa?"

"Huh?" I said, caught off guard.

"You heard me."

I started to tell him nobody, but lying to Malachi after

everything that had gone on was not a good look, so I swallowed and released a deep breath through the side of my mouth. "That was Ameen."

"Ameen?" Malachi frowned. "Ameen was just on your phone?"

"Yeah."

"And you were talking to him right here in my face?" he said evenly.

"It wasn't like that. He'd been calling here over and over again for weeks and—"

"Oh, so he's been calling here and you haven't said anything to me?"

"I didn't want you to get all pissed off, like you are now."

"Nah, I'm cool. Believe me, I'm straight."

"What do you mean by that?"

"Listen," Malachi said, "did Ameen threaten you?"

"No."

"Did he ask you to be his girl?"

"No. He apologized and said he wouldn't be bothering me again."

"Ai'ight." Malachi stood up and slid on his leather jacket. "That's wassup."

"Where are you going?" I said as he placed his keys in his pocket.

"I'm out." He walked to the door and opened it. "I'll see you when I see you." And he slammed the door behind him. I tried to go after him but he was too fast, and before I knew anything he was in his truck and had taken off.

I swear I couldn't move. I didn't know what the heck had just happened. One minute Malachi was cool and the next minute he was hot, pissed off, and gone. My heart thundered in my chest and my hands started to shake. I picked up my cell phone and called Asha, but no one answered, and then I called Courtney. "Two snaps up and a fruit loop, royalty speaking."

"Courtney," I said in a panic, holding my hurt feelings in my chest.

"What's wrong, Diva?"

I explained to him what happened and then I said, "I think Malachi just broke up with me."

"Ahhhh!" Courtney started screaming. "Oh no, oh no. Jesus, no. I knew you was gon' mess this up for us!" he cried. "Why, Zsa? Huh? Why?"

"What do you mean mess this up for us?" I snapped. "He was my boyfriend, what the hell are you crying for?"

"I live through your love life and this is not the ending I had in mind. You have to call him and get him back. We 'spose to graduate from Howard and have us a li'l girl named Shaquita in a few years. Don't do this, Zsa. Don't end my life like this." He started crying again. "You were wrong, Zsa-Zsa. Oh, Lord, oh, Lord."

"Okay, you know what," I said, "I gotta go. You trippin'."

I quickly dialed Malachi's cell phone number and prayed that he answered. After a few rings he picked up. "Yeah, what?"

"Look, before you say anything," I said in a hurry, "I'm sorry. I didn't mean to hide anything from you or to disrespect you. I love you, you know that, and I would never do anything intentionally to hurt you."

Malachi sighed. "You are a lot of work, Zsa. For real. I don't know what I'ma do with you."

"Love me." I gave a fake laugh, and when he didn't respond I said, "Pretty please."

Malachi laughed. "This is the second time I'm telling you this, but let that stunt you pulled be the last one."

"It won't happen again. I promise. So are you coming back?"

"Open the door," he said, "I'm already outside."

19

"Zsa, peep these shoes," Asha said as we browsed Neiman Marcus's shoe collection.

"Those are hot," I said, pointing at the pair of three-inch canary yellow stilettos she was holding. "How much?"

"Eight nine," she said.

"Oh, I want those," I said in glee. I swear, whenever I bought shoes it made me feel like it was Christmas all over again.

"I'm getting me some too," Asha said, "but I want the lime green ones."

We paid for the shoes and afterward we headed to the food court. Once we grabbed two orders of Bourbon chicken we sat at a small table in the center of the floor where we could see all the action. "Wait, Zsa, is that Jamil from school?" Asha asked.

"Umm-hmm," I said, "but that girl ain't his girl."

"Hot mess." She laughed.

"So," I said, "wassup with you and Samaad?"

"I love him so much." She blushed.

"I know." I smiled. "How did we end up with the perfect boyfriends, who are also cousins? Then that means our kids gon' be cousins too."

"Yop," Asha agreed, "and if we don't like our in-laws we'll always have each other to talk to."

We both cracked up.

"But I tell you what," she continued, "it will not be any kids anytime soon."

"Why do you say that?" I sipped my soda.

"'Cause."

"'Cause what? What you and Samaad not gettin' down like that?"

"Not yet."

"Why?" I curled my lip in surprise. "You're not a virgin."

"So, that doesn't mean that I wanna be in the sheets with every cat I meet. I'm just not feeling that, so we find other things to do. So what about you and Malachi?"

I shook my head. "Nothing's happenin', captain."

She laughed. "We could always get a job and occupy ourselves."

"When you fill out the application let me know, otherwise the check I get from my father's death benefits and what my mom hits me off with will suffice," I said.

"Whatever, you are so irresponsible. I'ma get me a job this summer. I have too much time on my hands."

"Asha, your daddy is a councilman."

"Exactly, so getting a job should be easy."

Asha was a mess. "Girl," I said as my cell phone rang, "did you see Courtney's Facebook page?" I looked at the caller ID and the number was restricted. This pissed me off because again it could be a thousand different people. A handful of which I didn't want to talk to. Forget it. I pressed the talk button, took a chance, and answered. "You rang?"

No one responded, but I could tell that someone was there because I could hear them breathing, and if I'm not mistaken it sounded as if they were crying. "Hello?" I paused. "Hello?"

Silence.

"Okay," I said into the phone, "I'ma hang up."

"Zsa." It was a hysterical male voice but I couldn't make out who it was. All I could tell is that they were in tears.

"Who is this?" I asked.

"Ameen."

"Ameen," I said, surprised. "Why are you calling me crying?"

"Hang up on him," Asha said. "Now."

"Wait," I mumbled. "Let me find out why he's crying."

"Don't be stupid, Zsa," she said.

"What, Ameen?" I snapped into the phone.

"Zsa, my mother died," he said.

My eyes practically bugged out of my head. I couldn't believe that. "Asha," I whispered, "his mother died."

"Okay," she said. "Give him your condolences and hang up on him."

"I can't do that," I said to her. "He really loved his mother."

"And your mother loved you when he left you in the park and beat up on the ground."

I rolled my eyes. Leave it to Asha. "Ameen"—I returned my attention to the phone—"I'm sorry to hear that."

"Man, you know she got sick all of a sudden." He sniffed. "But I didn't expect her to die. You know she really liked you, Zsa."

I didn't know what to say to that so I didn't respond.

"She really did." He carried on. "Her wake is tonight at seven at Cottons. Ai'ight, Zsa. I'ma get up." And he hung up.

I felt terrible for Ameen. I mean, me and my mother had our differences but I don't know what I would do if she passed away. "Asha—" I turned to her.

"Look, I don't want to hear it," Asha said. "You don't need to be kicking it with Ameen at any time."

"His mother died, would you chill?"

"He just wants you to feel sorry for him," Asha insisted.

"Well, I do," I said. "I know what Ameen did was wrong and I told you he apologized."

"You also told me Malachi bugged out earlier this week. So what's more important?"

"Malachi doesn't have to know Ameen's mother died."

"Okay, so let's move on."

"Asha"—I looked at my watch—"her wake is in an hour. Let's run over there real quick."

"Heck, no!"

"I have to pay my respects, Asha. He just told me his mother really liked me."

"Please, she treated you like garbage."

"Asha, are you going to come with me or not? Because I'm going."

Asha stared at me long and hard and then she rolled her eyes. "No, I'm not going."

"Fine, I'll go by myself."

* * *

"I don't believe I'm here with you," Asha growled as we walked into the funeral parlor. "This is crazy."

"We're only going to stay for a few minutes."

"A few minutes and that's it."

The funeral parlor was packed with people. Some of them I knew from being with Ameen and some of them I didn't. I spotted his son's mother right away. She looked at me and rolled her eyes. Whatever. Little did she know, but she could have Ameen.

"I'ma sit back here," Asha said. "You go up there"—she pointed at Ameen—"give him your condolences and let's bounce."

"That's exactly what I'ma do," I said as she sat down, and I headed toward the front of the room. I walked over to Ameen, who was sitting in a chair with his head in his hands. "Ameen." I tapped him on the shoulder. He looked up and a slight smile ran across his face.

"Zsa." He stood up and gave me a hug. "I'm glad you came, man, thanks."

"I just came to tell you I was sorry about your mother."

"I appreciate that, Zsa. And you know I'm really sorry about what jumped off between us. You're the best thing that ever happened to me and I messed it up."

"Ameen"—I started to feel uncomfortable—"this is not the time."

"I know. And I'm not trying to push up or anything like that. I just wanted you to know that."

"Alright." I felt nervous. Why? I don't know, I just did. "I'ma get going, Ameen."

He kissed me on the cheek. "Thank you for being here for me. It lets me know you still care."

That was definitely my queue. "Bye, Ameen. Take care."

I walked over to Asha and said, "Let's be out now."

"What did he say?" she asked once we got in the car.

"He was like, I'm glad you came."

"So why are you shaking?"

"I don't know. Like I started to feel scared standing next to him."

"You should be scared of him at all times. He hasn't changed, Zsa. No matter what he says and no matter who dies."

"I know," I said as we pulled off.

"Did he say anything else to you?"

"No," I said, deciding not to tell her about Ameen thinking I still cared about him.

"Good, and if he calls you again, you need to change your number."

"Asha, calm down."

"I'm *soooo* serious with you, because if I hear that you are talking to this dude again I'm telling your mother."

"You buggin'."

"I don't care if you get mad," she said. "You rather me tell your mother or tell Malachi?"

I rolled my eyes. "You know the answer to that."

"Ai'ight then, chill. Now, come on inside so we can go in my room and look at Courtney's Facebook page and laugh."

20

Me, Courtney, and Asha all sat in my room chillin' on a Sunday afternoon.

"Next year we should get matching tattoos for graduation," Courtney said, as we sat in my room listening to music and watching the falling snow through the window.

"Oole, Zsa-Zsa," Hadiah said anxiously, "can I get one too?"

"No," I said, "and don't ask again."

Asha tossed popcorn in her mouth and said, "What kind of tattoo are you talking about, Courtney?"

"Like maybe a strawberry." Courtney popped his gums.

"Oh, that would be so hot," Hadiah said in admiration. "When I get to be y'all age I'ma get mine right here." Hadiah pointed to the small of her back. "A tramp stamp."

"I'ma make you go in the other room," I snapped. "Say one more thing that's inappropriate."

I turned to Courtney. "I'm not getting a strawberry anywhere on my body." I frowned. "No."

"Well, what about," Courtney said, "a graduation cap with 'We in the house' written inside of it." He snapped his fingers.

"How about this?" Asha said sarcastically. "We should get a pair of pink panties tattooed in the middle of our chest. "Bam!" She snapped her neck. "That would be so hot!"

Me and Asha fell out laughing while Courtney stood up and said, "I don't appreciate y'all making fun of my tattoo." He unbuttoned his shirt and moved his boa to the side, showing off his boney chest. "This was a Superman symbol gone bad." He pointed to the tattoo in the middle. "My cousin did it for me as a favor. It didn't turn out right so I had him make it look like lace panties. Heck, I thought it was sexy."

I slapped my hand over Hadiah's eyes. "Oh, you wrong for even looking like that, Courtney," I said. "Oh, hell, no."

It's a good thing my cell phone started ringing because had I looked at Courtney any longer I may have passed out. I folded my hand in a prayer position and said, "Thank God. Saved by the ringing cell phone." I looked at the caller ID and it was an out-of-state number that I didn't recognize. I started not to answer it but then I changed my mind.

"Hello?" I said in my serious voice.

"Why you sound so serious?" A familiar male voice said. "You miss me?"

"Who is this?"

"Damn, I've only been gone for two days and you forgot me already? I'm hurt."

"Oh, my baby," I whined, realizing that it was Malachi.

"Oh, God," Asha said, "you gon' be on the phone forever."

"Whatever." I playfully rolled my eyes at her. "I miss you, Malachi."

"Yeah, we miss you," Courtney said.

"I'm not even going to respond to that," Malachi said to me.

"Where are you calling me from?" I asked him.

"Upstate New York."

"No, I mean whose phone?"

"Oh, my cousin's cell phone. I can't get a signal out here on mine. Tell me how much you love me," he said sweetly.

"I love you *soooo* much."

"Okay, I need to leave." Hadiah pointed to the door. "I've had enough of this love mess."

"That's our queue too," Asha said. "Come on, Courtney."

"Where are we going?" Courtney said. "I'm on the phone talking to Malachi." He cracked up laughing. "I'm just playing."

"Bye." I waved at Asha and Courtney as they walked out of my room. "Lock the door behind you." I returned my attention back to Malachi. "When are you coming home?"

"In two days," he said.

"That's a long time," I complained.

"I know, baby. But I'll be there. Listen, I have to get ready to go. I'll call you tomorrow. Love you."

"Love you more." I held the phone to my ear as Malachi hung up. All I could do was daydream about him being here with me. A few minutes later my cell phone started ringing again. When the number came up out of state I started grinning from ear to ear. "What?" I said, answering the phone. "You missed me too much to hang up?"

"Well, yeah, actually I do miss you."

This wasn't Malachi. "Who is this?"

"I've been gone that long that you don't even know my voice now?"

I snapped. "No, I don't, and if you don't tell me who you are, I'm hanging up."

"It's Ameen, Zsa. What are you doing?"

I rolled my eyes to the ceiling. "Why are you calling me?"

"Oh, I can't call you now?"

"Not really."

"Well, I missed you, Zsa. You know I don't really have anyone but you, especially since my moms died."

Suddenly I felt guilty. I hated this feeling. "Yeah, I know. How are you dealing with that?" I asked him.

"Day to day," he said. "Some days better than others. I miss her though, but I'm trying to get my life together, so I can hold it down for me and my sister, and my nephew, you know what I'm saying."

"Yeah, I hear you."

"And you know I got this job interview," he said, sounding proud of himself.

"You do?!" I said, a bit too excited. "That's real fly, Ameen. Good for you. Where's the interview at?"

"GameStop," he said with confidence. "The one in the mall. So I was wondering if you could take me or if I could use your car, you know what I'm saying?"

"No, I really don't know what you're saying. I know what you asked me and the answer to that is no and no."

"Then what I'ma do, Zsa? I'm trying to get on the right path."

"Where your friends at? Where are those chicks?"

"Man, to hell with them friends and them get-money chicks. They only want me if I'm in the streets and since I told them I wasn't hustling no more, that I was gon' try and make it on my own, they've been acting real funny."

"Well"—I paused—"I can't help you. And wait a minute, where is your car?"

"I had to sell it, to pay for my mother's funeral. She didn't have any insurance and everything was on me. So I had to do what I had to do. My moms was my world and now I'm just here by myself with nothing. So please, I'm begging you, for real, let me use your car. I swear I'll be back in like ten minutes."

"Ten minutes, Ameen, be for real."

"Not literally ten minutes, I mean like an hour. You can take me if you want to."

"I'm not getting in a car with you."

"Okay, well, let me use your car and I promise I'll be right back. I wouldn't disrespect you like that, Zsa. I mean, when you could've had me locked up for that argument we had in the park, you didn't, and I got mad love for you behind that. So I would never do anything that was disrespectful to you, and especially use your car and not bring it back on time."

"Alright, Ameen." I paused and sighed. "And you better be back here in an hour."

"Straight. Open the door, I'm outside."

"What?!" I snapped. "Oh, so you just assumed that I was going to lend you my car? You got a lot of nerve."

"Nah, it wasn't even like that. See, I was on the bus, and when you said yeah, I got off."

"You're lying, Ameen."

"Zsa, I'm not lying. Just please, come on, because if you don't hurry up I'ma be late."

I hung up on him and walked to the front door, where he was standing on my porch grinning from ear to ear. "Here," I said, handing him the keys, "and be back in one hour."

"I got you, ma," he said, opening the car door. "I got you."

I turned to go back inside and practically tripped over Hadiah, who was standing behind me. "Mommy gon' kick yo' behind."

"What I tell you about cussing?"

"Cussing is the least of your worries. You know ever since Mommy been going to carnivals in the evenings she be basing off."

"First of all it's counseling, not carnivals," I snapped. "So mind yours. Also. It's *my* car."

"So what, do you know what we went through behind you and that boy? Oh, no, I'm telling."

"You better not say a word." I looked at her and squinted my eyes. "Because if you do I'm not buying you anything else and I won't be taking you anywhere."

"Why would you do that to me?"

"Open your mouth and you shall see."

Hadiah rolled her eyes at me and stormed away. She was right, though. Why the heck did I do that? I know I should've said no. I walked back into my room and started watching the clock as if it were a television show. I needed to stay away from this dude and straight diss him, but I always felt guilty and he had a way of making me feel like I owed him.

"Zsa." My mother knocked on my bedroom door.

I jumped. She wasn't supposed to be home, at least not for another few hours.

"Come help me put away these groceries," she said.

I walked out of my room and into the kitchen where the table and the floor were littered with Pathmark bags. "How was your day, Ma?"

My mother looked at me as if I were crazy. "You never ask me about my day. What do you want and how much does it cost?"

"Nothing, Mother," I said playfully. "I was just wondering how your day was."

"It's been okay. Oh," she said, putting chicken into the freezer, "where is your car?"

"Umm." I stalled for a second too long. "Courtney. He had a job interview at the mall so I let him use it."

"An interview on a Sunday?"

"It's at the mall."

"I guess. And when did Courtney get a driver's license?"

"Umm, last year. Last month, I mean," I said nervously.

"Okay." She looked at me suspiciously. "Well after today don't let anyone else drive your car besides you."

"It's my car."

"But I paid for it and I pay the insurance on it. Now, don't start with me, because I'm not tolerating your smart mouth anymore."

"I didn't even do anything and you going off."

"I'm not going off, I'm just stating facts. Now I have a headache," she said as the doorbell rang. "Who is that? Are you expecting company?"

"No." I shook my head.

"Well, get the door." She poured herself a glass of juice and popped a Tylenol in her mouth. "I hope it's Courtney."

"Me too," I mumbled. I twisted the knob, opened the door, and it was Malachi. Malachi? What the heck was he doing here? Oh, God, this was the last thing I needed. "Hi, sweetie." I gave him a hug while standing in the doorway. "What are you doing here?"

"I came to surprise you. We were on our way back down here the whole time you and I were on the phone."

"Oh, okay," I said, still standing in the doorway. "Well, call me tomorrow. I'm sure you need your rest."

"Actually, I'm okay, but I'm sayin', you want me to leave or something?"

"No." I shook my head. "Not at all."

"Then why are you blocking the doorway?"

"I am?" I swallowed. "I didn't mean to do that. Come in."

Reluctantly I moved out of the way and I swear my stomach was doing back flips.

"Hey, Ms. Jazmyn," Malachi said, walking into the living room, "where is your car, Zsa?"

"Why is everybody concerned about my car? Dang. Courtney has it."

"Courtney?" he said, taken aback. "You let Courtney use your car? Why would you do that?"

"Same thing I said," my mother said, butting into our conversation. "Zsa, I'm going to lay down, my head is spinning."

"Okay," I said as Malachi and I headed into my room.

I was sweating bullets. I needed Ameen to bring my car

back and quick. I looked at the clock and Ameen's so-called hour was quickly turning into two hours, and by the third hour I was scared he was never coming back.

"Zsa." My mother knocked on my door and opened it at the same time. "What time is Courtney coming back with your car? It's going on eight o'clock. Nobody's interviewing for a job this late."

"It's the night shift, Ma."

"No," she said, "it's starting to look like the lying shift, Ma." She mocked me. "Don't make me call his mother. He got another hour and then I'm on the phone with Brenda."

"I'll call him." I sucked my teeth. Ever since my mother had been going to therapy she'd been beating her chest with me a lot more. Saying whatever she felt like saying, and if I say something that she feels is sarcastic she shuts it down. Hot mess. I picked up my cell phone and dialed Ameen's number. A recorded operator picked up the line. "The number you have reached is no longer in service."

How could Ameen's phone be cut off? I looked at my mother. "He didn't answer, let me try again." Instead I tried to slyly search through my caller ID for the number Ameen called me from and oh . . . my . . . God . . . the number had been erased. *Somebody shoot me.*

"Are you going to call him back?" my mother asked.

"Oh, yeah." I pretended to dial a number and then I pretended to be speaking into the phone. "Courtney, where are you?" I paused. "Well, you better come on, because it's getting late, and we have school tomorrow." I paused again. "Courtney, what did I say?"

"Let me speak to that boy," my mother said, and before I could protest she'd snatched the phone from my ear.

"Hello?" She spoke into the phone. "Nobody's up here." She looked at me strangely.

"Wow." I hunched my shoulders. "He must've hung up." I looked at Malachi and gave him a stupid smile, one he didn't return.

My mother smirked. "I'm going back to lay down, but if I come out here again and the car isn't here," my mother said, "I'm calling Brenda and that's that."

"Zsa." Malachi called my name as my mother slammed her room door.

"What?" I jumped.

"What are you so jumpy and nervous about?" Malachi asked. "You act like you're lying."

"Malachi, don't be accusing me of things, okay? You're the one who said you weren't coming back for two days."

"What does that have to do with anything?"

"So you're the one who lied to me?"

"Are you trying to start an argument with me?" Malachi frowned. "What, you want me to leave? That's not a problem." He grabbed his car keys.

"Malachi, I don't want you to leave," I said in a panic.

"Then what is the problem? Why are you acting like this?"

"That's it, Zsa." My mother stormed out of her room. "I'm calling Brenda, because I just remembered Courtney is sixteen. He doesn't have a driver's license."

"Ma, wait."

"What is she waiting for, Zsa?" Malachi pressed as someone pounded on the front door.

Thank you, Jesus.

I turned to them and smiled. "There's Courtney right

there. Now can you two go in the other room? I don't want to embarrass him, because I'm about to read him."

"Well, we'll be reading him together." My mother walked over to the door, and I tried to block her path. "What the hell?" she said. "If you don't move out of my way." She opened the door, and instead of Ameen standing there, there were two police officers at my door with the blaring red lights from their cruisers behind them.

I swear I was about to faint. "Yes, officers?" my mother said, "may I help you?"

"We're looking for," one of the officers said, "a Zsa-Zsa Fields."

"For what?" my mother said defensively.

"Is she here, ma'am?" the officer asked.

"She's right here." My mother pointed at me. "This is my daughter. Now, what is the problem?"

"Well, ma'am, we need her to come down to the station and answer some questions—"

"Questions about what?!" my mother snapped.

"We're trying to tell you, ma'am. We have a suspect in custody by the name of Ameen Jones. He crashed the car on the side of the highway and attempted to run. Don't worry, we caught him. But we also found drugs in the car, which he's saying weren't his, but were instead in the car when he borrowed it."

"I don't believe this," my mother said, pissed.

"I didn't have any drugs. He's lying!" I shouted.

"Well," the officer said, "that's why we need you to come to the station and give us a statement."

"Let me grab my purse," my mother said. "We will be right behind you, officers."

"Thank you, ma'am." The officers walked back to their car.

I turned around and looked at Malachi, who was grabbing his jacket and keys. I looked in his eyes and could tell he was hurt, which is why I couldn't let him leave. I had to explain or at least try to explain what happened. "Malachi." I grabbed his hand and he snatched it back. "It wasn't like that."

"You been playing me this whole time?"

"No." Tears filled my eyes and raced down my cheeks. "How could you say something like that? Ameen called me and claimed he had a job interview. He said he wanted to change his life."

"Zsa, you look so stupid to me right now. I swear to God, I wish I had never got with you. You were a better memory than anything else. I'm done. It's over." And he stormed out the door. My heart was in pieces and I was screaming at the top of my lungs, "Malachi! Don't leave!" But within a matter of seconds he was gone.

"Oh, no, you don't." My mother stormed into the living room. "Dry your eyes. You're grown, remember?" She called Hadiah, who had been sleeping in her room. "I want you to go next door and sit with Ms. Lucinda until Cousin Shake and Ms. Minnie get back."

"Okay, Ma."

After Hadiah left, my mother looked at me and said, "Let's go."

I felt completely out of my mind by the time we got to the police station. I didn't know whether I was coming or going, whether this was a dream or a strange part of my reality. All I knew is that my heart felt like a brick and my head was spinning. I gave the officers a statement and they informed me that my car was totaled in the accident. I swear, it was like at the police station, I knew physically I was there, but mentally I was a million different places. I needed to speak to Malachi and I needed to fix this. I needed the last five minutes we'd spent together back because if I didn't get this right, I had no idea what my life would be like.

I cried on the entire ride home. My mother was saying something to me. Something that sounded like a lecture but I don't know what it was, and I didn't care either, all I cared about was getting Malachi back.

By the time we arrived home, I flew into my room and dialed Malachi's number. He didn't answer, so I called him back and he still didn't pick up. I must've called him a hundred times and still nothing. I didn't care. I wasn't giving up so I called him again.

"What?" he said, answering.

"Malachi, it's not what you think."

"It's not what I think, you're right, Zsa, it's not. I thought you loved me, you don't. I thought you were faithful to me, you're not."

"I do love you and I never cheated on you. You have to believe me."

"You're a liar and we're done. It's over. It's always some rah-rah with you. Nothing is ever peaceful, so I tell you what, lose yourself, 'cause I'm done and that's for real." He hung up on me.

I tried calling him back at least a hundred times but he didn't answer. "Zsa." My mother called my name and entered my room at the same time.

"Not now, Ma," I said, wiping tears from my eyes. "I need to talk to Malachi."

"You don't tell me not now. Because it's right now!"

"I need to talk to Malachi!" I screamed.

"No, you need to talk to me. You have completely lost your mind. Here Ameen beat you, abused you, used you, and you're still messing with him?"

"I'm not messing with him!"

"Well, it sure looks like it. When are you going to say enough is enough? Huh? I knew I should've made you press charges on him."

"For what? You never followed through on any of the charges you pressed," I snapped. "Don't be trying to act like mother of the year now because you in counseling and now all of a sudden you wanna buck."

My mother walked up so close to me that I swear her breath was making my eyelashes blink. "If I didn't know that violence solved nothing, I would slap you! I don't know who you think you're talking to but I know who you're not talking to and that's me. I made some mistakes, yes, but I am your mother, not the other way around. You will not disrespect me and you will not stand in my face as if we are equals. You have a problem and it will be addressed. You are going to counseling. I don't care if you think it's for crazy folks, but you are going. Now try me if you think I'm playing. I'm not your girlfriend, I'm not interested in a compromise, and no, there's nothing you can say to make me change my mind. You so worried about Malachi, you need to be worried about yourself and your state of mind, because the way you're going, in a few years you are going to be a raggedy mess and I'm not having it."

"I'm not going to counseling!"

"Oh, no, then you got to leave." My mother took a step back. "Get your things and go. You so damn grown. You know all the answers." She grabbed my suitcases out of my closet and slammed them on my bed. "Then get out of here! Because I run this spot and what I say goes. Now if you don't like it, then deuces," she said mockingly, "because I ain't the one."

I couldn't believe this. My mother had warped into someone else, someone I was scared of. I felt like if I said anything I was about to catch a beat down. For a moment I was less worried about my breakup with Malachi and more worried about life with my mother. "You would put me out in the street?"

"You are my child," my mother said, wiping the tears that had formed in her eyes, "but I will not watch you be reduced to nothing. Now, I love you and this is your home, but if we don't go and work out the issues that we have here, then yes, you will have to go. Now you think about that." And she left.

I felt like a bomb had gone off and the only thing I could do about it was cry myself into oblivion.

21

Love, I thought you had my back this time . . .

—Keyshia Cole, "Love, I Thought You Had My Back"

My life was hell. I couldn't eat, couldn't sleep, and I didn't know whether I was coming or going. All I could do was think and cry. Cry and think. How did I end up here? How did my life wither into such a nightmare, where I finally realized what true love was, had the right man, the one I wanted for a lifetime, and in one split second of a bad decision he was gone and I had nothing.

I'd called Malachi a thousand times and he hadn't answered any of my calls or returned the kazillion messages I'd left him. *I feel like . . . like . . . like . . . I'm going crazy. Better yet, like I am crazy.*

I mean, I'd been hurt before and I'd cried a million times but this time I felt like somebody opened my heart, split it down the middle, and pissed inside.

I'd been up all night and although my eyes felt like weights there was no way I was staying home today. I got out of bed, showered, quietly dressed, picked up my car keys, and headed out the door. Once I was in my driveway

it clicked. I no longer had a car, which meant one thing: I
had to catch the bus. Jesus.

I pulled out my cell phone and called Courtney.

"I gotta take a who?" Courtney said, as if he were in
shock.

"A bus. It's a long story but I don't have my car anymore."

"Well, you need to go and get it, Diva, 'cause I can't
catch no bus. I don't even own a pair of sneakers."

"Well, Prince, I don't know what to tell you." And I
hung up. I really couldn't be aggravated with Courtney
today. I walked to the bus stop on the corner and hopped
on the bus. It was mad crowded with kids going to school
and people going to work.

The bus pulled up to the stop by Courtney's house and
he staggered on, looking a hot mess. His purple boa was
wrapped around his neck like a cyclone, he had rollers in
the back of his hair, and the three-inch boots he wore
looked to be leaning to the side, as his book bag fell down
his arm. "Driver," Courtney said, "I'm so upset. How much
is this thing?"

"Two dollars and seventy-five cents," the bus driver said.

"Oh, no!" Courtney wiped his brow as if he were due to
faint. "Y'all robbing people."

"Young man," the driver said, "are you going to pay?
Otherwise step off the bus, please."

"God bless you too," Courtney said, pulling out a hand
full of change from his pocket. "No need to be nasty." After
paying his fare Courtney walked to the back of the bus,
and I called his name. He flopped down next to me and
said, "I'm not speaking to you. You know that, right."

"No," I said, "I couldn't tell."

"Well, I'm not. And why are we on this bus? What happened to your car? We need it. That's it, I'm riding with Asha and Samaad tomorrow."

Suddenly and without warning I broke down and a river of tears fell from my eyes. "Zsa," Courtney said, looking around at the people who were staring at me and giving them a fake smile. "I know your dog died," was his attempt to play if off, "but it's okay."

"My dog didn't die," I said, "Malachi left me."

"Oh, Lawd!" Courtney shouted, and pretended to pass out on the seat. "No, Jesus. Not Malachi. No, not Malachi."

I looked at Courtney as he carried on like a church lady at her pastor's funeral. "Help me," he sniffed. "Don't take Malachi, Father. Not Malachi."

I wanted to punch Courtney dead in the face. "Shut up," I growled as we pulled up to the stop in front of the school. "You sound stupid."

"Don't be getting mad with me," he sniffed. "You the one messed our life up."

I ignored him, because I absolutely couldn't do it. At least not today. Tomorrow maybe I could entertain Courtney, but not today.

Once we arrived at school I didn't go in right away because I was hoping to catch Malachi before he went inside. Maybe if I spoke with him early it would give him time to think about us fixing our relationship.

I stood by the side entrance, and just when I was about to give up, I spotted Malachi pulling up in his truck. Although I knew what my plan was supposed to be, I had a million conflicting thoughts running through my mind, most of them telling me to keep it moving. But I couldn't.

I had to say something, anything that would make this right.

I walked over to Malachi once he got out of his truck, and he looked at me blankly. "Can I speak with you for a moment?" I asked him. "Please."

"Hurry up." He frowned. "I don't have that much time."

"I'm sorry."

"I heard that already," he snapped. "I thought you were going to say something new."

Was that a blade he just put to my jugular or were those simply words? I swear my mouth filled with blood and I didn't know what to say, but I was determined to think of something. "I know what I did was wrong." I paused. "And I really am sorry, but I never cheated on you. Ever. I love you and I want us to work this out. I just feel like if we had one more chance to do this again, I wouldn't mess up. So I am asking that you forgive me, please."

I stopped talking and Malachi stared at me. "That's it?" he said. "Are you done?"

"Yeah."

"Ai'ight." He stepped to the side and walked around me. "I'm out."

22

I need you . . . bad as the air I breathe . . .

—JAZMINE SULLIVAN, "I NEED YOU BAD"

It had been two weeks since Malachi and I broke up, and just when I thought undying misery may not have been my fate, my mother came and announced that today was the day we were to start counseling.

For real, for real, no lie, I was pissed. I thought she'd forgotten about it. I went from lying on my bed, nursing my broken heart, to sitting on the edge of the bed with my legs crossed and smoke rising from my ears.

No matter what, I didn't feel that I needed counseling. I wasn't crazy, and from what I'd heard and thought, seeing a therapist meant I was diagnosed as nuts and would be sent home with some psychotropic medication. Not. If my mother wanted to be labeled as a certified nut, then by all means help herself, but why on earth did she have to involve me?

"You may as well fix your face," my mother snapped while standing in my doorway, swinging her purse on her arm and juggling her keys in her hand, "because we're going." She stepped completely into my room. "And we're going now."

I sucked my teeth.

"Suck 'em again and you'll be carrying them in your hand while on your way to the therapist's office."

Dang? Why all of a sudden does my jaw hurt? For a moment I thought about voicing how I felt about the situation, but then again, maybe expressing how I felt wasn't worth the drama it was sure to bring.

I rose from the bed, grabbed my purse, and twisted my lips. "I hope this doesn't take long."

My mother didn't even respond. She simply walked into the living room, where Cousin Shake and Ms. Minnie were watching television. "Cousin Shake," my mother said, "Zsa and I are off to that counseling session I was telling you about for mothers and their firstborn daughters. Look out for Hadiah for me."

"Sure thing," Cousin Shake said. My mother walked out the door, and as I approached the threshold Cousin Shake said, "Zena the princess warrior."

I turned around. "What?"

He started laughing and twirling his index finger on the side of his head as if to say I was crazy. I rolled my eyes and slammed the door behind me. *I swear he is soooo inappropriate.*

I was silent for the entire drive to the therapist's office. All I could imagine were that the walls would be starched white with two gigantic couches sitting in the middle of the floor, one for me and the other for my mother.

We pulled into the parking lot of a brick office building, and once inside I noticed that instead of white walls, they were the color of wheat with beautiful African American artwork and African masks lining the hallway. I was careful not to look as if I was admiring the place too much, because I didn't want anyone thinking that I somehow wanted, or better yet needed, to be there.

The lobby was sprinkled with a few people, I guess waiting for their appointments with the other therapists that were a part of the practice. Nevertheless, even one person was one too many for me. All I could think was, suppose I saw somebody I knew? Dang, I had to get out of there.

"We have an appointment with Dr. Michael," my mother said to the receptionist.

A few minutes after we took a seat the receptionist said, "Mrs. Fields, Dr. Michael will see you now."

"Come on, Zsa," my mother said as I reluctantly got out of my seat and followed her like a sad puppy into the doctor's office. I have to say that the office was laid, red leather chairs, no couches, beautiful artwork and tons of degrees.

"You must be Zsa-Zsa." The doctor, who resembled Jill Scott, rose from her seat and said to me, "I'm Doctor Mya Michael." She held her hand out and pointed to the red leather wing chairs. "Have a seat."

"How are you today, Jazmyn?" Dr. Michael asked my mother.

"I'm okay, Doctor." My mother smiled. "And yourself?"

"I'm well," she said, taking a seat across from us. "Are we ready to begin?"

"Yes," my mother said.

I didn't answer. I figured if I could get away with keeping my mouth shut then I might actually be able to tolerate this place.

"Zsa-Zsa," Dr. Michael said, "I didn't hear your response. Are we okay to start?"

"Oh," I said, caught off guard, "yeah, I guess."

"I'll take that." She smiled. "Let's begin with what brings us here today."

"I feel that my daughter and I have some issues," my mother said. "And some things about our past that we need to discuss. I feel that they are affecting her and the abusive relationship she is in."

"I am not in an abusive relationship," I snapped.

"Why do you think your mother feels it was abusive?" Dr. Michael asked.

"Because." I hunched my shoulders. "She wants to assign me her life, like we're the same people, but we're not."

"Okay, so what makes you different?" the doctor asked.

"I fought back."

"You shouldn't have to fight at all," my mother said. "You should've never been in that situation. Just like I should have never been in my situation."

"Why don't we start from the beginning," the doctor said. "Tell me how your marriage was." She turned to my mother.

My mother smiled. "At first Zach was so wonderful and so sweet," my mother said as if she could see and smell my father. "He was the perfect gentleman, but he had a drinking problem, and when he drank, he would hit me."

I felt myself getting sick.

"The fighting didn't start right away," my mother continued, "it started with a slap, because I said something Zach didn't like. And then it went to him pushing me, and then it went to us fighting every Friday night, when the children were asleep."

Asleep? Did she just say asleep? "We weren't asleep and you know we weren't asleep."

"I know the fighting woke you up, but you always went back to sleep, after I would beg your father to stop hitting me."

"Are you serious?" I snapped. "Do you know how scared we were? Do you know we couldn't sleep because of the wall jumping and you screaming? Do you know we were scared as hell? Sleep." I swear I couldn't believe she said that. "We weren't asleep, we would sneak upstairs to Malachi's house, where it was quiet, and safe, and we didn't have to watch that damn wall jump!" I screamed. "Sleep? We were never asleep!"

My mother's mouth hung open. I could tell by looking in her face that she had no idea of what I had just hit her with. "You used to do what?" she said with tears in her eyes.

"You heard me! We would go upstairs and wait for you to call the police, because you always did and you always dragged us into the nonsense. Always! I am nothing like you, because I would never do that to my children! Ever."

"I didn't know that."

"Whatever." I wiped the tears falling down my cheeks. Already I'd said much more than I'd planned to.

"How did you feel, Zsa-Zsa, when your parents would fight?" Dr. Michael asked.

"Like nothing," I said. "Absolutely nothing. Like I wasn't even good enough for my parents not to fight. I felt horrible. I was embarrassed all the time. My friends didn't come to my house to play. I couldn't have anybody over."

"That's not true. Yes, you could," my mother said defensively.

"When, Ma? Huh, when? Before or after he beat you? Before or after Daddy was drunk? Before or after he brought that nasty Chinese food that I hate!"

"You love Chinese food."

"I hate Chinese food. And you know why I hate it? I hate it because every time I had it, you and Daddy always fought, and when I ate it, or better yet when I smelled it, it made me feel like a scared little girl. I couldn't believe you had Kenneth bring Chinese food and then expected me to like him."

"I didn't know."

"Well, pay attention," I said. "Just like when I was in the hospital and you forced me to go to that group, like I was supposed to admit that I really did see myself in those girls!"

"Did you see yourself?" the doctor asked.

"Yes," I cried. "I did. And I don't ever want to feel that way again." I looked at the clock. "I hope this is over soon, because I can't do this much longer. I'd rather be home crying over my boyfriend."

"Do you want to talk about your boyfriend, the one that hit you?" the doctor asked.

"First of all, he isn't my boyfriend. And second of all, I hit him back when he would hit me."

"You should have never been in that situation!" my mother yelled.

"Yeah, well, I got it from you. Hell, I thought fighting was a part of a relationship. That's all I saw, that's all I knew."

"It doesn't make it right, Zsa," my mother said.

"I'm done with Ameen."

"But he keeps you in this web. He's an abuser."

"Look, I messed up when I let him use my car, okay? I get it."

"Why did you do that?" the doctor asked me.

"Because I felt sorry for him. His mother died and he didn't have anybody but me. I needed to help him."

"But why?" the doctor asked.

"Because he needed me."

"How do you know he needed you?"

"He told me that," I said.

"So everyone who says they need you, you have to be there for them?"

"Yes."

"Why?" she probed.

"Because how else will I fix it?"

"Why is it your responsibility to fix it or to fix them?"

"I don't know." I hunched my shoulders in defeat. "I just feel like I have to. I have always been there to fix whatever. When my little sister was scared and crying I took her away so she wouldn't have to be scared. I just feel like . . . like . . . I've been grown all of my life and that is what I have to do."

"I'm the mother, Zsa," my mother said.

"You didn't even know I didn't like Chinese food. Ma, please, all of a sudden you wanna be Mommy to me. Don't come now. You never cared before about how I felt. You moved us out of the apartment we lived in into this great big house so that you could pretend my daddy never existed, and now all of a sudden you care about how I feel? Please."

"I do care about how you feel, and I haven't tried to act as if your father didn't exist. That's not true!"

"Yes, it is. You don't have not one picture of him in the house. Not one!"

My mother was silent.

"You don't know anything about me."

"That's why I'm here. I want to get to know you. I'm sorry I haven't been all that you needed me to be. I'm sorry that I placed you in situations and made you face things that didn't belong to you. I am sorry, but I'm here and I want to begin again. And what I need you to understand is that it doesn't matter if you fight back, you shouldn't have to fight, period. That is not love. Love is easy and free, it's freeing. You owe it to yourself to know that any man you have to fight with is not worth having you. And hitting is not the only type of abuse. Having you feel guilty all the time is emotional abuse. You don't owe Ameen anything, but you do owe yourself a chance to be in a healthy relationship."

"Ma, none of us know what a healthy relationship is."

"We will learn together. That's what Derrick and I have been doing, learning together."

"You've been talking to Derrick?" I asked, surprised.

"Yes." She nodded. "Almost every day, and we're determined to get things on the right track. And that's why I'm here with you. I know it's going to take time and I know it won't happen in an hour-long session, but it's a start."

I sat back and thought about my life. I thought about all of the choices that I'd made and how I could somehow make different ones. All I knew is that anything had to be better than this. "Ma, I don't even know how to begin."

"You've already started," Dr. Michael said. "And a start is all you need to begin to heal."

"Alright, Ma," I said, wiping tears from my eyes. "I can't promise you anything. All I can promise you is that I'm willing to try."

"And that's all I can ask for." My mother hugged me tightly. "That's all I can ask for."

"Well, ladies," the doctor said, as the session came to a close, "I think we have something to build on here."

"And I do too." My mother smiled and hugged me once more. "And I do too."

23

Your lies ain't working now,
Look who's hurting now,
See I had to shut you down . . .

—SUNSHINE ANDERSON, "HEARD IT ALL BEFORE"

"Zsa," my mother called from her room as I stood in the kitchen washing the dishes, "get the bell for me."

"Who are you expecting?"

"Kenneth," she said in a hurry. "I'm still getting dressed." She slammed her room door.

I swallowed . . . hard. I knew this moment would come, but I wasn't expecting it to come at seven-thirty on a Friday evening, but whatever. I walked to the front door and looked through the peephole to be sure it was Kenneth. And yep, it was. I sighed as I opened the door and forced myself to smile. "Hi." I gave him a small wave. "Come in." I motioned my hand in an "after you" fashion, and he walked into the living room.

"How are you, Zsa-Zsa?" Kenneth asked, stopping me in my tracks. I was trying like hell to hustle into the other room. I knew I said I would accept that my mother had a boyfriend she wanted to marry, but I didn't say a thing about talking to him.

"I'm fine," I said to Kenneth without turning around to face him.

I started walking toward my room and he said, "Hey, listen, is it okay if I speak to you for a moment?"

My back was to Kenneth as I rolled my eyes to the ceiling. "Sure," I said, turning around to face him. "What is it?"

"I know we didn't get off to the best start, but I want you to know that I really care for your mother and I would never do anything to intentionally hurt her. And I hope that maybe one day you and I can be friends."

"Umm-hmm," I said, "and if I give you a chance . . . I'm not saying that I will . . . but if I do . . . and you hurt my mama it's gon' be a problem. I'm just saying."

Kenneth cracked up. "You sound a lot like my daughter. She has that same spice as you."

"You have a daughter?" I asked, sounding halfway interested.

"Yeah." He nodded. "She's a junior at Morgan."

"Really?" Now I was truly interested. "That's the college I want to attend."

"Well, maybe—I'm not saying you will"—he smiled—"but if you decide to give me a chance, I'll introduce you to my daughter and you can visit the campus and tour the school with her. She just pledged Delta, and I hear they have great parties for you young people."

"Interesting." I curled my top lip. "If I gave you a chance, I think I would like that."

"Well, I'll make arrangements for that to happen, just in case." He smiled.

"Kenneth." My mother smiled as she walked into the living room. "I'm sorry it took me so long. I know you said you had a surprise for me."

"For all of you, actually."

"For us?" I said. Now I was the one surprised.

"Yeah, and I think you're going to really like this," he said, walking over to the front door and opening it.

"What is it?" My mother rushed to the door and I walked behind her. I should've known it was something big when she started screaming, causing Cousin Shake, Ms. Minnie, and Hadiah to run to where we were.

I ran to the door and stood behind my mother, who was hugging some guy dressed in an army uniform, and that's when it hit me. "Derrick!" I screamed, hugging him and my mother at the same time.

"Wassup, li'l sis?" he said.

I couldn't believe it. I hadn't been this happy in what felt like forever. I looked at Kenneth. "How did you get him to come home?"

"I'm a captain in the army myself, and let's just say I have connections."

"Is that really Derrick?" Hadiah said.

"Yes!" I answered her, filled with excitement.

Hadiah ran over to Derrick and started hugging him as well. We were all engaged in a group hug, and I swear this felt like Heaven.

Once we were done hugging and kissing my brother, we went into the house and Cousin Shake said to Derrick, "You all grown up now, look at you." He gave him a bear hug. "Heard you was over there in Iraqi. You don't need no blessing oil, do you? Ain't bombs on you or nothin', is it?" He patted him down.

Derrick laughed. "Cousin Shake, you have not changed." He looked at Ms. Minnie. "Who is this pretty lady?"

"She ain't for sale," Cousin Shake snapped, "so get

that thought outcha head, souljah boy. This is my wife, Minnie."

"Nice to meet you, Ms. Minnie."

"You too, baby. We all family around here. Now give me a hug, with your fine self looking like Idris Elba."

"I need to cook," my mother said. "I know you want a home-cooked meal, Derrick."

"I sure do, Ma. I sure do."

My mother and Ms. Minnie went into the kitchen while my brother and I went into his room. He threw his army green duffel bag onto his bed and sat down on the edge. "So wassup, li'l sis?"

"Nothing," I said, not sure if I should really tell him about my life or not.

"You sure?" he asked me. And I could tell that his question was loaded.

"Yeah," I said, "I'm sure."

"So how come I heard that you were in the hospital behind some dude putting his hands on you? I left home and Mommy was the victim. Now I come back and it's you. That ain't cool."

"Look, I've dealt with this. You know me and Mommy went to counseling and I'm working through it."

"Listen, I didn't come home to judge anybody, but all I'ma say is this, don't you put your hands on anyone and don't let them put their hands on you, 'cause mainly I don't wanna kill 'em, and I will."

"It's not even that type of party."

"Alright." Derrick nodded. "You know I got you. No matter where I am in the world, I got you."

"I know," I said, walking over and hugging him. "I know. Now, about Kenneth, what's up with him?"

"He's cool," Derrick said. "You can give him your stamp of approval."

"Ai'ight," I said as we walked out of his room. "Straight."

Once we were back in the living room, the dining room table was set and a spread of southern-style food dressed the table. We sat down to the table, and Cousin Shake said, "I know dang gon' well you all not about to eat without thanking Julio."

"Julio?" Derrick frowned.

"Just roll with it," I whispered to my brother. "Roll with it."

"Now er'body hold hands," Cousin Shake said. We all stood up around the table and held hands. "Well, Jessie," Cousin Shake started to pray, "You are really in the miracle-working business. You have blessed us with Derrick coming home. The only one of Jazmyn children with a name that makes any kind of sense. We thank You for all that You have done, Lord. For without we would have nothing. Oh, and I guess we'll work on accepting Kenneth into the clan. Doesn't look like he's half bad. Well, we gotta go 'cause we need to eat. Now thank You for Patti LaBelle, Teddy Pendergrass, and Millie Jackson, 'cause they got a concert tomorrow night and I'm praying that they tear the house down, so me and my Minnie can be so charged up that we can make some good ol' love and rub our bodies to it—"

"Cousin Shake!" my mother said.

"Alright, Julio. Tell Moses and Martha and dem I said wassup. Amen."

"Welcome home." I hugged my brother again, once we were done praying. "Welcome home."

"I love you all so much," my mother said, and we began to eat dinner.

* * *

Once we were all done eating and had our share of
laughing, joking, and catching on old times, Derrick said,
"Alright, I'm going to bed. I had a long flight. So good
night good people."

"Good night, honey," my mother said.

"Night, Big Brother," me and Hadiah said simultaneously, and then laughed.

"I guess I'm go and lay down too," I said, skipping off
to my room, thinking of how I had to call Malachi and tell
him he needed to come by and meet my brother. I hopped
onto my bed, dialed Malachi's number, and that's when it
clicked I no longer had that privilege. I sat on the side of
my bed and tears filled my eyes.

A few minutes later I heard a soft knock on my door.
"Zsa." It was Derrick. "Is that you?"

"Yeah." I wiped my eyes and tried to play my tears off.

"Wassup?" He walked into my room. "Why are you
upset?"

"I'm not upset."

"Zsa, I just heard you crying." He walked over by my
bed and sat on the corner. "Talk to me."

"Well . . . my boyfriend and I are broken up . . ." I started
telling him the story from beginning to end about Malachi
and I ended it with, "Now I lost him."

"Zsa." Derrick wiped my tears. "You didn't lose him.
You love him and you made some mistakes. Take it from
your big brother, men love even harder than women. So, I
think if you went over to him and really, really talked to
him and apologized for what you did and let him know
that you understand how you were wrong, I think you
might be surprised with the outcome."

"You think so?"

"I know so." He kissed me on the cheek. "Now, if you'll excuse me, I'm going to steal some more of Mommy's chocolate cake."

"You better wait for me." I laughed and ran behind him.

Derrick and I stayed up practically all night, and decided at six AM to go to bed. By the time I stepped in my room my phone was ringing. I looked at the caller ID *Essex County Correctional Institution? Who is this . . . Oh, hell, no.* I shook my head. *It better not be . . .* I picked up the phone and it was a recorded operator saying, "Collect call from . . . ?" She paused and a male voice said, "Ameen."

"Press two," the operator continued, "if you wish to accept the charges; if not hang up."

I started to hang up. Really I did, because this cat had tons of nerve calling me after all of the havoc he'd caused, but then again, I wasn't going to hang up, I was going to give it to him. I pressed one and before I could say "Hello," Ameen ran off at the mouth. "Yo, Zsa," he said in a panic, "I gotta get outta here. For real, you a minor so if you take the weight, you won't go to jail. So I need you to come and see me so we can discuss how we gon' do this."

"Do this?" I said in disbelief. "I won't go to jail. Boy, I've already been in jail. I been locked up in a relationship with you and my punishment has been everything that has fallen apart because of you. I've been humiliated, emotionally mutilated, had my car totaled, my mother not trust me, I've been beaten up and left on the ground for dead—by yo' behind. I've been in the hospital, to counseling, and I lost the only man who has ever really loved me. And now all of a sudden you're telling me to take your charges? How about you take my charges? Take the pain, embarrassment, and humiliation you've caused me. How about you take the bullcrap back that I've had to deal with and place it on your back. You do the time for that, 'cause I'm done. If anything, you're getting off easy."

"So what are you saying, Zsa? You not gon' take the charges?"

"Ameen, go play with your cellmate." And I hung up on his butt.

24

Nothing really matters
I don't really care what nobody tells me
I'm gonna be here
It's a matter of extreme importance
My first teenage love affair . . .

—ALICIA KEYS, "TEENAGE LOVE AFFAIR"

I'd been restless all night. The nerves in my back and my belly flipped like crazy, and the thoughts running through my head about Malachi—and whether I was woman enough and strong enough to stand face-to-face with him and tell him that I loved him and wanted him back, drove me crazy.

I knew that my brother had said that sometimes boys needed time . . . but what the heck was "time"? Was it like that space nonsense that all the boys asked for?

True story and for real, for real, I was confused as hell about how I needed to get Malachi back. But one thing I knew for certain was that I had to have him and I had to have him now.

It was seven o'clock in the evening and I lay in the center of my bed, wondering if time was always this slow, and then I remembered, yeah, it was, especially when you wanted something or someone desperately but didn't know how to go and get it. I rolled over on my side and figured that if I lay there any longer I was going to cry, scream, or both, none of which I wanted to do. I had come a long way since Malachi and I had broken up— heck, I'd come a long way since my life began. I knew now what healthy was. I knew what love was and I knew love didn't hurt, it wasn't confusing, complicated, or any of those things. Love was easy, free, and it felt good, all the time. It's the things that people did in the name of love that caused the damage.

That's what I had done. I'd taken advantage of the love Malachi had for me and now I was paying for it. It killed me when Malachi wouldn't talk to me, wouldn't look at me, and when he said to me, "What is it going to take? For me to talk to you real crazy in order for you to leave me alone?" And that's when it clicked, when I'd gotten it. I needed to step to left and let life take its course. But now waiting and falling back, stepping to left and all of that had my heart weighing a ton and the butterflies in my stomach on fire. I needed to fight for him, and if he tossed me out—or told me to get out—then at least I would know that I tried one last time.

I rose from my bed and quickly freshened up. I showered, brushed my teeth, and pulled my hair back into a single ponytail. I threw on a pair of Juicy Couture skinny leg jeans, a hot-pink V-neck T-shirt with a rhinestone princess crown in the center, and hot-pink stilettos. I slid my wifey ring into my purse, grabbed the keys to my just-received car, and was out the door.

The usual ten-minute drive to Malachi's seemed to take forever. The cars were moving slow, and it seemed that I caught every red light there was. Maybe this was a sign that I needed to turn around and go home. But then, if I did that, my tomorrow would be filled with a bunch of what ifs and I was tired of "what if" holding up my life.

But then . . . suppose he had a girl at his crib? Then I would look real stalkerish. Okay, maybe I need to pull to the side of the street and call him. Not. If he sees my number he may not answer my call.

You know what, heck with it, seeing as I was already on his block and pulling up in front of his house. I had nothing to lose so I was going for broke. My feet felt like they weighed thousands of pounds as I nervously walked onto his porch and rang the bell. A few minutes later Matthew opened the door and a surprised look ran all over his face. He twisted his neck from side to side, as if he were on the lookout for someone. "What are you doing here? I know you ain't down with the get down."

"Huh?" I said, taken aback. "What are you talking about?"

"Oh, you don't know?"

"Know what?"

"Never mind. I guess it's none of my business, anyway."

"What's none of your business?" I swear this little boy was pissing me off. "What are you talking about?"

"My brother—"

My heart jumped. "What about him?"

"Man, he's downstairs gettin' it in with like three, four, maybe even five girls."

I couldn't believe this. Now I was feeling stupid. "Are you serious?"

"Man, Zsa, they down there wildin' out. I think he broke up with you 'cause he was trying to get busy with the neighborhood. So I tell you what, don't even talk to that dude anymore. Come go in my room with me, my Spider-Man sheets got plenty of room, we can watch cartoons, some videos, eat some chips. What? What you need I got it all."

"Matthew." Ms. Karen called his name before I could decide if I wanted to clothesline this li'l boy or steal on him. "Who are you talking to?" She rushed to the door before he could answer her. "Zsa-Zsa"—she smiled with delight—"how are you?"

"I'm fine, Ms. Karen." I gave her a hug and a kiss. "How are you?"

"I'm okay, sweetie."

"I'm sorry I stopped by without calling, but I was hoping to talk to Malachi."

"You want me to go and clear the girls out of his room, Ma?" Matthew snickered. "So it's no rumbling going on?"

Ms. Karen popped Matthew in the back of his head. "What I tell you about playing so much? Don't mind him, that's his daddy's side of the family coming out."

"Watch it, Karen," Mr. Askew said as he walked past her and out the front door to their car. "How are you, Zsa-Zsa?" he asked.

"I'm fine, thanks."

"Take care." He waved at me. "Come on, Matthew, in the car. And Karen, not too long, please."

"Men," Ms. Karen said. "I'll tell you."

"You're telling me," I said, more to myself than to her.

Ms. Karen smiled at me and said, "Zsa-Zsa, I'm going to share something with you. I hope you don't mind."

"No, ma'am, not at all."

"When I was your age, I had a thousand things going on in my life. My parents had a terrible marriage. They argued, fussed, and fought all the time, so it made it difficult for me to recognize love, real love anyway. So when real love came I abused it, ran over it, and I took the man who was my one true love for granted."

Why are tears filling my eyes?

"I felt like," Ms. Karen continued, "he loved me, where was he going? But there came a time when he got tired of me messing up and he left me alone."

Tears were running down my cheeks.

"I was devastated," she continued, "and I didn't know what to do, where to turn, or how to get him back, but I knew I had to have him. So I took a chance, showed up at his doorstep." She paused and wiped the tears from my face.

"What happened?" I hunched my shoulders in defeat. "Did he turn you away and tell you to go home?"

"No." She pointed to her husband and son blowing the horn for her in the car. "I married him." She kissed me on the forehead. "Now I have to run."

I hugged her and said, "Thank you."

"You're welcome, honey," she said. "You're welcome."

I walked into the living room and locked the door behind me. For a moment I felt stuck in my spot. Wondering what Malachi was going to say to me, when he saw me stepping into his room. "Okay," I said to myself, "just be calm, Zsa. Talk real slow and easy. No, just get to the point. You know what"—I sucked in a deep breath and then let it go—"I'ma just see what happens."

The stairs leading to the basement creaked when I started walking down them.

"Who is that?" Malachi yelled from behind his closed door. I could hear his TV playing and the radio going as I stood there wondering if I should answer him or not. "Matt, if you come bustin' up in here again," he said, "I'm body-slamming you."

"It's not Matt," I said, opening the door and standing in the doorway, "and I really don't want to be body-slammed."

Malachi smiled, and then as if he'd just realized what he was doing, his look quickly faded into one that said he had better things to do. He picked up the remote and started channel surfing.

"You think I could like . . ." I nervously leaned from one foot to the next ". . . talk to you for a minute?"

Malachi didn't answer. He didn't even look at me. He continued to flip through the channels . . . but at least he didn't tell me to leave. "I'm sorry," was the only thing I could think to say that would keep the tears trembling my voice at bay. "I'm sorry I didn't show you that I loved you the way that I should've. But I didn't know how to. I never meant to hurt you, and I never cheated on you with Ameen. Ever. I loved you . . . and I still do. I just had so much going on with my mother and my life that I was all over the place. But now I'm focused. I went to counseling with my mom, and we talked about everything in our life. What we liked, what we didn't like, what hurt, and what we needed to change.

"I got it now. Love doesn't hurt. It's peaceful and it's fun, and it's you." I paused. My heart was on the verge of exploding. Honestly, I didn't know what hurt me more—

that Malachi was continuously watching TV or that I could tell by the look in his eyes that he was done with me. I was certain that my story would definitely have a different ending from Ms. Karen's.

"I love you, Malachi," I said, "and I'm here because there's no place I'd rather be than with you."

Silence. Other than the TV and the radio there was dead silence, and the silence actually had more volume to it than the program and the song playing. I felt so stupid—there I was showing up at his door unannounced and he was treating me like garbage. "So . . . like"—I chewed the corner of my lip—"you don't have anything to say?"

"Yeah," he said while waving his hand to the left, "you kinda blocking the TV, so you need to move over a little bit."

I was stunned. I swear I was frozen in time. Was this really it? The end? Him playing me like crazy and me leaving with my heart split open on his floor? I wanted so badly to scream, "I got it now, okay?! You don't have to push me away! I promise I won't hurt you anymore. I promise . . ." But judging by the disinterested look on Malachi's face, the chance I had was long gone, and now all that was between us was stale air. I couldn't look at him anymore and there was no way I was going to burst out into tears standing there. I was on it, but not like that. I did have some pride. I turned around quickly and practically ran up the stairs. I could feel the tears sitting in my throat like a ticking time bomb ready to explode, so I needed to hurry home or at least make it to my car so that I could scream and cry in peace.

Once I reached the front door I thought for a moment I

heard Malachi walking behind me, but when I looked and saw that it was his puppy, I hurried to my car and leaned against the door. Tears were everywhere, and the only thing I could think of was at least I didn't cry in front of him.

I held my head in my hands and cried myself into oblivion.

"You give up that easy?" poured over my shoulder.

My heart thundered in my chest. I wiped my face and looked up. It was Malachi leaning against the hood of my car.

"You wouldn't talk to me." I wiped my eyes. "I couldn't keep standing there."

"Come 'mere," he said.

Reluctantly I walked over and stood before him. "What I'ma do with you?" he asked.

"Let me love you," I said, and I knew it was bold and he could easily push me away, but I placed my hands around his neck. "And then you love me back."

"And why should I do that?"

"Because I wrote you this note."

"You wrote me a note?" he said, surprised. "And what did it say?"

"It said, 'You wanna be my boyfriend, circle yes or no.'"

Malachi stared at me, and I could tell that a thousand things were running through his mind. "It really hurt to be without you, but I couldn't tolerate you taking me through changes behind some other dude," he said.

"I never cheated on you with him."

"I know, but I couldn't swing with the way you were handling things."

"It won't happen again. I swear. I love you, Malachi."

Malachi paused and studied my face again. "And I love you, Zsa."

"So does this mean"—I pressed my lips against his— "that you gon' circle yes?"

"What difference does it make what I circle? Why is it so important to you?"

I sang against his lips. "It's a matter of extreme importance, my first teenage love affair." I stopped singing. "And other than that, at least at this moment, nothing else matters."

"I guess I don't have a choice then," he said, "but to circle yes."

My heart suddenly felt light, like all of what I'd gone through was worth arriving at this moment.

"Let's go inside," Malachi said, giving me a peck on the lips.

"Wait," I said, taking my cell phone out of my purse and flipping it open. "I just need to do one thing." I quickly dialed Courtney's number.

"I can't do it, Zsa," Courtney answered the phone somberly. "I have cried over losing Malachi enough. I think I'ma just go to church."

"Courtney, we're together again."

"Zsa, I know we had a secret fling in third grade, but when you're seventeen kissing under the kidney table no longer counts."

I sighed. "Courtney, I'm talking about me and Malachi. We're back together."

"JESUS!" Courtney shouted so loud that I had to take the phone from my ear. "There is a God. So we're back on again? You mean to tell me that little Shaquita will be born one day?"

"Yes, Courtney." I laughed.

"Okay, okay," he said, "so here's the new plan: Whatever you do don't mess this up!"

"Bye, Courtney," I said, and I could hear him singing as I clicked off the line and me and Malachi walked inside.

Questions and tips about what else?
Teenage Love and Relationships!

Hey it's me, Seven. I made a guest appearance in my cousin's book, *Teenage Love Affair*, but you may also remember me from my own novel, *Shortie Like Mine*, or the one that told my twin sister's side of life, *If I Was Your Girl*.

Anywho, since I've been away for a few books and off to college I have some love and relationship questions that people have asked me, and since teenagers seem to value my opinion, allow me to grace you with the answers.

1. Question: If he hasn't called me in a week, what do I do?

Answer: Hmph, call his friend and say, "Your boy is buggin'. So, wassup with you?" Psych, I'm just playing. What you really should do is keep it moving, don't call him, don't sweat him, and take it from me, stalking is not attractive—so don't do that either.

2. Question: What do I do if he has a girlfriend—or she has a boyfriend—but we're feelin' each other?

Answer: Okay, let me just put it to you this way: Don't be a rat, because being number two in line is not cute. Trust me he—or she—will cheat on you too. So what you need to do is tell them to step so far to the left that they're on the right. Please don't play yourself.

3. Question: I'm single and all of my friends have boos. What do I do?

Answer: Be thankful you don't have the drama. Take your time and look for someone who's cool and has something going for themselves. Being single isn't a curse, it's simply a time to be selective.

4. Question: How do I know when what I'm feeling is real love?

Answer: You know it's real when you dump him and want him back. LOL, just playing. Okay, you know it's real when it feels right. When you feel good about being with that person and you're comfortable with them. They aren't asking you to do anything that makes you uncertain or insecure. You know it's real when it flows . . . oh, and your parents like him or her. Otherwise, you may as well hang it up.

5. Question: I caught my boyfriend cheating. What do I do?

Answer: Attention: Don't bust the windows out of his car, do not put a Snickers bar in his gas tank, do not call the sideline chick, and do not—and I repeat, do not—confront the girl and pick a fight. This is when being a lady and having self-control counts. What you need to do is simply walk away. No ifs, ands, or buts about it. Don't take it as if the other girl (or guy) has won, because relationships are not a contest. Just leave, and trust me, it will save you a lot of heartache in the end.

6. Question: Do looks count?

Answer: They do if he's a bad mix of Lil' Wayne and T-Pain. Other than that, what's on the inside is what counts.

7. Question: I could swear I saw my boyfriend with another girl, but he says it wasn't him. What do I do?

Answer: Don't believe him, unless he has an identical twin. Then he might be telling the truth.

8. Question: How old is too old?

Answer: If your parents can press charges on him or her, then they are probably not the best choice.

9. Question: I want to break up with him. How do I do it?

Answer: Send him a text message every fifteen minutes to make sure he received it, remove him as your number one friend on MySpace, and put a neon yellow sticky note on his locker that reads, "Don't call me anymore." LOL! Okay, seriously, you need to be respectful and honest. Don't lead him or her on or give them false hopes.

10. Question: Can you please give me some tips on how to act on a date?

Answer: Ten tips on how to act on a date:

1. Paleeze, make sure your hair is done, there is no cold in your eyes, and your lips are not chapped or cracked down the middle.

2. If you are a girl, do not try and be a homeboy. And if you are a dude, do not try and be a gossip queen. Nothing says run the other way louder than this.

3. Do not be nasty or sarcastic. Use your table manners, such as, ladies, your napkins go in your lap, not tucked in your collar, and boys, if you feel the urge to belch, take your butt in the bathroom.

4. Keep the conversation flowing. Too much dead air time leads to thoughts of what else you could be doing.

5. Make sure he pays. Don't offer your money. Trust me, ladies—let's be old-fashioned on this one. You don't ever offer to pay unless there's a ring on it, and even then, you only pay half.

6. Dress cute but don't show too much. Cleavage is nice, ladies, but too much of a boob show does not say wifey type—it says ho. His mother will frown and hold a backroom conversation about you in two minutes flat when you step up in the house looking like you are a future video vixen. And boys, please pull your pants up. I mean, you don't have to wear them Jonas Brothers tight, but dang, I don't need a view of your underwear. And believe me, you can't come to any decent girl's house like that. The date will be over before it even starts.

7. Be honest about yourself but don't tell everything. Everyone is not worthy of your secrets. Keep some things close. For example, if you busted the windows out of your ex-boyfriend's car, you may want to keep that to yourself.

8. Stay classy at all times. Acting like a lady says wifey. And boys, if you act too much like a thug, I'ma get scared and start thinking that our date is a gang initiation. And if I'm too scared, I will be calling my daddy to come and get me.

9. Be outgoing. You could've stayed home and he or she could've dated your friend if you were going to be all uptight and everything.

10. And last but most important of all—have fun!

Hope this helps!
Love, peace, and hair grease!
Seven

HAVEN'T HAD ENOUGH? CHECK OUT THESE
GREAT SERIES FROM DAFINA BOOKS!

DRAMA HIGH

by L. Divine

Follow the adventures of a young sistah who's learning that life
in the hood is nothing compared to life in high school.

THE FIGHT	SECOND CHANCE	JAYD'S LEGACY
ISBN: 0-7582-1633-5	ISBN: 0-7582-1635-1	ISBN: 0-7582-1637-8
FRENEMIES	LADY J	COURTIN' JAYD
ISBN: 0-7582-2532-6	ISBN: 0-7582-2534-2	ISBN: 0-7582-2536-9
HUSTLIN'	KEEP IT MOVIN'	HOLIDAZE
ISBN: 0-7582-3105-9	ISBN: 0-7582-3107-5	ISBN: 0-7582-3109-1
	CULTURE CLASH	
	ISBN: 0-7582-3111-3	

BOY SHOPPING

by Nia Stephens

An exciting "you pick the ending" series
that lets the reader pick Mr. Right.

BOY SHOPPING	LIKE THIS AND LIKE THAT	GET MORE
ISBN: 0-7582-1929-6	ISBN: 0-7582-1931-8	ISBN: 0-7582-1933-4

DEL RIO BAY

by Paula Chase

A wickedly funny series that explores friendship, betrayal, and
how far some people will go for popularity.

SO NOT THE DRAMA	DON'T GET IT TWISTED	THAT'S WHAT'S UP!
ISBN: 0-7582-1859-1	ISBN: 0-7582-1861-3	ISBN: 0-7582-2582-2
WHO YOU WIT'?	FLIPPING THE SCRIPT	
ISBN: 0-7582-2584-9	ISBN: 0-7582-2586-5	

PERRY SKKY JR.

by Stephanie Perry Moore

An inspirational series that follows the adventures of a high
school football star as he balances faith and the temptations of
teen life.

PRIME CHOICE	PRESSING HARD	PROBLEM SOLVED
ISBN: 0-7582-1863-X	ISBN: 0-7582-1872-9	ISBN: 0-7582-1874-5
PRAYED UP	PROMISE KEPT	
ISBN: 0-7582-2538-5	ISBN: 0-7582-2540-7